# MEETINGS
## WITH
# JAKE AND JOE

# MEETINGS
## WITH
# JAKE AND JOE

ROGER W. BUENGER

3RB ENTERPRISES, LLC

Published by
3RB Enterprises, LLC
Florissant, MO 63034

Book design by Damonza.com

ISBN 978-0-9903080-1-0 (Paperback)
ISBN 978-0-9903080-2-7 (Hardcover)
ISBN 978-0-9903080-0-3 (Kindle)
ISBN 978-0-9903080-3-4 (ePub)

Printed in the United States of America

First Edition: April 2014

# Table of Contents

*The writing of this book has been a divine experience that can only be credited to my Creator, Almighty God. Everything in life begins and ends with Him. Inspired by a stray cat who came to live with my family, I created this tale by mixing events and aspects from myself and my own life with fiction. I believe the story literally told itself to me and I merely recorded it. In many ways, Henry Engel is a character very close to my own heart and I will forever be grateful that I know him.*

*To my Mom and Dad, THANK YOU for your unwavering support and the unconditional love you have given me throughout my life. You are the best parents any son could hope for. I love you both with all of my heart.*

*To Ryan and Rachel, this book is my gift to you. I hope it will be a constant and permanent reminder of how much I love both of you. Being your Dad is my greatest blessing in this life. 3RB!*

*To Michelle, as our adventure continues, I look forward to the next chapter with great anticipation. Finding one another again after all of the years apart has changed my life. I love you.*

*To Ayo and Fausto, getting to know you and be a part of your lives is a privilege I cherish. I love you both and am very proud that you are part of my family.*

*Thank you Joe. You have impacted the lives of everyone around you and we are forever in your debt.*

## CHAPTER 1

# Mail Call

A S HE STEPPED out his front door, Henry felt the crispness of the air despite the bright sunshine that was beaming through the leafless trees above him. It was early March, and in Lewis, Missouri that meant a tenuous dance between winter and spring. One day could be sunny with temps in the 70s, yet on the very next day you might find yourself below freezing and in the grips of a snowstorm. Such was weather in the Midwest. Natives always liked to say, "If you don't like the weather, hang around until tomorrow because it will change."

On this day, it was in the low 50s: *perfect jacket weather*, he thought to himself. His daily stroll to his mailbox would be a welcome stretch of his legs and he was looking forward to it. It had been a long and dark winter and he was energized by the prospects of the change in the seasons and the opportunity to spend more time outdoors.

This ritual journey was not just another "walk to the curb." His black asphalt driveway snaked approximately the equivalent of one and a half football fields down one hill and up another from front door to destination. It was no small thing for a 73-year-old man, but Henry Engel was in excellent health and not averse to *physical* exertion.

At 6'2" and 190 lbs. he was both well-built and in good shape. A thick head of dark brown salt and pepper hair, which he kept short and neatly combed, rustled in the light breeze. He wore copper-colored wire-rimmed glasses; they complemented his light-brown eyes, which sparkled when he laughed. His face was always clean shaven and his attire typically consisted of a pair of khaki pants, black or brown leather-laced shoes, and a button-down collared shirt. Generally, those who encountered him would perceive him to be a man ten years his junior due to both his appearance and demeanor.

Advancing off the porch, Henry zipped his khaki jacket halfway up toward his collar while duly noting a large limb that had broken off and fallen down from one of the towering oaks in the front yard. Removing it would be a task for the afternoon. He strode purposefully past "the island" (a patch of grass and trees so nicknamed because it was completely surrounded by a large circle of asphalt road creating a circular drive) and then headed on his way down the long hill.

Henry had dubbed the estate "Oak Forest" shortly after he acquired it. It was an ideal setup carefully created by the original developer. The entire lot totaled just under a dozen acres and was roughly half in forest and half in meadow. The home, set in a clearing high atop the large hill that dominated the estate, was a charming two-story Victorian that had been built just after WWII by a wealthy St. Louis businessman. It was complemented to the rear by a three-car detached garage and a spacious tool shed and was surrounded on three sides by a forest of oak, wild cherry, sassafras, and hickory trees. Perhaps the best feature of the place was the delightful wrap-around porch, which offered ample opportunity to sit and enjoy an evening breeze or sunset. At least Henry thought so. The forest to the front of the home had been intentionally thinned out to selected trees allowing a shady vantage to the sprawling meadow that lay beneath it. Offset to the right of the driveway at the base of the hill was a pear-shaped pond that signaled the end of the woods and the mid-point of the property before giving way to lush green open pasture.

Henry enjoyed the fresh air and was amused by the appearance of several cardinals rooting amongst the leaves on the forest floor. He had several well-stocked feeders positioned around the grounds and shook his head as he pondered why these particular diners had forgone the free meal he had provided in favor of working for their lunch. *To each his own*, he thought.

He slipped his right hand into his pants pocket and quickly found the large heavy coin he always carried with him and began to twirl it between his fingers as he strolled along. The silver piece was cool to his touch and had a smooth familiar feeling.

When he reached the bottom of the hill, the unofficial halfway point of his trek to the mailbox, he glanced at his watch and noted the time, 2:22 p.m. He could be sure the day's mail would be waiting for him as Lucy Dawson, his mail carrier, was a precise person bolstered by a healthy dose of obsessive compulsive disorder. Generally speaking, one could set one's watch by her. In Henry's case, 1:55–2:05 p.m. was his delivery time. She'd rarely be early. She'd never be late. Saturday delivery was at 11:30 a.m., give or a take a couple of minutes. He'd always meant to ask her what that was all about but didn't care enough to actually pursue it when he saw her. It was good enough for him that the mail always came and he could count on it.

Walking up the long incline toward the county road he glanced to his left at the stable, which stood idle. The original owner had owned horses and several acres had been fenced to facilitate their lodging and care. Henry had always maintained the building and the fence line but had never entertained the idea of actually owning even a single horse to live there. That was for another lifetime, which he had left behind long ago. However, he enjoyed the look of the building and felt the fencing gave Oak Forest a regal quality so he kept it for appearance's sake. Now, rather than housing horses, the stable served as a convenient garage for his 1967 International Harvester tractor and brush hog, which he used throughout the summer months to maintain the nearly six acres of meadow found on the estate. It also had become a catch-all of sorts for odd pieces of farm equipment or whatever else he was of a mind to bring home and put in there.

As he took the last few steps to the mail box, he surveyed the road in both directions. All clear, as usual. County Road 27 wasn't a bustling thoroughfare to be sure so the absence of traffic wasn't a shock. The presence of two cars at once—now that might have been.

He pulled the snugly fastened door of the oversized plain black metal box open and reached inside to retrieve its contents. As per usual, he exited with a handful of pieces of mail of varying sizes. Not a bad haul for a Thursday, he thought. He liked the mail. It usually contained one of the many magazines he subscribed to or something of interest. More importantly, it often brought checks from his many investments and business endeavors and sometimes even contained a new acquisition to be added to his coin collection, another of his passions.

"Hmm … no packages today," he muttered to himself and

returned the door to the closed position. He wasn't a bit surprised as he hadn't ordered anything recently but regardless he felt a twinge of disappointment, if only for a moment. He casually glanced down at the stack and quickly noted the end of an all-too familiar gray envelope sticking out near the bottom.

"Damn," he groaned after noticing it. It was the one thing he hated to find in the mail box. It was a link to a past he had left behind. Though letters just like this one had been periodically arriving for years, they were never welcomed. With the mail secured in his left hand, he began the march back home.

His usual practice was to sort through the items and identify anything particularly interesting as a pastime during the walk back, but today he was too busy taking in the sights and smells of early spring to care much. It could wait. Even the offending letter could not distract him. Right now he wanted to absorb the view of tiny patches of green emerging in the gray meadow and observe a red-tailed hawk soaring above him in total peace and solitude. He watched as it gently glided on the wind in a silent graceful circle.

*That's the perfect life*, he thought to himself as he gazed at the majestic bird. *On your own. Independent.*

It should surprise no one that he would feel this way. He *was* a hawk. He was a creature operating independently and on his own and very content to do it. He didn't need anyone else to care about him, and what's more, he didn't *want* anyone else to care about, either. Henry Engel was comfortable in his own skin and a loner, but he never felt alone. This isn't to say that he was a recluse; he wasn't. On the contrary, he went into town often for the things he needed or to enjoy a meal, and he spoke to whomever he had occasion to. He still traveled from time to time when it was required for his business interests or to attend a major coin show.

In addition, he had an assortment of casual "friends" with whom he interacted. However, they were really more like advanced acquaintances who could come and go from his life without consequence. That was where it stopped. No family, no wife, no children, no loved ones at all. Having lost his parents at an early age and then a beloved uncle when he was 19, there was no other person alive that he considered or acknowledged as a family member. He was alone on this earth. It was the path he had chosen for his life and he was ok with that.

A tremendously driven and successful businessman, he had instead devoted himself to the building of enterprises, investing, traveling, seeking adventure, and the like. He had learned a hard lesson about people, love, and betrayal as a young man and over the past 45 years had pursued a course that didn't allow for a repeat experience.

Despite that, professionally he was a true winner. He was a man of means and influence. He had banked millions and had sat on the boards of several leading corporations. He was often sought out by associates for his wise counsel and offered it freely whenever he could. In the world he had created for himself, he was well thought of and quite well respected. Overall, Henry was satisfied with his life to the extent that he ever really cared to analyze it.

Reaching the crest of the hill and approaching the house he now began to sort through the mail. Water bill, phone bill, a couple of likely candidates to contain checks, a *Smithsonian Magazine*, some junk mail advertisements, and the hand-addressed gray business envelope with no return address on it. The sight of the letter was met with another small groan and he quickly shifted it to the bottom of the pile.

Henry stepped onto the porch and after swinging open the front door entered into the house where he was greeted by the sweet smell of fresh-baked bread wafting through the air. He inhaled deeply to take in the full effect. It was delightful. He sat the stack of mail on the small antique table that stood against the dining room wall to his right and unzipped his jacket. After he removed it, he hung it on the hall tree and then reacquired the mail before walking down the entry hall past the stairs and toward the kitchen.

The hallway opened to a spacious breakfast room. A large oak table with six chairs stood on a tan ceramic tile floor beneath a slowly rotating ceiling fan. On the opposite side, a pair of French doors led to a gray stone patio and the back yard.

To the right of the breakfast room was the kitchen itself. It was rectangular in shape and the far wall was lined with both upper and lower honey oak cabinets. The upper cabinets ran the length of the room on either side of a double window and sported glass window pane doors allowing one to view the dishes they contained from the outside. The first floor had a nine-foot ceiling and this provided space above the cabinets where various antiques such as a cracker tin and a coffee grinder were displayed. The lower set of cabinets was capped with a deep gray granite countertop, which held a double-wide stainless steel sink that was positioned directly beneath the window.

At the far end of the kitchen a black and white stove/oven combination stood neatly beneath a matching microwave oven/exhaust hood unit. To its immediate right, a side-by-side white refrigerator provided ample storage and easy access to all. The wall was completed by a doorway leading to the laundry room and pantry, which also held the side entrance to the home. The near wall was composed of a door to the first floor bathroom and a large antique cupboard that lent an additional touch of nostalgia to the decor. In the middle of the kitchen, a granite – topped island stood beneath a brushed nickel three-bulb chandelier offering additional storage in the form of more cabinets and drawers. Two high-backed oak swivel chairs faced it from the near side. The seat on the left, nearest the kitchen table, was a favorite of Henry's.

He dropped the mail on the island and sat down to review it more closely. As he picked up the first envelope, Millie entered from the family room to his left.

"The bread smells terrific," Henry said, opening the conversation in hopes of scoring a piece of what was creating the delicious aroma.

"Of course it does. That's my grand mama's recipe; it always turns out. You want some Mr. Engel?" she offered with a smile.

His strategy had paid off. The quickest way to get a taste of anything Millie was preparing was to pay her a compliment.

"Yeah, I guess I could try a slice," he responded, coyly feigning indifference.

Millie pulled a drawer in the island open and withdrew a long slender bread-slicing knife from it. Noticing the pile of mail, she turned her attention to the freshly baked loaf of bread sitting neatly on a cooling rack next to the sink.

"You want butter on it?" she asked.

"Sure."

She deftly slid the knife through the middle of the loaf releasing the steam that had previously been trapped inside.

"My grand mama sure could make bread. When I was a little girl, she would bake every Saturday for the whole week and us kids would always hang around the back door of her house looking for a handout," she said, ending with a giggle. "You know, she used to bake a whole extra loaf just to give away to us each week as samples."

"Sounds nice," he said, not really understanding what it must have been like to have a loving grandma dote on him but being sharp enough to know an acknowledgement was expected.

"It was," she agreed as she opened the refrigerator and removed a clear glass dish containing a fresh untouched stick of butter.

"When you're little, you just don't realize ..." Her voice trailed off as she remembered the warmth of her grandmother and reflected on how children often times don't understand such things until they are much older and those loved ones are gone. She reopened the drawer in the island to retrieve a butter knife. As she did, she took a closer look at the pile of mail next to Henry and noticed he was intently assessing the water bill and not necessarily listening to her.

"You gonna open that one?" she asked, looking at the gray envelope that was halfway exposed from beneath the phone bill.

"Huh?" Henry replied, not sure what she had just said.

"I said, 'Are you gonna open that one?'" she repeated as she pointed with the butter knife to the gray envelope.

"The phone bill? Yeah of course," Henry responded slyly, knowing exactly what she meant but hoping to divert the conversation.

"You know which one I'm talking about and it ain't no phone bill. Why don't you go on and open it and see who it's from?" she persisted.

"I won't be opening it; mind your business," he snapped back, now feeling somewhat annoyed and no longer a bit playful. Millie's inquiry had struck a nerve.

"Mr. Engel, I've worked for you for going on 22 years and you've gotten at least 2 or 3 of those same gray envelopes every year for a good ten of them. Each time one shows up you throw it in the trash and never even open it. It's not my business but even my eyes can see it bothers you. Why not open one up and find out what it's all about and get it over with?" The words had just fallen out of her mouth. They were still resonating in the air when regret set in. She looked at him knowing she had just crossed a line that they rarely had ever approached during her tenure as his housekeeper. However, she also deeply cared about him and knew that something inside that envelope was a source of pain or angst and wanted to help him resolve it. Having said that, it was too late to backtrack now and she braced herself for what most likely was going to be a strong rebuke at best, and quite possibly at worst, an eruption. Those had been few and very far between but when Henry lost his German temper, it was better to be somewhere else.

He looked her in the eyes and slowly began to speak. "Millie, it's 23 years and I DO know who that's from. A long time ago I opened a letter just like that one … ," he paused before proceeding, "…and never again."

He stood from his seat at the island and with his right hand pulled the gray envelope from the stack of mail. With no sign of emotion he stepped over to the trash can, lifted the lid, and dropped the sealed letter inside, closing the lid behind it. As he returned to his seat, he exhaled. "Now, how about that bread?"

"Yes sir," Millie replied sheepishly as she opened the cabinet door just to the left of the sink, extracting a small white plate. She was glad the episode was over and felt extremely relieved that

Henry hadn't chastised her more vigorously for what clearly had been a breach of etiquette on her part. His personal business had always been off limits to her and she knew that.

\* \* \*

Millie James had come to work for Henry shortly after he completed his purchase and renovation of the home in 1974. Originally born in Georgia, she had moved to Lewis in 1972 when she was 33 years old to live with her cousin Jean and to help care for Jean's ailing mother, Millie's Aunt Bess. When Henry bought the estate, he spent eight months renovating it and upon taking occupancy later that year had posted a want ad both in the *St. Louis Post-Dispatch* as well as the *Lewis Gazette* seeking a housekeeper. Millie responded the first day that the ad appeared and Henry had been so impressed by her that he hired her on the spot. He then canceled the ads without seeing even a second applicant. She was exactly what he wanted.

Millie was an attractive woman. At 5'6" with a medium build, she possessed a pleasing figure. Her light brown eyes contrasted beautifully with her mocha skin and when she wore her hair pulled back from her face, her full lips and cheek bones were striking like those you'd find on a model featured in *Vogue Magazine*. She favored a knit top, blue jeans, and sneakers as her typical daily attire but could stun in a dress and heels when singing in the church choir or on other occasions when a more formal look was called for. Henry had noted on many occasions how pretty she was and wondered how it had come to be that she had never married but in keeping with his personal convictions, had intentionally neglected to share any of this with Millie. Her life was her business and he didn't cross lines. He didn't appreciate it if she meddled in his affairs and he returned the favor in kind.

Though theirs had always been an extremely cordial and comfortable relationship from the outset, it lacked the warmth one would expect to find between people after over two decades of near daily interaction with each other. Despite that, they had developed a perfect rapport, which allowed them to work flawlessly together like a well-synchronized machine. Henry knew that he could rely on Millie for everything he needed from her. She was an excellent housekeeper and a loyal and trusted employee who ran a perfect household up to the standards Henry expected.

She knew virtually everything about his tastes and preferences. After being together for such a long time, they generally no longer even discussed the daily menu. If Millie had a mind to cook it, Henry gladly ate it. If he ever made a special request, the next day Millie had it on the table. His clothes were always clean and ironed, neatly waiting for him in his closets and drawers. The floors were always spotless and dust was a rare commodity to be found inside the four walls of the Engel home. She was a hardworking perfectionist who took tremendous pride in her daily work. Her mother had taught her that anything worth doing, was worth doing the right way. Millie was the poster child for that philosophy and Henry greatly respected her for it.

Millie, in turn, craved security. In Henry she knew that she had found a job for life and was both well treated and handsomely paid for her time and service. Because of that, this job was priceless to her. It seemed less like work and more like caring for someone important to you. Being of service pleased her. She worked Monday through Friday from 9:00 a.m. to 5:00 p.m. and was available to Henry for special events such as a dinner party or weekend barbecue if he needed her. She cooked, cleaned, and did his laundry. She kept the home stocked with all of his favorite foods and whatever supplies were needed to operate the household. If she didn't obtain the groceries herself, she had them delivered. Henry never cared about the cost, he just expected it done. Millie complied.

In addition to her generous weekly salary, each year Henry would give her two weeks off and pay for her to return home to Georgia where she was born. After her aunt had passed away in 1983, her cousin Jean had moved to California and the trips back South were her only opportunities to spend time with family. She also enjoyed ample leisure time and a relaxed schedule when Henry was away on business. This had been a regular occurrence in the early years they were together and even now that he was retired still occurred occasionally. Many times, if things were in good order Henry would release her from her duties with a few words, such as "Millie I think we're in good shape. Why don't you take the rest of the day off," and she'd head home early. Despite this, in 23 years she'd never received anything less than her full paycheck from him regardless of the actual number of hours she had worked. If all of this wasn't enough, Henry also provided health and auto insurance and furnished a car for her as part of her compensation package. He was a man of means and was willing and able to pay for what he wanted. In Millie he had found a person he trusted implicitly to handle all of her duties and the administration of the home as she saw fit (within the guidelines he'd prescribed, of course) and he never questioned her household expenses. In short, Henry saw Millie as invaluable and she was both well respected and generously compensated as a result. Millie in turn treasured this and would never fail him. It was the perfect marriage.

\* \* \*

Millie lathered a pad of butter over the still-warm bread and set the plate next to Henry.

"Would you like some lemonade to go with that?"

"Please," he responded casually not looking up from the *Smithsonian Magazine*, which now held his attention. His voice was relaxed and calm and Millie was relieved to hear no tension in it. The moment had passed and she was off the hook. She was sorry she had pushed the issue with him. It wasn't like her to do so ordinarily. *Next time, I'll keep my prying to myself*, she thought.

# CHAPTER 2
## A Job Well Done

THE OVERHEAD PULLEYS whined softly under the strain of the weight of the large wood door as Henry pulled it to the right along its rails. Once open, he stepped inside the tool shed and across the dirt floor to the right side where several shelves held an array of tools including a well broken-in chain saw. The afternoon sunshine shone through the open doorway, negating the need to pull the chain dangling from the single light bulb suspended in the middle of the building.

The shed was original to the property, having been built at the same time that the house was constructed in the late 1940s. It was a rectangular 14' x 10' frame structure that had been painted white many times over the years providing a thick egg shell layer of protection. The charcoal gray shingled roof had been replaced only a couple years prior after a bout of hail storms had peppered it, and the other roofs on the estate, with damage. A lone window was located on the front, to the left of the door, and it was accompanied on either side by cornflower blue shutters that were painted to match the "barn style" door. Not coincidentally, the doors and shutters on the house and garage were painted to match. The tool shed served as a useful depot to store Henry's push mower and John Deere riding tractor, as well as all of the other gardening and landscaping tools needed to maintain an estate such as his.

He lifted the saw from its resting place and moved across the room to the work bench beneath the front window. Reaching into his tool box he retrieved a 5/8" closed end wrench and proceeded to loosen the two nuts that secured the chain guard to the sprocket housing of the saw. Once the nuts had been removed, he pulled the chain guard away and inspected inside to assure that the sprocket was clean and that the chain was properly seated on it. Often this area was a place neglected and it led to damage or premature wear reducing the life of a saw.

Henry was not one to waste much of anything. His days on his uncle's farm as a boy had taught him the value of a dollar and the necessity of extracting every last bit of value out of things. Though his bank account now warranted a different attitude, his upbringing wouldn't allow it.

Satisfied, he replaced the guard and secured it with the nuts. He then proceeded to fill the front reservoir with the oil it required to lubricate the chain during usage. Next, he removed the rear fuel cap and filled it with a 40:1 gas–oil mix until it ran over the top.

"Aww, damn," he scoffed at himself, less upset with the wasted fuel than he was with the smelly mess he'd made on the saw and the work bench. Gasoline alone had a strong aroma but the gas–oil mix required by a 2-stroke engine was downright pungent and once on you or your clothes, it permeated the air until it was washed away. He picked up a rag lying nearby and wiped off the side of the saw before swiping it across the steel bench top and clearing the small puddle he'd accidentally created. Tossing the rag aside, he grabbed his worn tan leather work gloves, picked up the saw, and headed out.

As he strolled across the back yard he admired the rear of his home. He was happy here. It had been a lucky stroke when he found it for sale all those years ago and he knew it. The peace and privacy he so valued was a natural byproduct of this oasis and he was acutely aware of it.

The estate had originally been a virgin tract of land that was one of many acquired by Allied Gas across the area in the mid-1940s. Most of the acreage around Lewis that wasn't forested was being used for farming or livestock and was commercially undeveloped.

At the time, the now natural gas giant was just a fledgling venture. A pair of entrepreneurs, backed by a group of deep-pocketed investors flush with cash from war profits generated by military manufacturing contracts, had done some test drilling and found rich pockets of oil and natural gas to tap. They saw an opportunity to accumulate a large amount of cheap real estate for their drilling and underground storage plans and seized it. The gamble paid off in Lewis, as well as other communities around the Midwest, and Allied had gone on to become a behemoth and the dominant supplier of natural gas to consumers throughout middle America.

When Allied was founded, the brother of one of its original investors had returned from the war looking to build a home outside of St. Louis and had taken a liking to Lewis. With a connection on the inside of the business, a deal was reached and the 12-acre estate that Henry Engel now owned was born and developed. The man and his family had remained here until late 1973 when he sold his business in St. Louis and moved his family to

California. Henry just so happened to be in the right place at the right time to become its next owner.

He surveyed the fish pond and waterfall, which stood still winterized under plastic sheeting and waiting to be opened for the season. He had put the water feature in a decade before as an accent to the large patio and pergola where he liked to grill outdoors. It could wait. It didn't contain any fish that needed care anyway. When he first put it in, a well-meaning business associate had given him a half dozen koi to stock it, but they instead quickly became hors d'oeuvres for the locals. The raccoon population that patrolled the area took care of that. Henry didn't lose any sleep over it as he wasn't one for pets of any kind. He'd only accepted the fish to be courteous in the first place.

Henry walked past Millie's white '94 Ford Taurus sedan as he passed the side of the house. When he first hired her, he'd mentally set aside that spot for her car even though there was ample space further back at the turnaround in front of the garage. Millie had initially protested that she had two healthy legs and no problem walking the additional 50 or so feet necessary to park back there. However, despite there being no actual parking space in this spot, Henry had insisted she park here as she often had groceries or other items to carry into the home. The proximity of the space to the side door made it an ideal choice. As always, Henry was the boss and there was no debate.

He arrived at the limb, which was lying just on the opposite side of the island from the front porch, and immediately realized it was much larger than he'd estimated at first glance. It was roughly 5 inches in diameter and maybe 12 feet long with several offshoots on it. It was dead wood that had been weakened over the winter months by the weight of ice and snow and had finally been brought down by a strategic gust of wind the previous night. It wouldn't be an issue to cut it up. That would only take him a few minutes and he was in no particular hurry. His meeting with Jake wasn't for another hour. However, he would need the John Deere and his utility wagon from the tool shed to haul away the firewood the job would yield. Oak was heavy and the wood pile was in the rear next to the garage, making carrying it there not an option. As long as he was already here with the saw, though, he figured he may as well go ahead and cut it up now, then get the tractor.

Henry bent over to set the saw on the ground so he could put his gloves on. As he returned upright his eyes tracked down the hill a ways toward the stable. He was tugging at the glove his right hand was seeking when he saw him for the first time. Off to the left, perhaps only 20 yards away he spied a pair of eyes watching him. They were peering at him from behind a clump of brush at the edge of the tree line where the woods thickened. He strained to see just what it was. *Wrong time of day for a raccoon or possum. What the hell is it?* His eyes strained through his glasses to get a clearer look and without noticing he took a couple steps forward toward the unidentified and uninvited stranger.

At that, the anonymous spectator broke from his position and retreated to a vantage a few feet further away behind a pair of twin oak trees. It was a small cat. Not just any small cat, but a small Siamese cat. It was marked with four dark socks, a dark tail, a cream-colored body, and a dark face bejeweled with two icy blue eyes. He was surprised because this wasn't something you'd expect to see 10 miles from town in the middle of nowhere. His next closest neighbor was three-quarters of a mile away and the

Fergusons weren't the sorts to have any cat, much less an expensive specialty breed like this.

"Get home!" Henry shouted. He had no want or need for a cat around and made it abundantly clear that squatters were unwelcome. He didn't care where it came from or where it belonged, he just wanted it gone from here. At the sound of his booming voice, the interloper exploded into a full sprint down the hill and dove under the fence. It dashed across the pasture and then cut in front of the stable where it suddenly wheeled and stopped in the open, staring back at Henry from what was a greater, and no doubt, safer, distance. Henry let out another "war whoop" directed at it but to no avail. The cat just stared back blankly at him. Henry then picked up his chain saw and with a single pull of the rope fired it up. With a couple pulls of the trigger he revved the motor like a biker showing off his new Harley and the deal was sealed. The little cat shot toward the far side of the stable and disappeared in full gallop on a trajectory toward the road and as far away from Henry as it could get.

"There you go," Henry chuckled to himself, "and keep going."

He proceeded to slice through the fallen branch in a series of cuts deftly executed with the skill of a surgeon. Over two decades as the steward of this estate, he had been provided ample opportunity to perfect his craft and he was as handy with a chainsaw as anyone could be. What's more, Henry enjoyed it. He liked to be outside and work invigorated him. In addition, each cut added to his ready supply of firewood so this little project was a win-win. In just minutes, he was done. He shut off the saw, admired his handiwork, and started back toward the tool shed for the tractor. As he did, something inside of him caused him to glance over his shoulder back down the hill and there it was again. Across the pasture, the little cat was positioned like a statue at the far corner of the stable. Curiosity had brought it back; fear had kept it at a safe distance.

"Son of a bitch!" he said aloud and shook his head. He was too far away to effectively frighten it so he continued on his way for the tractor and decided that when he returned if it was still there he'd head to the stable to make a more lasting impression on it. The last thing he wanted, or needed, was a resident cat around to deal with. Life had repeatedly taught him the consequences of investing himself emotionally in another. He was adamant that it would never happen again.

He put the saw back in its place and took the key for the John Deere garden tractor off of the nail inside the door. He checked the gas and oil levels and upon verifying that the air filter was clean he climbed aboard. Making sure it was out of gear, he depressed the brake, pulled the choke, adjusted the throttle, and turned the key. It hadn't been run in a while and he was pleasantly surprised that it fired right away. After pulling it outside, he dropped it into neutral and set the brake. He then hopped off and rolled out a small steel utility trailer to hitch to the idling tractor. A quick glance at his watch showed him that it was 4:15 p.m., still plenty of time to get this done. *No problem*, he thought. His meeting with Jake wasn't until five.

He had almost forgotten the little cat by the time he pulled up to the cut wood. A quick look indicated that it was gone from its place by the stable. Henry didn't feel compelled to waste time running down the hill to verify this and instead proceeded to load the trailer.

Within a half hour the last stick of wood was stacked on the pile beside the garage, and the tractor and trailer were back in their places inside the shed. Henry pulled the door closed and turned the key in the lock.

*Life is good*, he thought to himself as he walked up to the house. His job was finished, Millie had prepared fried chicken, mashed potatoes, and gravy and her world-famous homemade biscuits for dinner, and he'd be right on time for his meeting beforehand. "Well done, Henry," he gloated, "well done."

# CHAPTER 3

## "Hello Jake!"

HENRY FINISHED DRYING his hands and replaced the towel on its perch on the bar next to the bathroom sink. As he exited, he switched off the light and saw Millie pulling on her jacket.

"It smells great in here, Millie," he commented as he looked at the pots and dishes sitting on the stove containing his dinner.

"Everything is set up as usual," she replied, shrugging off the compliment with a smile. She liked to hear his praise but like a gifted athlete or actor, she had enough confidence in her own skills that such confirmations from him were unnecessary. She knew he liked the way she cooked because she was superb at her job and it pleased her. She just wasn't particularly preoccupied with hearing about it.

"Anything else you need today, Mr. Engel?" she asked.

"No, ma'am," he answered with a tone of satisfaction.

"All right then, I best be off," she said as she looked at the clock on the far wall of the breakfast room, which had just struck 5:00 p.m. "Time for me to go and for your meeting with Jake; I'll see you again." With that she was out the side door and on her way home.

"Goodnight Millie," he called behind her.

He stepped to the sink and opened the door of the cabinet beneath it. Reaching inside, his right hand found the object it was looking for. The neck of the bottle felt cool to his touch as he grasped it and pulled it out.

"Hello Jake!" he said with enthusiasm.

The 750 ml bottle of Jacob Patrick Jasterson's Bourbon was just two shots short of full, thanks to yesterday's meeting. He set the bottle on the counter and then opened the cabinet above and to the right of the sink where the glasses were neatly sorted and stacked by size. Selecting a suitable candidate he closed the door and swung around to the ice dispenser on the front of the refrigerator. He pushed the glass against the sensor and cube after cube tumbled downward until his glass was three-fourths full. He then placed the glass next to the whiskey bottle and removed the cap with his left hand while pouring with his right. Tipping the bottle for a three count he had exactly one shot of whiskey in his glass. There was no need to measure it; NASA couldn't have been more precise. Topping the glass off with water from the tap, his highball was complete. A spin of the ice with his finger and he was ready. His meeting with J.P. Jasterson was about to commence.

Lifting the glass to his lips, he took a long slow pull from it and swallowed with deep satisfaction. He had been having his "meetings with Jake" for nearly 50 years, as often as life allowed. Every day, at 5:00 p.m., exactly two highballs. It was a ritual he'd learned from a business mentor as a way to relax, reflect, and strategize and it had proved to be effective and enjoyable.

It was getting cool out now so he'd settle for a seat in the family room but typically, whenever the weather allowed, their "meetings" were conducted outdoors. He favored a seat on the front porch but had been known on rare occasions to switch it up with a position somewhere near the waterfall out back.

It was two drinks and done. Typically, meetings took about an hour or so. Henry often thought that he should patent the concept as many of his best ideas and business moves had resulted from an epiphany reached during a conference with his friend. However, regulation and enforcement of licensing rights for this might be problematic so why give the competition a chance to use his strategic advantage against him?

Henry crossed the breakfast room and passed through the doorway into the family room. He placed his glass on the table next to his favorite leather recliner and walked over to pick up the television remote off the nearby coffee table in front of the couch. Pressing the power button he sat down in his chair and exchanged the remote for his glass. After another generous swallow, the glass was half emptied.

He wasn't a particularly avid television viewer but he had grown accustomed to the company it provided. Rare was the time when he was indoors that either the TV or the radio wasn't on in the background. He liked to watch the St. Louis Cardinals play and was an NFL fan but hadn't quite jumped in on the Rams bandwagon yet. They had come to St. Louis in 1995 and though they'd already competed for two seasons in the Gateway City, they still felt like the Los Angeles Rams to him. Movies, on the other hand, were "a horse of a different color." Henry loved John Wayne films and owned virtually every one that was available to him on VHS. When he couldn't find something interesting to watch, he'd fire up his VCR and watch "The Duke."

Like a lot of people from his generation, Henry had grown up watching John Wayne on the silver screen. He was more than an actor to millions. He was an American icon and Henry could identify with the character traits that he embodied. Like Wayne, Henry had a strong sense of justice and integrity and couldn't tolerate what wasn't "right" in the world. He never intentionally wronged anyone and wouldn't allow it done to him in return. He was a gentleman and treated women with courtesy and expected others to do likewise. He was strong, yet gentle. Hard crusted, but with a tender side. He was a patriot. Like Wayne, he was a man's man. His appreciation for the actor also stemmed from his own male influences as a boy. Henry's father and his Uncle Ed (the man who'd raised him) were both just such men as well.

No Duke this evening, however, as the NBC nightly news had come on but Henry was deep in his own thoughts and hadn't noticed or cared. He was thinking about the letter that had come that day. It only occurred randomly a couple of times per year but each and every time one showed up it still disturbed him. He didn't let on to Millie, but she was right. The sight of that envelope and the handwriting on the outside had stirred emotions in a place Henry didn't like to go. After another sip from his glass, it was almost time to refresh it. It had been a very long time since it all had happened, yet it seemed only a moment ago. He was much younger then and he was a different person. He believed in people and trusted them. Before he had learned how to distance himself and control his emotions, he had been vulnerable. *I was weaker then*, he thought to himself. One day in 1953 had changed all of that.

"Hmmm," he hummed to himself noticing all that remained in the glass were a few melting ice cubes. He got up and headed to the kitchen for round two. He dumped the used ice into the sink and started fresh. As he poured the whiskey he noticed that dusk had set in. It was still light out now, when at this same time a week ago it had already been dark. The days were lengthening. Spring was on the doorstep. *Good deal*, he thought.

Stirring the ice with his finger, he glanced over to the stove. Millie's feast sat poised waiting for him to ravage it. They had long ago developed this current routine. She would prepare his dinner and leave it in various pots and containers on the stove or countertop so that he could eat it at his convenience. When she'd first come to work for him, she'd pleaded with him to permit her to stay later allowing her to serve him a hot dinner on the table and then clean up the dishes afterwards. She said that an important man such as Henry eating a warmed-up meal "wasn't civilized." However, Henry wouldn't have it. In his estimation, Millie already dedicated enough long hours to his service and he could tend to himself just fine. He had spent the better part of his adult life eating out of necessity between business meetings or on the run and he preferred to eat when he wanted it, to satisfy his own whims. She had a life too, he'd say, "so get after it and don't worry one extra second about me." He felt perfectly capable of rinsing off a few dishes and putting the remaining food away. The following morning she would load and run the dishwasher. It wasn't the typical behavior one would expect from a multi-millionaire but then again, Henry Engel was anything but typical. It was their system, and it worked just fine for both of them.

He peeled the foil back on the 13" x 9" Pyrex clear glass dish to sneak a peek at the golden fried chicken contained inside. He remembered a saying his Uncle Ed had been fond of when Henry was a kid on the farm and he said it aloud to himself, "What's better than fried chicken? More fried chicken!" He pinched a small corner between his right thumb and index finger and pulled a sample from the breast closest to him.

"Mm ... mm!" he cooed as he savored it. "Jacob, my dear Millie is the best," he exclaimed as he replaced the foil. This sort of personal commentary wasn't something Henry would have shared with Millie but when speaking with Jake, Henry could let his guard down. After all of their conversations over the years, Jake had never betrayed him yet.

As good as the chicken tasted and as hungry as he was, nothing could interrupt the second half of his meeting. Henry had priorities and mental health trumped hunger every time. He had a new coin magazine to peruse and he decided that now was a good opportunity to crack it open. He strolled back to the family room and once again found solace in his comfortable chair. The table next to it possessed a magazine/publication rack below the table top and Millie had neatly placed today's arrival, the latest *Smithsonian Magazine*, along with the others that had come this week in it. He thumbed through a couple of the half-dozen choices before he saw the cover of the *Coin Universe* he was searching for.

Henry had become interested in numismatics, or coin collecting, decades before after viewing the collection of a former friend. They were no longer in contact but Henry had cultivated what was originally a passing amusement into what now had become a raging passion. Since his pseudo-retirement from active business life, he had ample time and financial means to pursue this love of numismatics at the highest level. His current emphasis was devoted to studying early American Colonial and Federal coinage but he'd previously built, and still owned, many complete sets including one of the finest known sets of Buffalo nickels ever assembled. He possessed a particularly good eye for premium quality examples for their assigned grade and this gave him a competitive advantage in the marketplace. His expertise combined with his picky tastes had earned Henry a reputation within the hobby circles he moved in as an elite collector who had constructed a phenomenal collection.

Opening the cover he followed his normal protocol and scanned the table of contents for stories or news of particular interest. He would ultimately review every page of the issue but that would be either after dinner or tomorrow as time allowed. Right now, however, dinner was calling and the final segment of today's meeting would permit him to read something interesting if it caught his eye.

Henry selected a piece on page 35 relating to the origins of the United States Mint in Philadelphia as his target. He was a true numismatist. He was a student of the hobby as well as a collector and was always interested in learning something new to him. He adjusted the angle of his glasses to mitigate the glare from the lamp next to him and took another swallow from his glass, noting that there was less than half left in it.

Feeling relaxed, he then turned his attention back to the article. As he read through it, he quickly realized that it was somewhat parochial and didn't offer any new information or insight he wasn't already privy to. That was ok, however, as Henry was a "glass half full" kind of guy. Rather than see reading it as a waste of time, he felt gratified that he already knew as much or more than the author. This same attitude had served him well in his business life. Henry had succeeded where others had not because of his belief that everything had value. He could find opportunity where others only saw failure and had made that skill pay off handsomely time and again.

In any event, it had been another successful meeting with his friend Jake. He closed the magazine and laid it on the table as he rose. The last cool swallow of whiskey was sliding down his throat as he sauntered into the kitchen. He was hungry now and he placed his glass in the sink as he turned his attention to the dinner Millie had provided for him.

# CHAPTER 4

## "Socks"

THE NEXT MORNING Henry awoke to another bright and glorious day. He'd slept fairly well and was in a fine mood as he poured a cup of coffee for himself. Millie always set the timer on the automatic coffeemaker to brew for 7:00 a.m. That way, by the time Henry had gotten up, showered, and shaved, his morning coffee would be waiting for him when he came downstairs. Through the week, Henry didn't eat breakfast. It was a habit developed during his business life that he maintained into retirement. He'd managed to stretch his waking time back to 6:30–7:00 a.m. from its former 5:00 a.m. but the "lack of breakfast habit" was ingrained in him forever. Conversely, he enjoyed a robust breakfast on the weekends, but during the week, two cups of coffee splashed with cream were the norm.

Pouring the coffee, he noticed the dishes from last night's meal stacked in the sink. He'd have to remember to compliment Millie when she arrived today. She was a great cook, but her fried chicken and biscuits were always a treat to behold.

He peered out the rear kitchen window against the bright morning sunlight. Taking a swallow from his cup, he began mentally taking note of the early season chores he needed to accomplish, such as opening the waterfall and pond, when he glimpsed something small and light in color moving slowly back along the tool shed. Not completely certain as to what it was, he squinted to further focus his eyes on it. He now could see it more clearly. It was the little cat he'd seen yesterday, and he was sneaking along the edge of the building headed in the direction of the garage.

"Unbelievable," he murmured aloud. *What is wrong with this cat? Apparently the message didn't get through.* He took another sip from his cup and placed it on the island as he headed to the hall closet by the front door. Extracting his jacket, he moved through the kitchen and then the laundry room toward the exterior door on the side of the house. With a turn of the knob he was outside and stepping down the porch in the direction of the shed and garage.

He couldn't see anything. Where the cat had been a moment ago, there was nothing now. He walked back to the shed and then around the outside of it, but it wasn't there. He scanned the back yard, again nothing. Walking over to the garage, he inspected the area and it was all clear as well. However the cat had found its way back here, it now seemed to be gone. That suited Henry just fine. He got no thrill from running it off but he most definitely didn't want it hanging around either. He was walking back to the house still thinking about the stray cat when it sparked a memory of another stray animal with similar markings on its legs from his past.

\* \* \*

Henry couldn't really remember the day he first saw "Socks." He was only four years old at the time his father had brought him

home. Therefore, any recollections he had of him that first year
or two were likely more based on anecdotes that his older brother
Bill had told him years later, than actual clear memories of his
own. Socks was approximately a year old and at full size weighed
no more than 10–12 lbs. when they took him in. He had scruffy
medium brown fur, floppy ears, and four white stockings that
extended halfway up his legs. The name he was christened with
suited him perfectly.

Henry's father, Will Engel, worked at a fertilizer factory in
downtown St. Louis. It was backbreaking and dangerous work and
he toiled long hours to support his family. One day as he returned
home following his shift, he had noticed the small dog foraging
in a fallen trash can in an alley along Broadway. He had seen the
dog off and on for a couple of weeks and it looked as if it hadn't
eaten much in quite some time. He decided to take it home to his
two sons, Henry and Bill. Their mother, Esther, had passed away
just a few months earlier while attempting to deliver a would-be
little sister, and the Engel home had become a somber place for
the three of them. He hoped that this might be a tonic not just for
his sons, but for himself as well.

A clearer early recollection that Henry did have of the dog
was less pleasant. It was a memory of clutching onto Socks the day
the police officer came to Mrs. Watts' home. She was an elderly
next-door neighbor who looked after Henry and Bill when they
weren't in school and their father was at work. He remembered
vividly crying into Socks' fur as he processed the words that the
officer was telling Mrs. Watts. Their father had been killed, along
with two other men, in a terrible explosion at the factory. Henry
was seven years old at the time, Bill just eleven. Soon thereafter,

his father's brother came to take him, Bill, and Socks to Lewis, MO to live with him and their Aunt Mathilda on their farm.

When the black 1930 Ford Model A pickup pulled to the curb in front of the house, Henry remembered how anxious and afraid he'd felt but Socks kept straining at his leash to go to it. After Uncle Ed got out, Socks had broken away and run over to him. He treated him like a long-lost family member and likewise Uncle Ed engaged Socks enthusiastically. Henry had only spent limited time with his uncle on a few occasions and the warm affection that the man and the dog exchanged helped him to feel more at ease. Once their belongings were loaded, he recalled Bill sitting in the middle of the cab asking question after question about the farm. Meanwhile, Socks sat on Henry's lap with his head out the window as they drove together to Lewis and their new life.

\* \* \*

Returning to the kitchen, Henry draped his jacket over the back of the stool nearest the refrigerator. He felt the side of his coffee cup and was not surprised to find it cooler than he preferred. Taking the pot from its place on the warmer, he poured fresh hot coffee to top off the cup and stirred it in with his spoon. He glanced at the wall clock and saw that it was already 8:30 a.m. Millie would be along shortly. Raising the cup to his lips to take a "test sip," he again glanced out the window and was stunned to see the little trespasser had returned. It was now sitting right next to the tool shed where he'd seen it earlier before it had performed its Houdini impersonation and vanished.

"You've got to be kidding me," he exclaimed while putting the cup down next to the sink without ever having sampled it. Grabbing his jacket, he was out the door. Rounding the corner of the house he clearly could see his adversary facing him from across the yard not particularly seeming to be bothered by his presence. Apparently, without his chain saw he seemed less intimidating. He was mocking Henry, or so he thought. This agitated him and he broke into a gallop toward it while clapping his hands and hollering like a wild man.

"Hey, you! Get home!" he yelled with a volume and ferocity efficient enough to have cleared a small crowded movie theater just prior to show time. He was so focused on sending a definitive and lasting message that he didn't notice he had run directly over a small flower bed. Though it was not yet full of flowers, it did possess a cobblestone border that on this day would prove too much for Henry. As he crossed over it his right toe caught firmly and with one great lunge forward, he went down like a sack of potatoes as if tackled from behind. The outburst so shocked the little cat that it jumped straight up, and in mid-air turned three-quarters away from him so that when it landed again, it shot with legs scrambling across the yard away from Henry and off through the woods.

Henry didn't actually see any of this because he was too busy trying to gather his bearings and figure out what the hell had just happened to him. His glasses had been knocked off and flown several feet away but he could still see well enough because he really only needed them for reading. He lay face down for a moment as he took inventory of what may or may not have just broken on his body. The combination of adrenaline, anxiety, and embarrassment was a lot to handle for a man who hadn't yet had his morning coffee. Much to his relief, everything seemed fine and the only injury was to his pride.

He got to his feet and brushed himself off. Picking up his glasses he muttered to himself, "I'm going to feel that one tomorrow." He looked at the cobblestone and wondered how it had been able to reach up and grab him. The next thought that occurred to him was that he was glad Millie hadn't been there to see it. He imagined it was quite a sight to behold.

As he ambled sheepishly toward the back door, he paused briefly to look back in the direction he thought the cat had run. He couldn't really be sure because he was too occupied at that moment to notice but he sensed correctly that it was off to his immediate left through the forest. Shaking his head he began to chuckle. He wasn't beyond a good laugh, even if it came at his own expense.

*You win this round*, he thought to himself, rather amused at the spectacle he had just created.

Millie's car pulled up the drive at just that instant. She was early but thankfully not a moment earlier. Henry paused next to the spot where she typically parked her car and waited for her to get out.

"Well, good morning, Mr. Engel!" she said with a smile as she exited the car. "What's got you up and out so early today?"

Not wishing to divulge his bout of temporary insanity, he decided to employ the tactics any successful politician knew to use when cornered. He lied.

"Well good morning, Millie. Umm well, I was just getting a read on what needs to be done around here," he replied, sure that she'd see right through his weak and transparent attempt at diversion. He was certain she'd take one good look at him and be able to ascertain he'd been chasing a cat across the yard. Much to his relief, if Millie did see through him, she did not let on about it.

"Oh I see. Well I suppose it is that time of year again. Never too early to get a head start on a job," she said casually. *Hmm, not so fast*, he thought. Was she really indifferent or simply feigning ignorance to his ruse?

He opened the door for her and they walked into the house together. At that moment, he saw his opening to change the subject and move forward, and he seized it.

"Speaking of a head start, what are you doing here early? It's only quarter 'til nine. Millie, you know I've told you time and again you don't need to work as many hours as you already do. You surely don't need to start early."

As he spoke, she walked through the house to the hall tree where she hung her jacket and placed her purse by the base of it.

"Mr. Engel, you know it's Friday. Friday is my deep cleaning day. Got to have everything nice for the weekend for you," she chirped. Millie had long ago set aside Friday as a day to mop floors, clean bathrooms, and do general "heavy" cleaning on his house, which often didn't need it. She felt it was important everything was tip-top for him for the weekend. Henry never really questioned her on this but it didn't make a lot of sense to him because the house never really saw enough traffic to get all that dirty in the first place. That being said, since she had deemed Tuesday her "light cleaning" day perhaps it was he who didn't understand the beauty of her system. Regardless, it kept her happy so he didn't object.

She was typically perky but seemed to be in especially good humor today. Was it simply a good mood or had she perhaps been entertained by the spectacle of a grown man flying through the air and then left and returned in order to pretend she had just arrived so as not to embarrass him?

"You still haven't drank your coffee?" she quizzed him as she saw the near-full pot and the cup barely less than full. "Isn't it any good today? You want me to make another pot?" she continued.

She was on to him. He knew it for sure now. No one was that concerned about coffee.

"No need, it's fine; I just got a little sidetracked," he responded, picking up his cup. "Boy, the meal last night sure was terrific ..."

# CHAPTER 5

## Henry's Biggest Catch

"HEAVY CLEANING DAY" began as usual. Millie made an initial sweep of the entire house collecting any dirty laundry or towels she could find and started a load in the washer. With that underway, she preferred to start upstairs and work her way down. Her assault would begin in Henry's bedroom, which occupied the entire left side of the second floor. She would first clean the toilet, sink, and shower in the master bathroom. Next, she'd empty the waste basket and mop the tile floor. Upon completion of those tasks, she'd make Henry's bed, dust and polish the furniture, and conclude by sweeping the hardwood floors in the bedroom and the adjoining hallway. The rest of the second floor, consisting of two more bedrooms and an additional bathroom, required little attention. They were almost never used and their doors hardly were ever even opened. The original owner had several children and his family required this space but Henry did not.

Henry kept the bedroom on the front right corner of the house furnished in case he ever needed it for an overnight guest. In 23 years, that event had yet to occur. The rear bedroom had been converted into nothing more than a glorified storage unit and it was stacked high with all sorts of bric-a-brac, boxes of old magazines, and other various items that Henry had deemed "too good to throw away." Most of the things he accumulated ended up here or down in the overflowing unfinished basement.

Meanwhile, Henry spent the morning in his office. It sat in the front left corner of the first floor, beneath his bedroom, and was accessed from both the family room and entry hall by doors that permanently stood open. Along the front windows, a series of low-rise bookcases held a vast collection of books and resources related to numismatics and American history, two of Henry's favorite pursuits. His antique oak roll top desk was strategically positioned against the side wall so that he could easily gaze out the front windows to his left at his leisure. This had once been a formal sitting room and then a playroom for the previous owner's children but it now served perfectly as the command center of his empire.

To the right of his desk, along the inside wall, was a credenza that was designated for his computer, printer, and fax machine. Next to it, three file cabinets held the evidence of a life in business and his current important documents. Standing alone in the inside corner between the two doorways was a large black steel gun safe with a large brass dial, handle, and accents. Henry wasn't a gun collector. This was where he stored the rare coins not kept in his safe deposit boxes at the bank along with whatever other valuables he kept in the house.

A former employee had contacted Henry and asked him to review a business plan that he was formulating. The man was considering launching a business and wanted to hear what he thought his prospects for success were. Henry was always more than willing to lend his expertise to an aspiring entrepreneur and had consented to give it a look. He remembered and valued the help he'd received himself as a young man from his first boss, Mr. Schuetz, and saw mentoring others as a way to repay that kindness.

As he studied its pages he leaned back in his black leather chair and occasionally used a bright orange highlighter to stripe the sections of the text in front of him. At the same time, every so often he'd lean forward and take pen in hand to make notes on a yellow legal pad. Before long it was early afternoon and Millie was in his doorway asking about lunch.

"Are you getting hungry?" she asked.

Lost in thought, he was startled to see the clock read 12:25 p.m. already. "Yes, I guess it's that time, huh? Gimme a few minutes and I'll be in. I've almost got this licked," he replied and redirected his attention to the final section of the proposal.

"All right then. Do you want that leftover chicken from last night heated up or shall I make you a sandwich?" she said back to him, already halfway across the family room and heading to the kitchen.

"The chicken!" he called back, remembering the previous night's meal with fondness.

"I thought so," she said quietly to herself as she passed the table. It was set for one and the leftovers from last evening's chicken dinner, *already heated*, awaited Henry. As usual, Millie was on her game.

A few moments later, he strolled into the room happy to see everything waiting for him. Millie sat on the stool closest to the refrigerator eating half of a tuna salad sandwich and paging through the *Lewis Gazette*.

Henry took his usual lunch seat, the chair closest to the French doors, and began to fill his plate from the assorted dishes on the table in front of him.

In all of their years together, Millie and Henry had never eaten a single meal at the same table. Moreover, it wasn't often that they even ate at the same time or in the same room. Typically, Henry ate around noon at the table or at his desk, while Millie preferred to graze off and on throughout the day while attending to her duties and when she did sit down to eat something, it was always on the stool she currently occupied.

Their seating arrangement wasn't some sort of racially motivated issue; neither Henry nor Millie held one iota of prejudice toward the other. It wasn't sexism, class warfare, or one of Henry's rules either. In fact, it wasn't even something that they had ever even spoken one word about. It was simply the way they did things from day one and neither of them gave it a second thought. It was just routine and it felt normal to them.

"I noticed this morning the disposal's been leaking. When I was underneath there, I saw Jake got a wet foot," she said looking at the cabinet below the sink where Henry stored his whiskey bottle and Millie kept her cleaning supplies.

"No kidding? Well we certainly can't have that," he replied with false indignation.

"Yeah, it wasn't a huge puddle but if that keeps up that wood will get to warping and then it'll seep down and start to pop up the tile," she said as if predicting the eventual demise of civilization as they knew it.

"Yep, we'll get after it," he agreed. "I've got a couple of other things I need done so I'll get a hold of Louis and see when he can take a look at it. Good enough?"

"Good enough," she answered with a tone of approval as if *she* was the homeowner.

Most of Henry's afternoon was spent doing paperwork in his office. There were checks to write and bills to pay. On the positive side of the ledger, there were several checks that had come in this week including a rather sizable dividend from an investment he held. Each needed to be recorded in his ledger, endorsed, and listed for deposit during his weekly Saturday morning visit to the bank. Equally as pressing, he had a letter to answer from an attorney regarding a zoning issue related to some real estate he owned. Also, there was an insurance proposal to consider and for good measure, if he got bored, a three-inch stack of prospectuses from mutual funds that he invested in, which had been accumulating for several weeks. The only interruption to his work was his walk to the mailbox just before 3:00 p.m., which brought two more small checks for deposit and the latest issue of *TIME* magazine.

While Henry was occupied, Millie moved around the first floor with precision. She cleaned, washed, stacked, sorted, dusted, vacuumed, mopped, wiped, and scoured everything in sight. Henry thought things were clean Friday morning. Millie made sure of it by Friday afternoon.

By 4:30 p.m. all was completed and for good measure a meat loaf was in the oven. She'd set the timer on the stove for 55 minutes and had written a reminder on a Post-it note and placed it on the microwave door at eye level for good measure. Green beans and sweet corn were already in pots sitting atop the burners alongside a handful of dinner rolls wrapped in foil needing only to be heated for a few moments while the meat loaf cooled. A bowl of cinnamon applesauce and a slice of peach pie she'd brought from home waited in the refrigerator.

Knowing that she was done for the day she walked into the office to check in with Henry. It was nearly 5:00 p.m. and time for her to go and for him to get to his meeting.

"Anything else you need from me today, Mr. Engel?" she asked with her purse in hand.

"No ma'am. I think we both have had enough for today, don't you?" he said while picking up a plain envelope from his desk and handing it to her.

Knowing that it was her weekly paycheck, she took the envelope from his hand. "You ain't lying," she exhaled in her thick Southern Georgia accent with a tired smile on her face.

"Thank you, sir," she said as she placed it in her purse and zipped it closed.

"No, thank you, Millie," he responded as he stood from his chair.

She turned and they both exited from the office. It was almost 5:00 p.m. and she was headed home to a hot bath and a good book. Henry had an important meeting to get to. Crossing through the kitchen, she paused and went over the instructions for his dinner as if he was a 13 year old and the timer and note might not be enough of a reminder. Satisfied she had done all she could to assure he was properly fed, and sensing she had beaten the topic to death she finished with, "All right then, you better get to your meeting. I'll see you again," and she headed out the door to her car. If there was a better housekeeper in all of the Midwest or a better person for that matter, Henry wouldn't have believed it.

Stepping over to the sink, he felt some stiffness in his back as he leaned over to open the cabinet door beneath it. Assuming it was from sitting in his office chair all day, he didn't pay much attention to it. However, when he stood back upright with bottle in hand, it pulsed again.

As he went for a glass from the cabinet, his eyes briefly glanced out the window and caught a glimpse of the flower bed where he'd performed his acrobatics exhibition that morning. He was quickly reminded of the fall which was the cause of his discomfort.

"Yeah, that was dumb," he thought out loud, mocking himself as he filled his glass with ice. Returning to the sink he added his perfect three count pour to it and topped the glass with water from the tap. Stirring it briefly with his index finger, the first installment of Friday's meeting was complete and he and Jake could get underway. He took a large swallow from his glass and upon the whiskey clearing his throat he let out a discernible "Ahh."

It was getting late in the day but after having spent the majority of it indoors in his office, he decided he wanted to sit outside for a bit. He opted for the front porch over the back patio in favor of the sunset that would be unfolding in the next hour. Cloaked in his favorite tan khaki jacket, he sat down on the aluminum park bench to the left of the front door and immediately could feel the cool of the metal through his pants.

"Not quite spring yet," he said to no one in particular. It was probably not the wisest move to sit in the cool air on a cold metal bench with a stiffening back, but at that moment he didn't care. It was the first outdoor meeting of the year and he immediately remembered why he enjoyed it so much.

As he sat there, he surveyed his surroundings while occasionally sipping from his drink and letting his mind clear. His thoughts drifted. The sun was lazily making its way down through the western sky opposite him. He could hear the song of the frogs floating up the hill from the pond below. This was the first evening he could recall hearing them this year and he was pleased because it was another confirmation that winter had ended and spring was breaking out all over. The sounds reminded him of another pond in Lewis and another time in his life.

\* \* \*

As a boy on the farm, Henry would lay awake at night and listen to the frogs in Old Man Janson's pond through his bedroom window. The Janson's farm was next to his uncle's and the pond, which was just over an acre in size, sat just on their side of the property line. It made for a good fishing hole and habitat for wildlife while serving to provide a ready water source for the couple dozen head of cattle that Mr. Janson kept.

Henry and Bill often went there to fish or to catch frogs in the summertime. One sunny Saturday afternoon in 1934, the brothers had decided to go fishing and had set up camp along a shady bank under a grove of trees. A dead elm that had fallen into the pond long before they were born provided good cover for fish and made it a favorite spot for the young anglers. The boys sunk their cane poles in the bank and sat, along with Socks, waiting for a strike while eating peanut butter and jelly sandwiches they had brought from home.

They had good fortune that day and landed several nice blue gill over the course of an hour or so. As Bill was retrieving another prize to add to their day's catch, Socks perked up and began to bark. Henry looked to see what had captured the dog's attention and saw that a young boy, approximately the same age as Henry, was walking toward them. He was blonde haired and blue eyed and just a little shorter than Henry.

"Hi!" he called out to them. "You guys catching many fish?"

"Yep, we've got a bunch on the stringer," Henry replied proudly. Bill was occupied with removing his latest catch and didn't look up.

"Nifty," he said, seeming not especially interested in fish as he turned his attention to Socks who by this time was at his feet and giving him the once over. "Is this your dog?"

"Yeah, that's Socks. He doesn't bite," Bill joined in now.

"Neat dog, hey pal!" the boy said as he knelt down and gave Socks an affectionate scruff behind his ears. Socks clearly appreciated the attention as he repaid it with generous licks to the boy's hands and face, which were met with giggles from the recipient.

"Hey, that tickles. Come on now," he said rising to avoid the kisses.

"I'm Henry and this is my brother Bill. We live over there," Henry said as he pointed through the trees and across the field to his uncle's house and barns.

"Yeah I know," the boy answered back. "My grandpa told me. He said you guys used to live in St. Louis; that's where I live. My name is George. My Dad runs a shoe factory there. I come out here sometimes in the summer to spend time with my grandpa and grandma."

George spoke as he walked over to the elm that protruded out into the water. He climbed over the petrified exposed roots that had been unearthed when it fell and onto the trunk. It was smooth and silvery gray, having shed its bark many years before. As he did, a couple of lounging turtles, which had been sunning themselves on the far end of the log, slid into the safety of the water.

"Why don't you guys fish out here?" he called, pointing to the end of the tree that extended roughly 30 feet out into the pond.

"We can't," Henry answered with a tone of embarrassment.

"Well, why the heck not?" George asked as he walked further out onto the log. "This is a great spot!"

"Our uncle won't let us," Bill stepped in. "We can't swim."

"I'm afraid of the water," Henry confessed without being prodded to do so.

"Oh, makes sense to be afraid if you can't swim I guess," George responded without any judgment in his voice as he walked out onto the fallen tree. "I can; my Dad taught me when I was little but lots of guys can't, so what? Hey, how old are you guys?" he called out, changing the subject as he sat down to remove his shoes so he could swing his feet in the water.

"I'm nine and he's thirteen," Henry answered back.

"No kidding? I'm nine too!" George replied excitedly as he removed his socks and placed them on top of the shoes, which were now resting next to him.

Bill decided that a jug of lemonade was worth a walk back to the house and took Socks along as a companion to retrieve it.

"Keep an eye on those poles!" he instructed Henry as he and Socks trotted away across the field.

"Yeah, I got it," Henry acknowledged sitting down on the bank between the poles.

"I'll help!" George chimed in. From his vantage point out on the log he could see the tips of both poles and add a second pair of eyes to stand watch. He gently swirled his toes in the water and continued his conversation with Henry.

A few moments had passed when suddenly the pole on the

left began to bob up and down with small random whips of motion.

"Hey, I think we've got something!" Henry cried out to George and stood to grab the pole. At that instant, George noticed the other pole had begun to bounce more violently than the first one.

"You've got two somethings, Henry! Look!"

Henry grabbed the first pole and began to bring the fish in as he cried out to George, "Hey, get over here and grab this other pole!"

George jumped to his feet with great enthusiasm. As he raced toward shore, he knocked his socks and one of his shoes into the water. Henry was battling the fish on the first pole when he heard the thud of George's head against the log. It was an eerie, dull sound, like a dropped melon smacking the floor. By the time he looked over at him, George's lifeless body had flopped sideways off the log and slid into the water, face down.

"George!" Henry shrieked in terror. He flung the pole away and sprinted to the base of the tree, which was just a few yards away. He stopped frozen in his tracks when he got there, looking at the water. George's motionless body floated 15 feet away from him.

"Help!" he screamed as he looked first to his uncle's house and then in all directions.

"Please help!" he cried out again. The Janson place was over a hill and there was no way to see or tell if anyone could even hear him. He looked back at George, then at the water. *There is no time*, he thought. *No time. It's up to me.*

With all of the courage he could mobilize, he climbed up over the roots and onto the log. He was terrified but the adrenaline of the moment had empowered him. Without another thought, he dashed in an instant across the tree to where George was floating. He could see a red tinge of blood on the wood where George's head had struck the log. George was only a couple feet away from him now but it was just outside of Henry's outstretched arms. He was starting to feel lightheaded as he hyperventilated from both his fear of the water as well as the horror that George must be dead.

At that instant, George's left leg jerked a few inches to the side and his torso twisted slightly. Henry could see a faint cloud of red in the green water surrounding his head. George was still alive!!

He dropped to his belly and reached as far as he possibly could stretch, almost slipping off the log and into the pond himself. With the last inch of reach he could possibly muster, his finger tips on his right hand were just able to grab George's left index finger. He yanked with all of his might and jerked George toward him. Having now taken a firmer position on the fallen tree, he grabbed George's wrist and rolled him over as he pulled him to the log. George had a small gash over his right eye that had swollen closed to the point where it was only bleeding slightly now.

He was starting to regain consciousness and was coughing violently as his lungs cleared of the pond water he'd ingested. Henry couldn't lift him out of the water because he wasn't strong enough. *George is practically the same size as me*, he thought. *How can I get him out of the pond?* He hatched a plan to pull George along as he crawled atop the log toward shore, all the while keeping George's head above the water.

A moment later, they made it to shore. Henry jumped down off the log to pull George, now conscious and crying, completely out of the water and onto the grassy sloped bank. He was going to be ok. Henry had saved his life. This boy, named George, would be the biggest catch Henry ever made.

* * *

The sun was nearly lost over the horizon as Henry realized he'd lost all track of time. He looked at his glass, which now only held a few bits of melted ice and water and stood to head inside for his refill. As he opened the storm door, he could hear the melodic beeping of the timer on the stove and smell the aroma of something burning.

"Aww dammit!" he exclaimed as he rushed down the hallway and into the kitchen where a thin haze of smoke hung around the lights over the island. The clock on the wall read 5:50 p.m. Whatever happened from here, he'd be damned if he'd let Millie find out that after her timer, her note, and the redundant instructional seminar he had *still* burned his dinner. Hurriedly he set his glass on the counter and grabbed a pair of oven mitts from the drawer next to the sink. He expected he would find a baked brick when he opened the oven door but was relieved to find the damage manageable. While the juices had indeed baked away leaving a black smoking residue in the bottom of the glass pan around the meat, other than some crusty edges, the lion's share was still largely edible even if it was a little drier than he would have preferred.

With disaster averted and seeing Jake still sitting and waiting for the second half of their meeting, Henry figured he had the whole weekend to deal with the incident before Millie returned on Monday. He would air out the house and soak the pan in baking soda overnight but for the moment that could wait. Business had to come first.

# CHAPTER 6

## Off to Lewis

T HE FOLLOWING MORNING, Henry steered his navy blue 1996 Ford Explorer out of the driveway at 7:40 a.m. headed toward Lewis. As he did, he took his travel cup from the center console and took a swallow of the fresh coffee before replacing it. Next to him, in the passenger's seat, his briefcase occupied its usual place. Resting on top of it was a yellow legal pad on which he had jotted a short list of items that he intended to purchase while he was in town. He adjusted the volume on his radio and turned the heat on low to remove the overnight chill from the cabin.

Lewis was located roughly 10 miles to the southwest, just a short 15-minute drive through the countryside. The town was originally founded in 1813 as a small military outpost constructed during the War of 1812. It was given its name in honor of Meriwether Lewis, the famous explorer and soldier who had died just years before, in 1809. However, none of the present-day inhabitants could explain why his was the name selected for this place as he had never even set foot here. In any event, a small monument with a plaque bearing his likeness stood in the town square and served as an occasional photo opportunity for a random tourist who happened to be passing through or as a backdrop for some teens in homecoming attire.

Following the war, the small fortification had been abandoned but a trading post and farming community of a few dozen people had taken root. The sleepy little town grew slowly over the next 130 years until the appearance of the Allied Gas Co. and the big money it brought with it changed the landscape. The boom that occurred in the area in the late 1940s and 1950s would triple the footprint of the town itself and nearly quadruple the population.

Modern-day Lewis was home to 3,753 residents according to the sign posted outside of town. It was hard to tell, because the city limits extended over a vast area and things were spread out, but no one seemed to care or had ever questioned why the sign had gone unchanged for years.

It was essentially divided into two sections unofficially referred to by the locals as "Old Town" and "New Town." Old Town was composed of the buildings built on the original site where the fort had stood, with many dating from 1900–1920 and one, the Lewis Bank & Trust Building, dating all the way back into the late 1800s. They were lined up and down either side of Main Street and sprawled over two city blocks. Around this middle stood many of the oldest homes in Lewis as well as its original church, Calvary Lutheran built in 1848, and the town's only cemetery.

A quarter mile south of the end of Main Street, New Town began. Over the past five decades it had been the site of all of the commercial growth in the area. Currently, it held most of the modern offerings one could hope for in a small town. There were ample retail outlets of all sizes, kinds, and varieties as well as several restaurants and diners including a brand new McDonald's, which was especially popular with the younger citizens of Lewis. With two gas stations, two grocery stores, three taverns, and a Walmart, Lewis could hold its own with any other small town in middle America and now seemed downright metropolitan to those who had lived there all of their lives.

Saturday was Henry's day to conduct his banking affairs and any business that he needed to attend to in Lewis. He generally only visited the bank once per week and liked to arrive there around 8:00 a.m. After completing matters there, he would always head over to The Eager Beaver Diner for breakfast. When that was concluded, he'd visit Hendrick's Mercantile and/or Walmart for whatever odds and ends were needed at home. After that, if the need presented itself, he'd pay a visit to Lou's Barber Shop for a haircut. Sometimes, if in the mood, on his way out of town he would swing past his favorite ice cream parlor, The Old Farm Dairy, for a two-scoop cone to enjoy on the drive back home. The whole endeavor typically chewed up the morning and put him back at Oak Forest by early to mid-afternoon.

The morning was somewhat overcast but the sun occasionally broke through the clouds to Henry's left illuminating the patchwork of fields and forest along the graying asphalt. Just shy of one mile down the road from his mailbox, he passed the Ferguson place on his right and looked over to see if anyone was moving around outside. It was a small one-story frame home with a detached two-car garage and he noted that all was quiet.

He hummed along with the country music playing on the radio while looking outside to assess the progress that spring was making in its annual arrival. A few miles further down the road, about three miles outside of Lewis, he passed the Janson farm and the former site of his Uncle Ed and Aunt Mathilda's home. He saw the pond where he had saved George's life so many decades before.

\* \* \*

Henry remembered that after that day, he and George had become best friends. George didn't have any siblings but Henry became like a brother to him. In the summer when George came to stay with his grandparents, the boys were inseparable. During the school year, they would take turns visiting each other as well. George would sometimes come to Lewis, and at other times, Uncle Ed would drive Henry to St. Louis to stay for the weekend with the Schuetz family. The Schuetz's enjoyed having Henry in their home and over time George's father, in particular, grew very fond of him.

George Schuetz, Sr. was an exceedingly successful business-man. He was the second-generation owner of the Schuetz Shoe Co., which George's paternal grandfather, Joseph, had founded in 1883 when he immigrated to America from Germany. The thriving business was a major employer in St. Louis and it pro-vided Mr. Schuetz with both a generous income and a great deal of power and influence within the local business community. Joseph Schuetz was still living in those days and Henry recalled how the elder man would often come to George's home for din-ner and to discuss business with his son, George Sr. The men would stay at the dining room table, long after the dishes were cleared, puffing on cigars and discussing every facet of the opera-tion. They would always encourage the boys, Henry and George Jr., to listen in on their conversations. Henry didn't realize it back then, but the principles and strategies of business that he learned from the Schuetz's would be invaluable to him and would propel him to a successful career of his own. He also hadn't realized that he and George were being groomed for positions within the Schuetz Shoe Co. that they would eventually assume. *Those were good men and good times*, Henry thought to himself.

*   *   *

Henry pulled off of the county road and onto Main Street right on schedule. He would be at the bank at 8:00 a.m. sharp and felt satisfied with himself as he downed the last drops of his coffee. He rolled through Old Town admiring the classic architecture of the buildings. He could remember how it was when he was a boy growing up here and it wasn't so very different today. A few of the businesses had closed or relocated into New Town but for the most part it still had the same look and comfortable feel it had back then. He liked that. It was what had brought him back here to live. It was charming and comfortable and he had a history here. Due to his business travels, he had seen the world and what it had to offer and it had come up wanting when compared to Lewis. He looked off to his left and saw the Calvary Lutheran Church and Cemetery. He had a history there too. It was the place where he had gotten married. It was also the place where he had laid a loved one to rest.

He passed out of Old Town and through the brief cluster of homes that transitioned like a time machine to the New Town section of Lewis. Seemingly to further cement the psychological transformation from past to present, the name of the street changed at the end of Old Town from Main Street to Hughes Avenue, though the same piece of pavement made one straight continuous run through the heart of town. The city fathers had voted unanimously for this tribute back in 1960 in homage to one of the founders of Allied Gas Co. The honor was bestowed on a man named Johnny Hughes who had donated a large sum from his business profits to build a community center, which was still in widespread use today.

As Henry proceeded, now on Hughes Avenue, the first commercial building he came to was the "new" Lewis Bank & Trust building. This free-standing structure, erected in 1978, replaced the original site of the banking enterprise, which stood in Old Town and now was known as the "old" Lewis Bank & Trust building. That former location was currently owned and maintained by the local chamber of commerce and served as a civic museum. Not only was the Lewis Bank & Trust the oldest bank in Lewis, MO dating back to the late nineteenth century, it also was the oldest business in town.

Henry engaged his turn signal and steered the Explorer smoothly to his right and into the empty parking lot, easing it gently to a halt in the space closest to the door. He looked at his watch and nodded approvingly as he saw that it read 7:59 a.m. He placed the gear shift in park and turned the key to kill the engine.

Just then, a slender young woman with sandy brown hair wearing a light blue blouse and tan slacks appeared in the bank doorway to unlock the door. She was a familiar figure and he immediately identified her as Amanda Knox, a conscientious 28-year-old employee with aspirations of running the operation someday. She was as much of a fixture on Saturdays at the bank as Henry was, having missed only two over the course of the six years she had been employed there. Henry admired her responsibility and enthusiasm for her job and always enjoyed their exchanges.

He grabbed the handle of the dark brown leather briefcase

next to him and exited the vehicle. As he pulled the front door of the bank open, he could smell the aroma of fresh coffee brewing in the reception area.

"Well, good morning Mr. Engel!" bubbled the attractive young lady who had just unlocked the door. Her face radiated a broad smile and her bright blue eyes projected a genuine excitement about being at the bank early on a Saturday that perhaps only Henry could relate to.

"Good morning, Amanda," Henry replied. "How are you today?"I'm just great, sir, thank you. How about yourself?" she said as she straightened some brochures that were standing on a rack just inside the door.

"Ohhh, I may not be hitting them all out of the park," he said with a mild laugh while pausing briefly, "but I'm still swinging!" Following the exchange he continued toward the teller windows.

"Good morning. How are you today?" The forced monotone greeting came from Sara Hamilton, the middle-aged heavy-set woman sitting behind the counter. In contrast to Amanda, she rarely ever worked on a Saturday morning and did not seem happy about being there on this one either. Her lack of pride in her work was evident and she never even bothered to look up at Henry as she sorted through her cash drawer. Her demeanor might have been the result of her long marriage to the reigning town drunk, Eddie Hamilton, or due to her general discontent with her own lackluster existence. Regardless, she wore her misery on her sleeve and had no intention of disguising it for anyone.

"Good morning, I'm just fine," Henry answered in a decidedly less friendly tone than he had just been using with Amanda. He had no use for Sara and didn't mind if she knew it. Every time he had ever encountered her she was either surly or busy telling whomever was within earshot how bad her day was and how hard things were for her. In his estimation, she was a professional "loser" who thrived on the attention she believed it garnered her. He surmised that her lot in life was largely the consequence of her own decisions and he could not tolerate people who played the "victim card" rather than accepting responsibility and working toward improvement.

He himself had come from a very difficult childhood, had experienced great losses, and had worked hard to earn everything that he now possessed, mostly with a smile on his face. Just after his father had been killed, Uncle Ed had told him, "Henry, you can let this beat you or build you. Lots of folks have a hard life. It's an *excuse* for failure, not a reason. Life is what *you* make of it." These were the most important words that anyone ever said to him.

"Hi Henry!" called a man's voice amicably from the doorway of a large private office to the left of the counter. "I thought I heard you out there. Please c'mon in."

The voice belonged to Tom Donaldson, who was the president of the bank. He was a short, husky man, in his early fifties. He had lived in Lewis his entire life and Henry had attended school with both his father and mother. Whenever they met, Tom greeted Henry with the respect and warmth afforded a person who has known you and your family for a lifetime. The fact that Henry was the bank's single largest depositor also certainly didn't hurt matters either.

"How are you today, sir?" Tom asked as the men shook hands.

"I'm doing pretty well. How about yourself, Tom?" Henry responded as he sat down in one of the two matching burgundy leather cushioned chairs facing Tom's desk. He placed his brief-case next to him on the seat of the other.

"I'm doing fine, thanks," Tom said as he moved around to the high-backed black leather chair stationed on the opposite side.

"Hey, I was just talking to Dad this week and he was asking about you. He asked me to say 'Hello' and to give you his best the next time I saw you."

"Oh yeah?" Henry said raising his eyebrows as he slid the brass latches open on the briefcase. "That's awfully nice. Please pass along my well wishes to him and your mom too when you talk to him. Are they still down in Florida?"

"Yeah, going on five years now. After Dad retired from Allied he said he was going to find someplace warm to sit around and drink beer and I guess he meant it." At that, both men laughed.

Henry pulled a large manila envelope from his case and laid it on Tom's desk. Inside of it were all of the checks that Henry had accumulated this week along with a completed deposit slip.

"This all we have for today, Henry?" Tom asked as he stood and picked up the envelope.

"Yes sir, that'll take care of me," Henry replied.

"Very good; you want a cup of coffee while you wait?" he asked as he paused at the doorway with the envelope.

"No thanks, Tom, already had a cup and I'm off to breakfast after this. Thanks though."

"You bet," Tom called back as he circled behind the counter. He proceeded to the vacant teller's window next to where Sara was waiting on the morning's second customer. Henry slid his right hand into his pocket and slowly rubbed the large silver coin he carried with him between his fingers as he waited. It only took a few moments for Tom to process the checks and prepare the receipt. Once that was done, he opened the drawer beneath the counter to retrieve the amount that Henry had indicated on the slip that he wanted to receive in cash rather than deposit.

Returning to his office, Tom paused to count out the green paper bills on the desk in front of Henry. With both men satisfied that the amount was correct, he then handed Henry a bank envelope to carry the funds in. Henry pulled five twenties, three tens, and four fives from the stack to carry in his wallet. He put the remainder into the envelope, which he then placed into the briefcase.

"Are you going to visit your safe deposit boxes this morning?" Tom asked, knowing that Henry more often than not did just that during a visit to the bank.

"Nah, not this trip. Maybe next time," he responded while getting to his feet with his briefcase in hand.

Henry actually had 11 safe deposit boxes in the bank. Inside of them he stored all sorts of documents and valuables including a substantial quantity of gold and his most prized physical possessions, his rare coin collection. Periodically, he would swap out portions of the collection to take back home where he could view, study, and enjoy the pieces in person. While those coins were in his possession, he kept them stored in the safe in his office. When it suited him, he'd return the coins to the bank vault and withdraw another group for a visit. Lewis had little crime to speak of at the time and almost no one short of Lucy, his mail carrier, and Millie likely even knew that he collected coins. However, Henry's collection was valued at just over seven figures so he believed the extra security measures were warranted.

If Tom knew anything of this, he most certainly never let on to another living soul or ever said a word of it to Henry. He had prepared many cashier's checks payable to coin dealers on Henry's behalf over the years but never spoke a word of it to anyone. He simply did as directed and treated a $50,000 check the same as if it was for a few hundred dollars. It was good business and Tom Donaldson, like Henry, was a good businessman. Privacy was of the utmost importance at the bank and if there was any reason why Henry kept the lion's share of his valuables there, it was because of this, and not because of any personal relationships he had with the bank president or his parents.

The two men walked out from the office and exchanged a few more words before parting company with another handshake. An older couple stood behind a young man in line waiting for their turn at the teller window. When they saw Henry, they exchanged greetings with him. There were few people in town who didn't know who Lewis' most affluent citizen was and, of that number, the vast majority thought well of him.

As he strolled toward the main entrance, he once again passed by the coffee pot in the reception area and its delightful aroma permeated the air. He was getting hungry now and was glad that breakfast was his next order of business. Reaching for the door, he heard a voice call to him from behind, "Have a great day, Mr. Engel!"

It was Amanda. She was seated at a desk on the far wall serving a customer yet had still made the effort to wish him off.

He turned to her and with a wave and a wink called back, "Will do. Hope you do the same, kiddo." *She is a sharp girl*, he thought to himself as he walked outside. He expected that someday he'd be visiting *her* in the big office.

# CHAPTER 7

# "What's in a Name?"

THE EAGER BEAVER Diner was located three blocks down and on the opposite side of Hughes Avenue from the bank. It anchored the northern end of a retail strip plaza originally constructed in the late 1950s that was now known as the Landmark Center. The name of the complex was ironically appropriate due to the fact that the diner's vintage towering steel and neon sign depicting a cartoon-like grinning beaver complete with baseball cap was one of, if not the most widely recognized features in all of Lewis.

Over the years, many businesses had come and gone from this site but the diner always remained continuously in operation and in virtually the same configuration from day one. In addition to the eatery, the current tenants now included a hair and nail salon, an insurance office, and a Laundromat.

"The Beaver," as the locals called it, was a popular destination in Lincoln County with a glowing reputation in and beyond the city limits. The food was excellent and affordable and the atmosphere friendly and warm. It was nearly impossible to find a man, woman, or child in Lewis who hadn't ever been there at least once. In addition to the more casual patrons who occasionally frequented the diner, a robust group of "regulars" kept it an active and going concern. For many of these people, their daily or weekly visits to The Beaver were seen as an integral social event of the highest priority. Over the years, much business had been conducted, gossip exchanged, and even a few marriage proposals tendered inside its walls. If one wanted to take the pulse of Lewis, this was the place to do it.

Henry turned into the parking lot just after 8:30 a.m. Several cars and trucks were clustered against the front and side of the building, so he opted for an open spot across from the door against the curb facing the street. *It looks like a better early crowd than usual for a Saturday*, he thought as he shut off the engine and exited the vehicle.

As he crossed the lot, he could see several of the usual suspects seated inside through the full-length front glass windows that extended along the entirety of the otherwise brick building.

The entrance was a single glass door on the far left corner of the establishment. Just to its right stood a pair of newspaper boxes selling the latest editions of the *Lewis Gazette* and the *St. Louis Post-Dispatch*. Immediately inside the door, a short counter with a cash register extended five feet out from the end wall. After a break the width of a doorway, the counter resumed and ran parallel to the front windows before cornering and turning at a ninety-degree angle to the rear of the large rectangular room. Six stools sat along the face of it and two more were positioned on the end. At the turn of the counter, a three-tiered lighted glass display case held slices of a variety of fresh baked pies to entice the customers.

Behind the counter, a swinging door and a large serving

window provided access to the kitchen. A rear countertop supported several coffee pots as well as a soft drink dispenser and various other necessary appliances while providing shelter to stacks of clean dishes stored beneath it.

Past the counter, two rows of five square tables with four chairs each were flanked on the back and end walls by a series of brown vinyl booths.

The décor was pleasant, clean, and well lighted. In recent years, the wallpaper, which had become yellowed from cigarette smoke, had been replaced by a fresh coat of light almond paint and the walls were decorated with a series of photographs and mementos from the town's history. Of particular pride to the local populace was a photo, plaque, and letterman's jacket that had been mounted in the far rear corner of the diner over a booth. This was done to memorialize the town's lone state basketball championship, which Lewis High School had captured in 1976. A member of that team, Charlie Heinz, had made that spot his personal oasis and often could be found occupying the table several times per week.

As Henry pulled open the front door, a woman he was acquainted with was approaching to exit. He stepped aside quickly to hold the door open for her.

"Good morning, Henry, thanks very much," the woman said with a smile as she passed through the doorway.

"You're welcome; have a good one."

He had barely taken a step inside before he was greeted by Suzy Grainger, the daughter of the founder and current proprietor of The Eager Beaver. She was a plump woman, in her early forties and had grown up in this place. Her father Gus, now retired, had built it from the ground up and she and her daughter Jenny currently continued the family legacy.

"Well, there he is!" she announced with a sweet country accent and a broad smile. She was sorting through some receipts on the counter near the cash register.

"Well, hey there, young lady!" Henry shot right back with equal enthusiasm. "What do you know?"

"More than yesterday and less than tomorrow," she quipped.

"Smart girl ... smart girl," he laughed.

A voice called to him from the third seat at the nearly full counter.

"How ya doing, Henry?" asked a gray-bearded older man with a deep voice. He had put down his newspaper and was now peering over the top of his cup of coffee at him.

"I'm good, Hank," Henry responded as he stepped toward the man. "What's new?"

Though they shared the same name, neither would ever have dreamed of being referred to by the other's moniker. While Henry was an accomplished and polished businessman, Hank Fitzgerald was a "good ole boy" who had made his living as the town's go-to auto mechanic. Nearing retirement, he had slowed down a bit and now allowed the three others in his employ to handle the lion's share of the work, generally only stepping in to troubleshoot a tough problem.

His shop had handled Henry's automotive issues exclusively since Henry moved back to Lewis and the men knew each other well. Though they came from different backgrounds, they shared a common respect and liking for one another.

"Aww, not too much I s'pose. We've had a couple nice days, huh?" Hank continued.

Typical to any small town, when there wasn't any particularly pressing news or hot gossip to share, the conversation could always rest on the recent local weather.

"Sure have," Henry replied as he slapped Hank on the shoulder and moved toward his usual seat in the diner.

It was well known at the diner that on Saturday as well as most Sunday mornings Henry could be found in the first booth past the counter along the back wall. He had sat there religiously for years and the staff always made sure the table was set for him with both a local and a St. Louis newspaper waiting. As he made his way to his seat, he exchanged greetings and casual pleasantries with the assortment of other people gathered there, all of whom he knew. Before he could get comfortable, Suzy's daughter Jenny was filling his cup with fresh black coffee and placing a small steel pitcher of cool cream on the table in front of him.

"There you are, Mr. Engel," she said with a smile.

"Thank you, dear," he responded as he lifted the little pitcher to add cream to his coffee.

In a moment, Jenny reappeared with a tray that held Henry's breakfast. She placed a platter in front him that was dominated by a steaming three-egg, ham, and cheese omelet. Two crispy strips of honey maple bacon adorned the top of it. Next, she placed a second smaller plate with shredded golden hashed brown potatoes to his left. Finally, she sat a third plate with two slices of wheat bread toast to his right along with a small bowl containing several pads of butter that were individually wrapped in silver foil.

This was Henry's standard Saturday morning feast. He had eaten the same breakfast here on Saturdays since before Jenny was born. Suzy always made sure it was hot, ready, and waiting for him. Within moments of his arrival it appeared on his table each time, like clockwork. This scene was in stark contrast to his Sunday morning breakfast, which tended to have very little rhyme or reason and was a more relaxed affair. On Sundays, Henry would typically sip coffee and pore over the menu before ultimately settling on a selection that had piqued his interest.

He was halfway through his meal and scanning the *Gazette* when a man and two boys sat down at the table nearest to him. He immediately recognized the man as Louis Benhardt, one of the town's firemen.

Louis was a strapping 36-year-old man with a broad frame and square jaw. He was six foot tall with dark brown eyes and a matching dark brown head of hair that he kept cropped close to his head and flat on top. He was a husband and father of four, known to be one of the hardest working souls in town. Well-liked by everyone, he was affectionately nicknamed "Louis from Lewis." He and his wife Sandy, a schoolteacher at the elementary school, struggled to support their four boys aged three to thirteen. So, in addition to his full-time paid position at the firehouse, Louis took on any odd jobs he could to help make ends meet at home. He was a sort of "jack-of-all-trades" and Henry would hire him from time to time to do work at Oak Forest.

"How are we doing today, Mr. Engel?" the younger man asked.

"Hi Louis, good morning boys. You're just the man I need to see."

"Oh yeah? What's going on?" Louis inquired.

"Well, it seems Millie's been seeing some leaking from my disposal," Henry responded as he took a sip from his coffee cup.

Jenny approached Louis' table from the other direction and unwittingly interrupted their conversation.

"How's it going, fellas?" she said as she greeted them and sat a couple of menus down.

"We're doing just fine Jenny, thanks."

"Where's the rest of your crew today?" she asked him as she rested her hands on the open chair at the table.

"Sandy took the little ones with her to see her mother in Troy today so we decided to get out and see the world ourselves," he answered.

As Henry redirected his attention to his breakfast he could overhear their conversation. He remembered that Sandy was from Troy, MO, which was a larger town located just to the northwest of Lewis. He also took note of the behavior of the two boys, Josh age 13 and Sam age 11. They sat quietly and patiently waited for their father to order their breakfast. They were polite kids who had better manners than many of the adults Henry knew.

Jenny hurried off with their order and Louis, not missing a beat, swung his head back around to Henry.

"Sorry about that," he apologized. "So, you say the disposal is leaking?"

"Yeah, I don't know that it's a real big deal but maybe you could take a look at it. I've got a short list of a few other things that could use some attention. Do you think you would have a couple hours one of these days to head out to my place?"

Henry had made it a practice to accumulate odd jobs for Louis. Many times it was work he could easily accomplish on his own but he preferred to put a few dollars in the hands of a family that could use it.

"No problem. I'm off duty until Monday; I could come by tomorrow afternoon if it's ok."

"Well, I don't want to take you away from your family on a Sunday," Henry countered.

Louis shook his head and looked back in a way that indicated to Henry that his need for income had to trump his desire for family time right now.

"No, really it's fine. I'm happy to do it. How does two o'clock sound?" Louis was shrewd enough to know that Henry sometimes "created" work for him in addition to his real needs. He sincerely appreciated it and in turn always made himself available to Henry at a moment's notice.

"All right then," Henry replied. "Two it is."

Jenny brought two bowls of cereal along with two glasses of juice to the boys and a cup of coffee to Louis. Henry had seen this sort of breakfast before. When times were lean after his mother passed, his father had often had a liquid meal while he and his brother Bill had something to eat.

He exchanged a few more words with Louis as he finished his own breakfast and then polished things off with another half cup of coffee. Sensing it was time to move forward with his agenda for the day, he got his bill from Jenny. Once he had left her tip on the table and said his goodbyes, he proceeded to the cash register.

Suzy recognized that he was ready to pay and stepped behind the counter to meet him.

"Everything ok today, Henry?" she asked as if he was a first time customer.

"Fantastic, as always," he replied as he handed over his ticket along with two twenty-dollar bills.

"Great," she said as she rang in the total. When the drawer opened, she was ready to get his change when she realized he had given her two twenties instead of one.

"Uh-oh, one too many, Henry," she said as she tried to hand it back to him.

"No, put that toward our favorite fireman's tab. See that he gets one of those omelets and the boys get some pie to go too," he instructed while refusing to accept any change from her. "And let's keep this between us, ok?"

Suzy realized what Henry was doing and her face got even brighter than it had been a moment before.

"Well, that's a wonderful thing to do. Don't worry, I'll take good care of them," she whispered back to him.

"Good deal. I'll see you tomorrow."

"Yes sir … I'll look forward to it!"

Henry turned to leave and at that exact moment met the face of a man that he despised coming through the door. It belonged to John Everett. He was a couple years older than Henry and they had known one another dating back to childhood. John had an arrogance and air about him that rubbed Henry the wrong way. He was loud, sarcastic, and a braggart without the credentials to back it up, in Henry's opinion. If John had made the gesture that Henry just had, he was the type that would have erected a billboard in town in his own honor announcing it.

Henry hadn't spoken to John in over 50 years and whenever possible did not even acknowledge his existence. Though John didn't understand why, he knew precisely where he stood with Henry and made little effort to address the issue with him. Henry, on the other hand, knew exactly why he felt the way he did about John. He had overheard a disparaging remark that

John had made about Henry's fiancée and from that moment forward hated him. It usually took a lot to get on his wrong side but once there, Henry could hold a grudge with the best of them.

"Henry," the man muttered in a low deadpan voice as their eyes met for a second.

Henry looked through him as if no one was there and remained silent as he stepped past and out the door.

"Jackass!" he grumbled softly to himself as the door closed behind him. For whatever reason, on this day, Henry had chosen to speak to John after all.

# CHAPTER 8

## Magical Moments

THE NEXT COUPLE hours of Henry's Saturday were devoted to casually browsing through two of his favorite haunts in town, Walmart and Hendrick's Mercantile. He had only a short list of needs to acquire but when his time allowed he enjoyed just strolling up and down the aisles and scanning the selections hoping to run across something new or different he hadn't seen before that might be of interest to him. He found the contrast between the big-box chain store and the "Mom and Pop" business to be a delightful clash of cultures.

The Walmart in Lewis was just 12 years old and stood as a beacon of progress and expansion in New Town. Its massive structure was spacious and offered a broad selection of items including the latest innovations, fashions, and trends, in volume at low prices.

Conversely, Hendrick's Mercantile founded in 1904 was a stalwart in Old Town that served as a nod to Lewis' past. It was a two-story red brick building with a small covered frame porch that extended along its front. Its two floors were crammed to their ceilings with shelves filled with an astonishingly diverse cross-section of all sorts of goods neatly arranged. From old-fashioned penny candy to kitchen gadgets to pruning shears, it was all here. Though many folks in town had predicted its demise when progress marched into Lewis, Hendrick's had withstood the onslaught and kept its doors open with one-of-a-kind merchandise and friendly personal service unsurpassed elsewhere.

Henry had conquered Walmart and was finishing his tour of Hendrick's as he headed up the final of aisle of the store, past the penny candies, toward the cash register. The sight of the endless bins of assorted treats triggered a memory he hadn't visited for a very long time.

* * *

He was reminded of another day, when as a boy he and George had been in this very same aisle agonizing over which treats to spend their collective fortune on. It was April in 1936, and he was 11 years old at the time. Between them, they had scraped together 13 cents with which to splurge and the decision on what to buy was being hotly debated. It was a somewhat sunny morning a lot like this one when he had heard the bell jingle atop the door indicating someone was entering or leaving. His back was to the entrance as he faced his friend but when he noticed George's eyes light up at the sight behind him, he turned to see what the fuss was about.

There, just a few steps away, the most beautiful girl Henry had ever seen had mysteriously appeared. She had big brown eyes and flowing auburn curls that were pulled back from her face and tied with a blue ribbon into a ponytail behind her head. She wore a yellow sundress with tiny blue specks embedded in it and stood a few inches taller than either boy did. A tiny silver cross hung from a thin chain around her neck.

She was looking at the candy, just as they were, when she sensed the two pairs of eyes they had trained on to her. Slowly looking to her left at the two younger boys gawking in her direction, she spoke: "Umm ... hi there?" in a somewhat curious and embarrassed tone. She wasn't used to this sort of unabashed attention back in Peoria. Back home, she was just one of the gang. *Don't they have girls in Lewis?* she wondered to herself.

Neither boy said a word in response to her greeting. It was as if some sort of spell had momentarily bewildered them and suspended their wits.

"My name is Mary. Who are you guys?" she asked while turning her attention back to the selection of candy in front of her.

Suddenly regaining his composure and sensing the need for a reply, George had stepped in and introduced them to her.

"I'm George; this is Henry. Who are you?" he asked, not fully comprehending that she had just told them her first name.

"Like I said, my name is Mary, Mary Elizabeth Winters. My pop is Doc Winters; we're moving to town today," she answered while picking up a couple of pieces of bubble gum and taffy from the bins on the shelf in front of her.

Henry recalled that he had heard Uncle Ed and Aunt Mathilda discussing the fact that Doctor Travis, the only physician in Lewis, had accepted a position in Kansas City and was leaving town. Being a kid, he didn't really pay much more than passing attention to that conversation but now could reason on his own that this girl's father was his replacement and the new doctor in town.

"No fooling? That's swell!" George said approvingly. "Say, how old are you?"

"I just turned 13. How about you guys?"

"I'm 11, so is Henry," George answered for both of them while tapping Henry on the shoulder as if to prod him to speak. "Neat" she said as she looked back over her shoulder at an older man who was clearly her father standing at the cash register waiting for her. "Oh, gotta go. See you fellas around." She turned and scurried to the man's side where he paid for her candy as well as a few items he had set on the counter.

Henry never uttered a sound. He had stood there mute as he attempted to gather himself. Before he could muster the courage to say even a single word to this mystical creature, she was gone. That was the first time he ever laid eyes on Mary Elizabeth Winters and it changed his life forever.

\* \* \*

Leaving Hendrick's with a small sack of treasures, Henry climbed behind the wheel of his Ford Explorer. He assessed his mood and his degree of hunger as he started the engine and concluded that neither warranted a drive back through town for an ice cream cone. The Old Barn Dairy, his favorite ice cream parlor on the face of the earth, could wait until another day.

Turning off of Main Street and onto County Road 27, Henry headed the vehicle toward Oak Forest. The early morning clouds had mostly moved on by this time and the noon sun was high in the sky and shining brightly. It was a pleasant and enjoyable drive that passed quickly. In short order, he could see his mail box just ahead on the right-hand side.

He slowed the SUV and turned gently into the driveway bringing it to a stop just past the mailbox. With the engine running, he moved the gear shift into park and opened the door to get out and retrieve his mail. He wondered what Lucy had brought for him.

As he opened the mail box door, he looked down across the property and instantly recognized the persistent feline trespasser that had suddenly become quite the nuisance in his world. The little cat was sauntering along the driveway at the base of the hill headed up toward Henry's house.

Henry quickly collected the mail from the box and hopped back into the Explorer, dropping it onto the seat next to him. He threw the vehicle in gear and gunned the motor, accelerating swiftly down the driveway toward his nemesis. The little cat sensed the approaching danger and immediately broke into a headlong sprint up the hill. Henry had never witnessed a cheetah in flight in person but he estimated that this creature must be part jungle cat. At first, it followed the driveway but as Henry closed in it reached the crest of the hill and cheated fate by shooting off of the asphalt and across the island, beyond Henry's immediate reach. He pursued along the driveway to the right-hand side of the island while keeping his eyes locked on the fleeing varmint crossing the ground to his left.

His SUV cleared the back corner of the island just as the little cat did. Sensing Henry's close proximity, in a moment of panic it turned abruptly from its path toward the rear of the house and directly on a right angle in front of him.

"Whooooaaahhh!" he exclaimed as he slammed on his brakes. The vehicle jerked to a stop with enough force to throw the mail next to him all over the floor.

"What the hell was that?" he blurted out loud. He looked around outside but didn't see the cat anywhere. *That can only mean one thing*, he thought to himself. He hadn't intended on harming the animal. In fact, he realized just then that he hadn't really any idea what he was going to do if he had caught up with it in the first place. All he knew was that he wanted it gone, as in off the property, not dead.

He stepped out of the Explorer and around to the front as he took a second look over the surrounding area for any signs of the little cat. Not seeing or hearing anything, he felt a bit badly that he had brought harm to it. He knelt down on the asphalt and peered underneath expecting to find an unfortunate sight. Very much to his surprise, there was nothing there. No grim scene of an injured or dying animal. No cat at all in fact. He couldn't believe it. He stood and walked to the rear and repeated the exercise to get a second look from a different vantage to confirm it. Again, there was nothing there. He was actually relieved.

"Incredible," he muttered to himself as he stood and brushed off the knees of his pants. "That's just … incredible," he said a second time, trying to understand what had just happened.

In disbelief, he looked around a final time at the front of the house and surrounding grounds but there was no doubt that the cat was gone. Houdini had done it again. It certainly must have cost it one of its nine lives, but it had beaten him once more with a dramatic disappearing act. What made it even worse, Henry thought, was that for a few moments he had actually felt a little sorry for it. In a split second, Henry had gone from genuine relief that the cat was ok back to seething aggravation at its very presence on his property in the first place.

Composing himself, Henry opened the front passenger's door and retrieved the mail from the floor. He noted that there was nothing of importance amongst the day's haul as he laid the small stack of correspondence on the steps of the side porch before getting back into the SUV. Henry pulled the Explorer back to the tan three-car garage and up to the white door on the far left. With a push of a button on the opener, which was fastened to the visor above his head, he raised the door. While he watched it rise he recalled how he had refurbished the garage and replaced the original large manual sliding doors with the modern vertical doors and openers he enjoyed today. *Money well spent for sure.* When the door was fully open, he pulled into the bay and brought the vehicle to rest in its usual spot.

To the immediate right, a white 1994 Lincoln Continental stood passively awaiting its next journey. Henry used this car for any long trips he chose to take as well as all of his business excursions to St. Louis and Chicago. The latter were becoming all but a memory as he had intentionally stepped away from active involvement in his business interests over the past couple of years. These days, he contented himself with investing and consulting and had decided to leave the "managing" and the daily stress attached to it to someone else.

In the far right bay, his prized antique truck stood safely under a gray cover. He occasionally took it out of the garage on a nice day for a brief run around the county to keep it "fresh." Beyond that, it stayed put with the exception of the annual July 4th Independence Day Parade through downtown Lewis. He and the truck had appeared in the celebratory event every year since the nation's bicentennial in 1976. Being a patriot in the truest sense of the word, Henry loved the 4th of July in general and was always as tickled to drive in the parade as the locals were to see his vintage vehicle. Seeing that all was well, he dropped the garage door and walked out the side entrance headed for the house.

The balance of Henry's afternoon was devoted to cleaning up the yard and preparing for the imminent planting and mowing season. He raked a few errant leaves, changed the oil in his John Deere tractor and push mower, and turned over his garden and several flower beds with his shovel. The only interruptions had been a few moments taken to wash down a ham sandwich with a glass of lemonade and the scrubbing of the previous night's scorched dish to remove any incriminating evidence Millie might use against him. Before long, it was time to wrap things up and head to his all-important meeting. Henry returned the shovel to its home in the tool shed and pulled the door closed with plenty of time to spare.

\* \* \*

"Jake, old buddy! How's it going?" Henry asked gleefully as he poured the brown liquor over the ice cubes. After the customary three count, he tipped the bottle back and placed it on the counter before filling the balance of the glass with cold water from the tap. With his right index finger he gave the contents a quick spin and then took a generous swallow while still standing at the sink.

"Ahhhh, you *ARE* a good man," he proclaimed with emphasis. He walked with glass in hand toward the front door. It was a tad warmer outside now than it had been the evening before and he had decided on the front bench as his perch for today's conference.

Henry settled into his seat and put his feet up on a red plastic milk crate that some wise man had strategically left there earlier in the day for just that purpose. He was feeling good. It had been a full but enjoyable day and he ran back over it in his mind while savoring his drink. The weather was nice, he had accomplished everything he had set out to do, and had a terrific breakfast to boot. Damn good day, he concluded. The only drawback had been the momentary interaction with John Everett at The Eager Beaver and upon recalling it, Henry once again murmured "Jackass!" just to reiterate the point he had made earlier to himself.

The first half of his meeting went by quickly and it didn't take long before he was back at the sink setting the agenda for the second session. He was thinking of what he might prepare for himself for dinner when he noticed the light flashing on the answering machine. It sat on the end of the counter closest to the kitchen table and he was puzzled as to who might have called him and when. He hadn't recalled hearing the telephone ring but couldn't remember if he had checked it when he had gotten home from Lewis either. With drink in hand, he pushed the button to retrieve the message and was greeted by a beep and then a robotic voice.

"You have one new message, received at 8:47 a.m. Saturday ..." After a slight hesitation and another beep, the message began to play.

"Hi there Mr. Engel, it's me," said the familiar voice he knew so well. "I was just sitting here thinking that I maybe had forgot to tell you I left you a lasagna in the freezer that I thought you might like this weekend." It was Millie. *Good God*, he thought, *she can even tell the future*. Did the woman have no limitations? The message went on for several minutes to provide explicit instructions for heating the entree and to suggest what might be appropriate side dishes to eat with it. Henry could only shake his head and smile. She never ceased to amaze him.

Now that his dinner dilemma was solved, he turned the

knob on the oven to the temp Millie had directed and headed back outside to continue his meeting while it preheated. He sat down on the bench just as a pickup truck on the road roared past and off through the hills. He figured it was likely some teenagers from town. They typically didn't get out this way much through the week but on Friday and Saturday nights, especially as the weather warmed up, a few of them were prone to turning the outlying roads into their own personal speedway. Every few years, it would end in tragedy for some unfortunate souls. Nevertheless, the allure of speed and the open road mixed with hormones and beer overwhelmed their underdeveloped common sense and a never-ending stream of new immortals took their turn at tempting fate.

Henry listened to the sound of the pickup fading into the distance. He tried to compare it to the time in his life when he was younger and first running up and down on many of these same roads. *Times were different then*, he thought. So was he. His early life had been hard and he was mature past his years by the time Uncle Ed had taught him to drive in his 1930 Ford Model A truck. It was the truck that had brought Henry to Lewis when he was seven after his father was killed. It was also that very same truck that had brought him back here after a 30-year hiatus and had led him to buy this place.

After Henry had moved away from Lewis and expanded his world beyond the state limits of Missouri, he always subscribed to the *Lewis Gazette* wherever he was. It was a tie to his past that he could never seem to let go of. By keeping abreast of the daily events, progress, and news of the town he had in a sense lived vicariously here his entire life. He knew information of the births, marriages, and deaths of the residents better than many of the lifers who never had lived elsewhere. Many of his meetings with Jake over the years had been dedicated to catching up on the local news.

It was during one such meeting in early 1974 that Henry had noticed the advertisement in the *Gazette* for a farm sale that was scheduled for March of that year. Farm sales were auctions held either to liquidate the estate of someone who had passed or to sell off property when someone had sold their farm or lost it to the bank. They were typically one – or two-day events, depending on the size of the sale, and were social gatherings of the highest order drawing people from all over the surrounding area.

Henry had seen many such ads over the years in the *Gazette* but this was the first time that something published in the list of items for sale had piqued his curiosity. He made arrangements to adjust his work schedule and made the trek back to Lewis to attend the sale. From the moment he set foot in town that day, it had felt comfortable to him. It was like putting on an old pair of shoes you haven't seen in years. They still fit. Much had changed, but more had remained the same. He ran into old friends and acquaintances who still remembered him. He also felt an advantage as he saw many new faces that he recognized from the newspaper but who had never laid eyes on him before.

At the sale, he had immediately confirmed what he had already suspected. The 1930 Ford Model A truck being sold was originally his Uncle Ed's. *How on earth could that be possible after all of these years?* he wondered. That answer and the mystery of how it had come to be owned by this party was something he learned after the fact. However, when he first saw the old pickup, now in woeful disrepair, he had instantly been able to identify it by the dent in the front fender that he himself had caused during one of his driving lessons. Then and there he resolved to buy it at any price and once the auction began, no one was going to best him.

From the first call by the auctioneer, Henry had thrown aside auction etiquette and simply stood with his right hand in the air never flinching. Several other bidders had an interest in the lot but it quickly became evident to all in attendance by his "statue of liberty" strategy that it was going to be Henry's no matter the cost. No matter who bid against him, he persisted until all competitors had lost their spirit to continue. By the time the gavel fell, the price was nearly twice the original estimate but Henry had never wavered and the prize was his. He would have gladly paid more if necessary. It was a magical moment for him.

It was shortly following the conclusion of the bidding that Henry had first met a fellow named Hank Fitzgerald who owned a garage in town. Hank had struck up a conversation with Henry to find out why he was so enthralled with the worn-out Ford. After learning about its history and what it meant to Henry, he had enthusiastically endorsed an associate in St. Louis as the ideal person to restore it to its original glory.

Later that same day, Henry had decided to take a drive out past the site of the old farm. He had been enjoying the scenery and had cruised well past it when he came upon a "For Sale" sign along the road in front of this place. He remembered this area as undeveloped and was both stunned and interested to see the oasis the current owner had created in the wilderness. Like the truck, it needed some work but by the time he had driven back to town he had decided that this place had to be his. The next afternoon, an agreement in principle to make Henry its next owner was in place. By the following spring, Uncle Ed's fully restored and pristine 1930 Ford Model A truck stood in the garage as well. It felt good to Henry to know that it was still standing back there right now.

His drink was finished and he reasoned that the oven was most certainly ready by this time, so Henry declared the meeting a success and headed inside to prepare his dinner.

# CHAPTER 9

## Time and Patience

HENRY CHECKED THE watch on his left wrist and saw that the gold hands indicated that the time was 1:41 p.m. It had been a leisurely Sunday thus far and he didn't feel especially motivated to get involved in any projects at this point. *Louis is set to arrive at 2:00 anyway*, he thought, so he adjusted his position in his recliner and flipped the next page of his *Coin Universe* magazine. A few moments later, he glanced through the window nearest his chair to gauge the weather. It was decidedly cooler out today but despite the fully overcast skies the forecasted rain had not yet arrived. Momentarily he wondered how any profession such as meteorology could be taken seriously when an accuracy rate of less than half the time seemed to be the accepted norm. *After all*, he reasoned, *they start out with a 50–50 chance of being right and still miss the mark more often than not. Any trained monkey could do that.* With a chuckle to himself he redirected his attention back to his periodical.

Thus far things had proceeded pretty much according to plan. He had spent last evening catching up on his reading and then enjoyed watching *The Horse Soldiers*, one of his favorite John

Wayne movies. Having slept fitfully through the night he had risen just after 7:00 a.m. and by 9:30, was seated at his usual table at The Eager Beaver and studying the menu over a cup of coffee. Ultimately, he had gone with the biscuits and gravy, which were particularly tasty on this occasion. After breakfast, he had come back home and spent a little time filing away some papers on his desk before settling into his chair to finish the numismatic publication he had started the night before.

At five minutes past two, a robust knock on the front door indicated that Louis had arrived. Henry stood and walked into the breakfast room. He peered down the hallway toward the front door, which was standing open. Through the storm door he could see the smiling face of the man he was waiting for.

"C'mon in!" Henry called while motioning with his right hand for him to enter.

"What do you say, Henry?" the man called back as he opened the door and proceeded into the home.

"Just a little bit cooler out there today, huh?" he asked sarcastically, knowing that Louis was surely aware of the obvious precipitous drop in the temperature overnight.

"Yeah it is," the younger man replied as he walked down the hallway toward Henry. "I don't know about you but I am ready for spring."

The men met at the edge of the breakfast room and exchanged a firm handshake. Henry had always admired a man with a firm grip and it was no coincidence that Louis was Henry's kind of guy.

Louis unsnapped and removed his red nylon jacket, which was emblazoned with "Lewis Fire Dept." in large yellow letters on the back. While he draped the windbreaker over the nearest chair at the kitchen table, Henry pulled a 3" x 5" note card from his shirt pocket, which had a handful of jobs listed on it that he wanted Louis to attend to.

"Say Henry, when did you get a cat?" Louis inquired casually.

The question caught Henry, who was deep in thought, somewhat off guard.

"A what? A cat? I don't have a cat … ," he mumbled while studying his list intently.

"Sure you do," Louis pressed forward, a little confused. "I just saw it out front. A little Siamese cat?"

The light bulb that popped on over Henry's head must have been blinding to Louis and visible for miles around.

"Noooo! Where?" he exclaimed in disbelief as his attention rapidly moved from the list to this inconceivable news.

"It was sitting on your front porch when I pulled up and then it ran around the side to the back yard," Louis reported without really understanding Henry's reaction. He knew he had never seen a pet around in the years he had been coming here but never really had thought about it or realized Henry apparently didn't like cats very much.

"God daaaammn!" Henry blurted out with extra emphasis on the second word. He wasn't a particularly profane man but he did wield a healthy off-color vocabulary when the occasion called for it. He apparently had not only failed in running off the problem, but now the intruder was becoming bolder and had even had the audacity to come onto *his* porch. The situation had spiraled out of control. Something drastic had to be done.

"Is there something wrong, Henry?" Louis asked, trying to make sense of Henry's rage.

"Yes, there is. A couple of days ago this cat showed up and I've been trying to run it off but obviously that isn't working."

"Where's it from?"

"Damned if I know, Louis. It's a fancy breed so it surely can't be from around here but it doesn't seem too interested in moving on either. I've just about broken my neck trying to get rid of it," Henry stated, remembering his fall in the yard and screeching halt in the driveway.

"Huh, that's really weird all right," Louis acknowledged as he walked over to the French doors and gazed outside looking for the cat he had just seen moments before.

"I can understand why you don't want it around here. I hate cats. Always have. They're shifty and devious. I'm a dog man."

Henry was absorbing what he'd just heard and was weighing whether or not the fact that this creature was a cat had anything to do with his disdain for it. *No*, he thought, *it is just that I don't want something hanging around that relies on me for anything. I know where that can lead to and I'm not going there.* If he had wanted a cat in his life, he would have gotten one. This was an unwelcome intrusion into his personal space. This animal would be trouble and would need care. It had to go.

While he was pondering all of this, Louis continued to speak, sensing Henry was really getting worked up about the situation.

"Henry, if you'd like, I'll be more than happy to take care of this for you," he offered. Louis was acutely aware of how generous Henry was to him and his family and felt he owed him a debt of gratitude that he would gladly repay in any way he could.

"Seriously? That'd be terrific. Honestly though, I don't know what you could do that I haven't. This thing is hard-headed as hell."

"I've got the 12-guage out in the truck. I'll grab it and see if I can't take care of this real quick; then we can get started on that list," he said as he reached for his jacket. Louis was an avid sportsman and Henry realized that he intended to take care of his problem the way he and Bill used to deal with varmints on his Uncle Ed's farm. *The old-fashioned way.*

Suddenly, Henry once again felt compassion that he didn't expect to find inside himself for this strange feline. It was the same way he had felt yesterday when he thought he had run over it with his Explorer. He didn't want to put a "hit" out on the little creature. He just wanted it to move on and to go somewhere else and be someone else's cat.

"No ... no thanks, Louis. I really appreciate it but we can't do that," he quickly interceded. "I wouldn't feel good about something like that."

Louis was a bit surprised at Henry's objection but felt relieved as he had gotten no more thrill out of the idea of hunting the cat than he did when he knew he had to enter a burning building. When a tough job needed to be done, he was the one you could call on and count on. However, his preference was that he would never be needed for those situations in the first place.

"Oh, ok ... well, whatever you want to do, Henry," he said, replacing the jacket on the chair. "Honestly, I don't think you'll have to deal with it for very long. It didn't look to me like an outside sort of cat. Besides, with the coyote population and all of the hawks and owls around here, something will get it one of these days if it doesn't move along on its own first."

The words hung in the air for a moment as Henry wrapped his head around them. Louis was right. There was no reason for him to get so bent out of shape about a strange cat or as a result to have blood on his own hands. Nature would take its course and in short order he wouldn't see it around anymore. This did not mean he was planning to tolerate it lying on his porch or was accepting it as a resident. It simply meant that there was no good reason to chase it all over the place like a deranged mad man either. In due time, it would be gone one way or another. He concluded that he would wait it out and his problem would solve itself.

For the next couple of hours, Henry and Louis moved around the house and outbuildings addressing little issues Henry had noted that needed some form of attention. Millie's prime concern, the garbage disposal, was first on the list and turned out to be nothing. It simply required a little effort with a wrench to tighten the bolts that held it to the sink. In moments the pesky leak was eliminated. It was all downhill from there.

The completion of Henry's "to do" list went quickly as the men engaged in lively conversation on topics ranging from sports to politics to events in town. Before long, everything Henry had intended to tackle was finished and Louis was on his way with a generous check in hand to compensate him for the time and effort spent during his visit.

As the dark green Chevy Silverado was heading down the hill, Henry stood on the front porch watching him drive away. He thought to himself that this was the one fault he had with his young handyman. How could a person of Louis' caliber drive a Chevrolet? Being a "Ford Man" himself, it was beyond his comprehension. He shook his head and turned to go inside.

Though the expected precipitation had never materialized, the cold gloomy weather outside wasn't very inviting so Henry opted to spend the balance of his afternoon indoors. It was just past 4:00 p.m. and there was still time to accomplish something before his meeting with Jake so he decided to pull out some of his coins. From time to time, he enjoyed looking over whichever specimens from his collection he currently had stored at home in the safe and this was a perfect opportunity to do so again.

Henry stepped into his office and over to the heavy black steel door of the safe in the near corner. With his right hand he nimbly rotated the large brass dial on the front, first to the right ... then to the left ... and once more to the right ... stopping precisely on "13." With his left hand he dropped the brass lever to the side of the dial downward and pulled the large heavy door open toward him.

Inside the safe a series of shelves had been installed and boxes of varying sizes and shapes sat upon them. Each contained some sort of valuable or memento that Henry preferred to keep safely locked away. On one of the middle shelves, several long narrow 2" x 2 ¼" x 9 ½" black cardboard boxes were stationed. On the end of each box was a small piece of masking tape with a single identifying cursive word written on it in black ballpoint pen. He carefully studied the selection available to him before reaching for a box that had been labeled "Buffaloes."

He wheeled with the box in hand and moved across the room to his desk where he sat it down in front of him before taking his seat. After he had switched on the desk lamp, he carefully removed the lid from the box to reveal the top edges of a perfectly organized row of cardboard "flips" stored within.

A coin "flip" is a 4" x 2" piece of thin cardboard that has a finished white exterior side, like a dress shirt box, and a gray unfinished interior side. Two holes are cut to the exact diameter of the coin specified and sit at an equal distance on either side of a center seam. The interior unfinished side has a thin film of cellophane that extends across it and serves as a windowpane for the holes. A collector places a coin on one side, and then folds the other half over on top of it. Once closed, the flip is 2" x 2" and is stapled along its four sides to seal the coin inside where its obverse and reverse can be readily seen through the windows. The "flip" provides protection to the coin as well as a means to label it because it can be written on.

In this box, Henry had assembled a complete set of Buffalo nickels. Struck sporadically from 1913 to 1938, James Earle Fraser's magnificent design had earned this name due to the representation of an American bison on the reverse and the metal on which the coins were struck. However, some also referred to the coin as an Indian head nickel due to the obverse design, which features the head of a stoic and noble Native American. Whatever the name, Henry had always loved the coin series due to its artistic excellence, high relief, and the truly American subject matter it depicted.

The coins in the set had been arranged in sequence according to date and mint mark from the first issue in the series to the last. He pulled open the center drawer of the desk where among various other items he kept an assortment of magnification devices. In this instance, he selected a large 5x glass that had a black metal rim and handle and looked akin to something Sherlock Holmes might have utilized while solving a mystery.

He extracted the first flip from the front of the box and held it in his left hand under the lamp while positioning the magnifying glass he held with his right hand over the coin. On the front of the flip, "1913-P Ty 1" and "Gem Mint" had been written in blue ballpoint pen. He admired the razor sharp detail on the obverse of the highly lustrous and satiny piece. This particular example was easily an MS-67 with claims to a 68, making it a competitor for the finest known specimen from that issue.

Coins are universally graded using a numerical system called the Sheldon Scale, which was first introduced by Dr. William H. Sheldon in 1949. He devised the system to assess a coin's level of preservation as well as to differentiate it from others in its class according to several factors. In the 1970s, the American Numismatic Association (ANA) chose to adopt it as the preferred way to grade coins and the rest was history. The Sheldon Scale ranks coins on a numerical basis from 1 to 70, with 1 being the poorest condition and 70 being theoretical perfection. The lower grades, Poor 1 to About Uncirculated 58, are used to evaluate the degree of wear seen on a particular coin. The upper grades, Mint State 60 to 70, are reserved for coins that exhibit no signs of any wear from circulation. In this category, coins are graded by factors such as strike, luster, eye appeal, and the absence of surface marks caused by handling at the Mint or while in transit in large bags with other coins. In most cases, only modern products of the United States Mint can hope to approach perfection and therefore collectors constantly compete for the very best condition coins in a series they can find.

Henry's set of nickels had been painstakingly assembled over the past 30 years and included only the finest examples of each issue that he could locate. He had spent hundreds of hours attending coin shows and auctions as well as thousands of dollars to acquire these pieces. As he replaced the first coin and selected the second, he could recall where each one had been purchased. If ever he forgot, he kept a log in a journal where he recorded the date, seller, and price paid for each coin in the set.

One by one, he removed, viewed, and replaced his trophies. He had performed this exercise so many times over the years that he had memorized the characteristics and nuances of each piece. This was an especially advantageous skill because he was uniquely equipped to identify an upgrade to an issue in his set if he came across one without having to lug the set along everywhere he went. Lately, this occurrence had become less frequent as the quality of his set escalated. The last such incident had been nearly two years prior when he happened to see a particularly well-struck high-grade 1924-S nickel sitting in a dealer's case at a show. He had paid a premium for it but was pleased in the end. After returning home with the coin and comparing it to the one in his set, he had confirmed that this example was superior in every way to the one he had. This triumph was a rare and exciting victory for Henry and exactly what drove him with such passion to constantly enhance his collection.

It hadn't always been this way. Henry was not born a numismatist. In fact, his current status was a product of environment and not genetics. When he was in his late teens, George had shown Henry his own small collection one day in his bedroom in St. Louis and Henry had felt unimpressed.

"So, you mean to tell me that you paid a buck for that quarter? Man that guy must have seen you coming, George!" Henry had needled his friend. Undaunted, George continued over time to talk about his collection with Henry and the seeds were gradually planted. By the time Henry was in his mid-twenties they had taken root and eventually over time had grown and flourished into what presently could be fairly called Henry's greatest enjoyment in life.

While returning the 1937-D to its place in the rear of the box, he happened to notice that his watch read 5:12 p.m. He was shocked at how quickly the time had flown by and promptly stood to head off to his engagement. Henry had been so engrossed in his coins that he was late for his meeting with Jake that day.

"Alright fellas, we'll continue this shortly," he said aloud to the box of nickels as he left the room. It wasn't often that he was late for a meeting but he reasoned that it would be ok in this instance. Jake knew Henry loved coins and was just the type of friend who would understand his tardiness and make an exception.

# CHAPTER 10

## *The Hunters*

HENRY RETURNED TO his desk with a full glass in hand to finish his run through the set of Buffalo nickels. Before he sat down in his chair, he casually looked out the front window at the sun that was beginning to set and took a swig of his drink. While the whiskey was still lingering on his lips he noticed something that didn't belong in the yard. It was the little Siamese cat back again. This time it was stationed out on the island opposite the front door. It was frozen in a prone position, perpendicular to him, facing to Henry's right. His immediate inclination was to rush out the front door and scream something harassing at the beast but he then quickly remembered the new edict he had established. Just hours earlier he had decided to take a more passive approach to this situation. In light of this detente, he held his ground and simply watched it despite his urge to do otherwise.

The wee predator was attentively fixated on something just out in front of it. Its body was straight as a board and flat along the ground. Henry was puzzled by the position it was in and couldn't see anything to explain what it was looking at. For several moments, man and animal were still. His curiosity wouldn't allow him to turn away and he took another swallow from his glass without diverting his attention from the story developing in front of him.

Just then, the rear end of the little hunter began to fiercely wiggle with energy. Its long body recoiled for a split second into a ball of muscle and then lunged forward landing a yard from where it had started with a definitive pounce. It seemed to have captured some sort of quarry as it had both paws overlapped across a point in front of it and its tail was flailing wildly in jubilation. Suddenly it looked directly at the window Henry was standing behind. If he had not known better, he would have sworn that the creature was looking directly into his eyes.

\* \* \*

The scene reminded Henry of another that he had once witnessed. It was while he was on an African safari in 1967. He was 42 years old at the time. A pair of business associates had organized the journey and they had successfully persuaded him to go along. The ultimate point of the adventure was to be a lion hunt and the men had hired two locals, twin brothers named Jombo and Timbo, to serve as their guides. They had not experienced much luck in locating game and time was soon running short. In light of this, the party had decided to split up in a last-ditch effort hoping that one of them might get a chance to take a shot at the intended trophy.

Henry had ended up alone with Jombo while the two other travelers ventured off in the opposite direction with his brother. The pair set out early on the second to last day and by mid-morning the experienced eyes of the guide had picked up the trail of a small pride of lions heading to the east. He instructed Henry that the cats would have likely fed overnight or in the early morning hours. By afternoon, they would be resting somewhere on the savanna under the shade of a tree to get relief from the hot African sun. This would allow the men to close the distance on them and possibly provide the opportunity for the trophy shot that Henry had come such a great distance for.

Jombo proved to be a wise and savvy guide. As predicted, by early afternoon, he had spied a group of lions sleeping far off in the distance under a lone scraggy tree surrounded on all sides by a sea of pale wild grass. He observed that the approach to this position didn't afford the men much in the way of cover and advised Henry that they should take a different strategy. He knew of a small water hole a short distance further east and deduced that the lions would eventually have to make their way there. He led Henry to the hole while giving the pride a wide berth so as not to give themselves away.

The topography of the area around the water hole was most certainly more advantageous for the hunters than that of the savanna. A pair of ten-foot-high rock formations on the southern end would provide an ideal perch overlooking all of the approaches and also would afford them some measure of protection as well. It was perfect, thought Henry at the time.

The men took their positions and waited. Over the course of the next few hours, many creatures wandered to the relief of the water's edge but not any lions. Henry passed the time by gently twirling the large coin he always carried with him between his fingers. It was an attempt to keep his mind off of the sweltering heat that was made more unbearable by the baking rocks they were crouching amongst. Henry had been hot in his life on the farm, but nothing before that day had come close to the discomfort he was experiencing. In contrast, Jombo looked cool and comfortable. The tall slender man was a product of this environment and seemed unfazed by it. Henry had just about decided to give up the position when Jombo motioned toward the distance with his hand.

Henry looked in the direction indicated and was awed by the sight of the pride approaching from some 50 yards away. Three females were flanked by a pair of cubs. Just off to their left, Henry's prize sauntered with the regal purpose of a king. He slipped his coin back into his pocket, raised his gun into position, and waited patiently. The large-caliber rifle could easily drop the male from where he was but it was approaching him and closing the distance so he opted to wait to shoot rather than risk a miss.

Jombo sat in silence waiting for Henry to take his shot. He knew that it got no better than this. The stars had aligned and his American companion would have an ideal, almost surreal, opportunity to complete his mission. In short order, much to their astonishment, the entire pride was less than 20 yards away from their position and lapping water from the edge of the hole.

The male lion was truly magnificent. He stood nearly four feet tall at the shoulders and was almost ten feet from tip of nose to tail. Jombo would later estimate his weight to have approached 500 lbs. His mane was full and gorgeous, his colors were golden perfection. Henry was mesmerized by the animal's perfect combination of power and beauty. Sensing that the moment would quickly pass, Jombo nudged him gently to break the spell and indicate it was time to act. Henry trained the sight of his rifle onto the chest of the beast and took a slow deep breath to steady his hands, which were trembling rather noticeably with excitement.

It was just then that something occurred that neither man would ever forget.

Precisely as he was preparing to squeeze the trigger, the imposing brute looked up from his refreshment and directly into Henry's eyes. How it could possibly have known exactly where he was and yet have acted so calmly? Could it have sensed its imminent demise and yet remained so cool and unaffected? Henry could not explain these things even now. However, there was no question in the minds of either man that it was absolutely true. The lion had made direct eye contact with him as if it knew everything without previously having offered any indication whatsoever that it was aware of their presence. What's more, it had remained stoic and detached.

For a few seconds, there was a connection forged between them. It was a defining moment in Henry's life and it left him flabbergasted. He removed his finger from the trigger and just admired the majesty and dignity of his adversary and the magic of the moment he had just experienced. He had gone from hunter to partisan. He had decided to live and let live. This was not a trophy that he wanted to take or one he could have been proud of later for doing so.

Jombo never uttered a word. Rather than implore Henry to act, he too was bewildered by the events he had just seen. The lions continued to drink for a few more moments and then one by one moved off in no special hurry. The male was the last to leave but not before throwing a brief glance back in Henry's direction. Perhaps it was in appreciation for the pass it had been given or an acknowledgement that the hunters would be allowed to leave peacefully as well. There was no way to know. The men sat in stunned silence as the pride moved off and out of sight. Henry would never see that lion again and it was the last time in his life that he ever hunted anything other than coins.

\* \* \*

The little cat looked at Henry with the same nonchalance the great lion had exhibited. It was inexplicable how the feline had sensed he was there but just the same, the palpable feeling that it certainly knew of his presence was unmistakable. Just like the lion, the little cat almost seemed to be saying, "Yeah, I know you are there. I have to live my life and it's up to you to choose how to proceed from here. So be it." After a few seconds more had passed, it looked down to whatever it was holding and bent to put it into its mouth. Henry couldn't see what it had captured, but it was contented to pick it up and slowly stroll around the side of the house and out of his sight with the urgency of a browser on a Sunday afternoon stroll through Macy's.

Perhaps it was the conversation with Louis or the recollection of his intrigue in Africa that brought it about, but from then on Henry's feelings toward the cat softened substantially. The following morning, after Millie had arrived she made note of the cat to him for the first time as she was hanging her jacket in the hall.

"Say Mr. Engel," she called to the family room where he was seated. "Have you seen that little ole cat that's out in the yard?"

Henry was prepared for a trap. He was still uncertain as to whether or not she might have seen the cat before and remained unconvinced that she was oblivious to his flop in the yard while pursuing it. He knew Millie to be a cunning and cool customer so he proceeded with caution.

"Cat? What cat?" he responded slyly.

"There was a little Siamese cat on the prowl back by the big garage just now when I pulled up," she responded as she stepped into the room with him. "Nice looking little thing too. He saw me but didn't pay me too much mind and went around in back of it."

"Huh? You don't say?" Henry continued the charade.

"Yeah, I thought maybe you might've seen him. Kinda surprising to see something like that out here, don't you think?"

"Yes, it sure is. Well, it's not hurting anything so we'll just let it move along on its own," he instructed while trying to think of a way to change the subject. "No reason to get too worked up about a stray cat."

Millie was a little surprised by his indifference to the sighting but seemed generally satisfied with Henry's answers and she turned to leave the room.

"Do you smell something burnt?" she asked as she walked into the breakfast room. This was most certainly not the topic Henry was looking for as an escape from the cat conversation. *How in the world could she possibly still smell the stench of the over-baked meat loaf from Friday night?* he wondered. He had gone to great lengths to air out and scrub down the crime scene. The woman simply wasn't human. She was part blood hound. In a desperate attempt to divert the conversation away from that subject he blurted out, "So, what kind of cat did you say it was?"

Over the next several weeks Henry observed the cat on a regular basis moving about on the property and made no attempts to interact with him or to drive him off. The urgency to dispatch the animal from the premises was gone. The "witch hunt" mentality that had consumed Henry previously was a distant memory. In fact, if anything, he had begun to grow accustomed to having the creature around.

However, none of this was an indication that Henry had adopted the cat as his own either. There would be no assignment of a name or providing him with food and water as a caregiver would. It was simply a newly established mutual respect between two parties who had come to an agreement that they could coexist in harmony.

Likewise, the young cat seemed to have made peace with the arrangement as well. He somehow sensed that the porch of the house was off limits to him and he made no attempt to violate the boundary. He was quite satisfied with traveling around the grounds and generally paid no particular attention to Henry other than to give him a wide berth whenever the two encountered one another. He seemed to be doing surprisingly well for himself also. Henry noticed that he was growing and had added some weight to what was originally a very scrawny frame.

# CHAPTER 11

# Of Cats, Mice, and Men

MARCH GAVE WAY to April and by mid-month spring had defeated winter and was in full command throughout the countryside. Generous rains and warm sunshine had unlocked the pent-up energy that had been stored during the previous months, creating an eruption of growth at Oak Forest. The dormant grass had transformed into an ocean of green while the foliage on the trees was becoming thicker with each passing day. The color and contrast provided by the blooms on the redbud and dogwood trees was spectacular to behold.

Henry was an avid gardener and with the last frost of the season in the books, the vegetable garden behind the house was shaping up nicely. It was in exceptional condition with seeds for radishes, lettuce, and spinach sown and cabbage, cauliflower, and broccoli plants already in the ground. In the next wave he would add sweet corn seed as well as tomato and green pepper plants to the mix. In addition, the seeds for his flower beds were also sown and right on schedule. The last couple of years had seen colder and wetter than expected weather in March and April but this season's return to normalcy was greatly appreciated.

The days passed quickly for Henry as there always seemed to be something that needed to be attended to at this time of year, but he loved every minute of it. He had cut his teeth on the farm and the fresh air and physical activity invigorated him.

Equally as thrilling for Henry was an annual coin show held each spring in St. Louis that he had been attending for years. He enjoyed attending other shows and auctions around the country from time to time but this multi-day event was the highlight of Henry's numismatic calendar. The St. Louis show was always held over the third weekend in April from Thursday through Sunday. It attracted scores of nationally known dealers as well as a plethora of collectors from throughout the Midwest. As a result, the volume and diversity of the coins available there was enormous and it afforded Henry a key opportunity to land upgrades for his collection.

During the previous weeks, Henry had devoted a great deal of time and energy to reviewing his numismatic holdings. He had pored over his coins deep into the night on multiple occasions while jotting remarks in a small blue spiral-bound notebook. Along the way, he had prepared a box containing 34 coins from various series that had been identified as potential candidates for replacement with a better example for one reason or another. If the trip yielded even a 10% turnover he would consider it a victory as finding better coins than those he owned was becoming increasingly difficult all the time as the quality of his collection escalated.

The morning of Henry's departure arrived and he withdrew

the Lincoln Continental from the garage and brought it to the side of the house for loading. It was a slightly overcast day and he suspected rain might be in the forecast though he hadn't bothered to watch the news to find out. After noticing a film of dust on the white finish of the exterior he thought to himself that he wouldn't mind driving to St. Louis in the rain in exchange for a free rinse off of the auto.

Around Lewis this was referred to as a "hillbilly car wash" and in light of his desire to arrive at the coin show prior to its opening it would have to do for today. He went back into the house and made his final preparations for the trip.

Waiting for him on the countertop of the island was a cinnamon coffee cake Millie had baked for him the day before and a full thermos of hot coffee he had just filled. His briefcase, which held his coins, notebook, and other important reference materials he had selected to take along, stood on the stool closest to the door. Henry made a final sweep through the first floor making certain he had everything he intended to take along. Satisfied that all was accounted for, he collected the remaining necessities from the island and headed out the door, locking it behind him.

He knew that Millie would be out to check on things each day that he was gone, as was their standard procedure, so he felt quite comfortable leaving without any of the anxiety that someone might feel about leaving their home unattended for a few days.

Once everything was stowed inside the car, Henry took his place behind the wheel and paused for a moment to clean his glasses. Convinced they were as clean as they were likely to get, he replaced them on his face and started the engine. He took a quick look around the car as he buckled the seat belt just to see if perhaps the cat was in the neighborhood but he was nowhere to be seen. *Hard telling where he is*, Henry thought.

One of the great mysteries that surrounded the cat, in addition to his origin, was where he slept at night. In the six weeks he had been hanging around, Henry still had no clue where he bedded down. He simply appeared in the morning and disappeared in the evening and try as he might to solve the riddle, thus far he had been unsuccessful. In addition, he couldn't figure what was the great attraction of Oak Forest that kept it here and how it seemed to be feeding itself to the extent that it looked downright well nourished. It seemed to Henry that his furry cohort Houdini still had some tricks up his sleeve.

He slipped the vehicle into gear and eased it down and out of the driveway. He was in great spirits and even to this day, became genuinely excited whenever he had the opportunity to attend a coin show. *It is going to be a good weekend*, he thought. Perhaps he would get lucky and be able to land some nice coins. Either way, the fun was in the hunt.

Shortly after noon, Millie pulled up alongside the house and brought her car to rest in its usual spot. She exited the vehicle and glanced around briefly before opening the rear driver's door to remove a bag of cleaning supplies she had purchased for Henry before heading inside. *All seems quiet*, she thought.

She was in a good mood as usual and was humming one of her favorite church hymns, "What a Friend We Have in Jesus," as she entered the kitchen. After placing the sack on the counter, she stepped over to the cabinet, which was above and to the left of the sink and opened the door. She removed a dinner plate and turned and put it on the island. She then moved over to the bread box, which was next to the stove and removed two slices of sandwich bread from the loaf inside. With these in hand, she pulled open the refrigerator door and retrieved a half-gallon container of milk from the top shelf.

Returning to the island she proceeded to break the bread up into small pieces roughly the size of a dime and scattered them about the plate. She then removed the lid from the jug of milk and poured it slowly over the bread until it was saturated. Satisfied that all was in order, she picked the plate up and walked over to the French doors. While humming more loudly now, she used her free hand to unlock and open the near door before stepping outside onto the patio. Turning to her left, she placed the plate against the house below the bay window that sat at the rear of the family room.

The window was cantilevered, which is to say it extended out on its own beyond the support of the foundation of the house, and sat just inches above the ground. Millie had discovered weeks ago that the little cat was living beneath it and had been regularly sneaking food to it there when Henry was away or otherwise occupied. At first, she had been compelled by compassion for the creature and the realization that without help it would perish. Despite Henry's directive to ignore it, this was something that her conscience would not allow. Her plan had been to nourish and then capture the cat and remove it to safety before finding it a good home, all without his knowledge. However, the plan had now evolved into something entirely different.

As the plate came to rest on the stones, a little black head popped out from beneath the window.

"Well, there you are!" she said with excitement. "I was wondering where you were at, Hobo."

It was a nickname she had given him almost immediately due to his transient status, another clear violation of Henry's decree. As she returned upright, the happy customer came out entirely and stepped up to the plate without hesitation. He was extremely comfortable with Millie as he completely understood that she was the source of his meals. He was also as completely enamored with Millie's skills in the kitchen as Henry was and eagerly devoured the feast she had provided for him.

Millie crouched down next to him and gently stroked his head and back a few times while he ate. His purring was so strong that Millie wondered how he could breathe between that and swallowing his meal.

"We're all clear for a few days, boy," she said with a wide smile. "Mr. Engel is away until Sunday afternoon so we don't have to sneak around until then *and* you get some special treats this weekend."

Because of her work schedule, her clandestine "Meals on Wheels" program was typically restricted to five days a week. However, she had figured a way around the Gestapo for that as well. She had been smuggling handfuls of dry food and throwing them underneath the window on Fridays so that Hobo would have something to eat on the weekend. For water, he simply drank out of the waterfall at the edge of the patio. She had it all worked out and so far Henry didn't have a clue.

"Don't you go thinking bad of him," she continued gently. "He's a good man who's got a lot of hurt deep down inside that don't leave no room for love. I don't know who done it, but whoever it was sure got him good. You just hang in there. He'll come around. He needs you, he just don't know it yet. Any man whose best friend is a bottle of whiskey can certainly use a cat. Besides, we're all he's got." She gave her friend another gentle stroke as she reflected on what she had just said.

As Millie stood up, the little cat had just finished cleaning the platter and was beginning to groom himself. He was meticulously washing his face by first licking his right paw and then rubbing it along his nose and mouth. It was a procedure he repeated again and again dozens of times before switching to the other paw in order to clean the opposite side of his face. He looked healthy and had grown since she first saw him, she thought to herself. She felt good about her efforts even though she took no pleasure in defying Henry. In this case, she reasoned, the end justified the means.

After he had sufficiently bathed himself, the little cat made one rub along Millie's legs before walking with great satisfaction across the back yard toward the garage. Millie picked up the plate and went inside feeling almost as gratified as Hobo did.

\* \* \*

Henry returned home mid-Sunday afternoon feeling like the cat that had swallowed the canary. It had been an extraordinary trip and he had experienced unprecedented success at the show. He had been able to locate and acquire a whopping nine upgrades to his collection. Seven of these came from a long-time dealer friend who had recently been retained to disperse the holdings of an elderly client. Many of the pieces had been off the market for decades and the dealer had set aside a group of several dozen coins that were exceptional for Henry to consider. After settling on which of these he was interested in, Henry had been able to strike a fair deal in cash and trade to complete the transaction. To find so many upgrades and of such high quality all in one place was literally the chance of a lifetime in Henry's estimation and he seized it.

In addition to his good fortune finding coins of interest on the bourse, he also had a great time refreshing relationships with dealers and collectors that he had met over the years. Several leads were obtained and the groundwork for one potential trade had been laid as well. Finally, he had enjoyed meeting with Jake and several hobby friends on Friday and Saturday nights at his favorite steak house in St. Louis and the meals afterward were terrific.

Once Henry had unpacked his travel bag, he went downstairs to unload the briefcase, which was resting on his desk. The box containing his coins was placed in the safe and the reference texts he had taken along were returned to their homes on the book shelves. It was only 4:15 p.m. but Henry was in such good humor that he decided to break from etiquette and start his meeting a bit early today. He was sure Jake wouldn't mind and besides he was tired from the weekend's events and did not feel like doing much of anything else at that point. So, he decided it was his best option and to no one's surprise Jake did not put up a fight; he too was more than willing.

Henry and Jake strolled around the outside of the house for a few moments inspecting the grounds before settling onto the bench on the front porch. *Everything looks good*, he thought. The afternoon was pleasant and sunny with a light warm breeze occasionally whispering through from the southwest and it felt good to let his mind and body completely relax.

As he sat and enjoyed his drink, it occurred to him that he

hadn't seen the little cat before he left on Thursday morning and thus far hadn't spied him upon his return. It was somewhat unusual as he seemed to show up every time Henry was outdoors. Perhaps he had finally moved along? Maybe something had finally gotten him? Before Henry could chase down these thoughts any further, the missing party sauntered up the driveway as if on cue.

He proceeded along the edge of the asphalt at the far side of the island headed toward Henry's left and on his way to the rear of the house. Henry watched with interest as he continued. About halfway, he paused and looked in Henry's direction for an instant before taking an abrupt turn across the grass toward the front of the house. He appeared to have caught a glimpse of Henry sitting on the porch and had decided to move closer to investigate. As the feline crossed the island Henry could see a large lifeless field mouse dangling from his mouth.

The animal continued toward him until he had crossed the near side of the circle drive and halted on the sidewalk a few feet short of the porch. With the mouse still hanging from his mouth he looked at Henry briefly with a sort of puzzled look. Henry was surprised by this direct contact and didn't know quite what to do or how to interpret it. The two watched each other intently for a bit before the hunter made the first move and dropped his trophy onto the ground before lying down next to it.

Henry did not have a lot of experience with cats while growing up but the businessman inside of him knew when a peace offering was being made. The cat was showing him his prize, paying him respect. He was reaching out to him. It was something Henry hadn't expected or prepared himself for and he wasn't quite sure how to react.

"Well, aren't you just the hunter?" Henry asked him. As the words slipped from his mouth he realized that he had just crossed a line that he had previously not dared to approach. The cat seemed to respond to his voice as it squinted its eyes submissively for just a second while whipping its tail excitedly on the cement surface.

This was the first time Henry had truly gotten a close-up look at the fellow. His eyes were a sparkling crystal blue color and quite stunning, like a deep pool of water glistening in the sun beneath a tropical waterfall. Increasing the effect, his narrow face was a rich satiny black, which provided the ideal contrast to make the hue even more spectacular. He was lean and muscular and clearly well nourished. Despite the fact he lived outdoors day and night, his coat was clean and well groomed. In short, he was extremely handsome. Henry wondered why he hadn't really ever noticed that before. In all the times he had chased him away early on or more recently had looked at the cat, he had never really *seen* him.

"So, tell me, just exactly where are you living?" he asked while bringing the glass to his lips for another swallow. It was a question that had perplexed Henry and as long as they were going to exchange a few words he was going to broach the topic. Unfortunately, the cat wasn't forthcoming about his sleeping arrangements and for now that answer would remain a mystery.

Henry finished his drink and sat for a time just looking at his counterpart. He was in no rush to move and break up the encounter. After all of his objections and angst about this cat, he now found himself strangely fascinated by it. He was unique and strong. He was independent and self-sufficient and he was damn good looking too. *Hell, he's just like me,* he thought to himself. The comparison made Henry smile and chuckle aloud.

"Well sir, if you'll wait a minute here I have someone I'd like you to meet." As Henry stood the cat did as well moving from a prone position to a seated one. He looked with curiosity as Henry opened the door and went inside.

Henry poured himself another drink and headed back for the porch. As he opened the storm door he immediately saw that the visitor and his prize had disappeared. He was a little disappointed he was gone and rather surprised at himself for feeling that way. He drank from his glass while looking around in all directions from his position just outside the front door but could see nothing of the cat. *Houdini has done it again*, he thought.

As he stepped over to the bench he felt something beneath his right shoe and moved his foot to see what it was. He was shocked to see it was the deceased field mouse. The hunter had placed it there as a form of tribute to the master of Oak Forest.

"Well, I'll be damned!" Henry mumbled to himself in astonishment at the gesture that had been made, albeit in a somewhat grotesque fashion. The cat had reached out to him. He had decided to be the bigger man and had humbled himself to break the ice. Beyond that, he had given Henry something of great importance. After all, in the wild, food was life itself. However, though he had exhibited great character and courage, he had left the gift and vamoosed just in case the recipient did not share his enthusiasm for improving the relationship.

Henry used his foot to slide the corpse off the porch and

onto the grass before taking his seat. He hoped that after a while the cat might return for it. He needed to eat and Henry needed it gone.

He continued his meeting for the next half hour or so while he digested what had just transpired. It seemed quite clear that this cat had no intention of moving along any time soon and he was quite self-sufficient, thriving in fact. It had come as a surprise to Henry, but he couldn't help but like him. They had gotten off to an extremely rocky start but somehow had found an amicable existence that each seemed to be adjusting to. Maybe having a cat around wasn't so bad after all.

# CHAPTER 12

## A Name Makes It Real

SEATED AT HIS favorite spot at the island in the kitchen, Henry was deeply engrossed in his newspaper when he heard the sound of the side door opening. He had lost track of time while studying the articles but there was no need to check the clock now; it was 9:00 a.m. and that was Millie arriving.

"Well hello, young lady!" he called to her cheerfully.

She closed the door and entered the kitchen with a bright smile on her face, genuinely pleased to see him as well.

"Hello yourself!" she responded as she passed him on the way to the hall tree to hang her jacket and put down her purse. "How was the coin show?"

"Outstanding, better than I could have hoped for actually."

"Well that's wonderful!" she replied at the good news.

"Looks like it was all quiet around here, huh?" he asked.

"Yes sir, it sure was." She had returned to the kitchen and now was moving toward the cabinet to the right of the sink to retrieve a coffee cup for herself. As she did, she noticed the index card lying on the window sill with a short list of items scribbled on it. This was a system that they had devised many years ago. When either of them thought of something that was needed for the household, it was jotted onto a 3" x 5" index card and put onto the sill. When it came time for Millie to shop for Henry's groceries or household supplies she would take the list with her and replace it with a new blank one. It had proven to be a highly effective method to assure that the house was stocked with everything either of them needed or desired.

She did a quick scan over the list, which included the usual suspects but was startled at the fourth entry, which was discreetly nestled between hand soap and paper towels. Could it be true? Was it some sort of aberration? She had to take a second look just to be certain, but there it was. Cat food. She could hardly believe her eyes. She was so surprised that she dared not even comment on it for fear of derailing a major shift in Henry's policy that she hadn't truly deemed imaginable.

Millie casually put the list back on the window sill and stepped over to the coffee pot to fill her cup as coolly as she could. She glanced at Henry who was reading intently as she was already making plans to swing past Walmart on the way home to acquire the goods noted on the card. This was an opportunity she intended to seize upon before Henry changed his mind.

Meanwhile, Henry had prepared himself for a reaction from Millie. He feigned deep concentration on the newsprint in front of him as he peeked past it and watched her study the list. Surely she had seen the notation for the cat's food and he had a neatly prepared speech all ready to go. He planned to defend his change of course and explain that it was simply a short-term humanitarian gesture. He was even a little bit chagrined that she didn't mention it to him and therefore had denied him the chance to utilize the well-thought-out and rehearsed oratory on her. He watched as she filled her coffee cup and almost brought up the cat himself but then thought better of it. If she had not noticed the request for cat food there was no reason to cross that bridge with her right now. He'd deal with it later.

When Millie arrived the following morning with two Walmart bags in hand, Henry was a bit confused. She didn't typically make a shopping trip until later in the week, unless he had specially requested it, so as to economize the effort and get everything needed in a single outing. He quickly surmised that she must have had special need of some sort of cleaning supply and dismissed his concern.

Just as he had been the day before, he was again perched at the island and was scanning the daily newspaper with a cup of coffee in hand. His affection for the local news was so great that he had made a special arrangement with the publisher of the *Lewis Gazette* to have someone drive out each day to Oak Forest and throw that day's edition on his front porch just after sunrise. It was a luxury that a man of Henry's means could afford and it was worth every penny to him.

He tried to appear indifferent to her presence as she unloaded the bags but he was carefully eyeing their contents as she unpacked them. She was making small talk all the while about nothing particular and did not seem the least bit curious about his special request. Once the bags were empty, Henry gathered that she somehow had missed the requisition for the animal's food because it clearly was not among the purchases. She slipped back into the pantry to put away a couple of items and Henry felt slightly indignant at her oversight. How could a woman of her considerable talents for this position have missed something so simple? He had rehearsed his speech a half dozen times more overnight about the obvious duty he was obligated to perform in feeding the cat and she had yet again denied him the chance to perform it for her.

Just then, Millie re-entered the kitchen holding a 5-lb. bag of Purina Cat Chow in her hands.

"What did you want me to do with this?" she asked him as disinterested as if she were holding a sack of potatoes. Henry was caught completely off guard both by her demeanor as well as the package she held. She hadn't overlooked the cat food after all.

"Umm, yeah … good," Henry stammered while trying to appear unaffected himself. "How about we put a bowl of that out on the side porch for that cat that's been hanging around."

"Ok," Millie answered with virtually no emotion as if he had just mentioned a shirt that needed ironing.

*Ok?* Henry thought. Was that all she had for him. *Ok?* He had braced himself for a scathing inquisition as to why he was now going to feed the cat he previously was trying to run off and whether that meant it was staying on permanently. However, Millie offered no opening to broach that topic. In fact, she did not seem fazed at all. She simply opened the bag and poured a portion into a medium-sized plastic margarine bowl that she had saved for use for just this sort of purpose. Henry was puzzled by the lack of any reaction but opted to once again avoid the topic rather than pursue it even though he had his brilliant explanation at the ready.

"How about instead I put it out back on the patio?" she asked. "I think I've seen him out there before and besides, he seems to be afraid of that porch. Is that ok?"

*If you only knew*, Henry thought. The little cat wasn't as afraid of the porch as she might guess. It certainly had not bothered him any on Sunday when he delivered the mouse to Henry's feet. He knew more about the cat than she did, he thought, but he would let her have her way on this point. In a day or two when the contents in the bowl had not been touched, he could more subtly move it to the porch without her recognition that this was more than an act of compassion on his part. It was indeed an acceptance of his furry cohort as a welcome friend rather than charity to a trespasser who was just passing through.

Over the next couple of weeks, Millie's suggestion for the site of the cat's food bowl had worked out surprisingly well despite Henry's skepticism. In addition to the cat getting a good meal each day, a side bonus for Henry had been the discovery of where the little Houdini had been living during all this time. It was quite a surprise to both he and Millie to learn that the creature had made its home beneath the bay window behind the house. What a stroke of luck and genius it had been that Millie had placed the food bowl near that spot and it had enticed him out of his secret hiding place for all to see. Henry had been equally surprised to see how quickly the little cat had taken to her. Almost immediately, it had responded to her bowls of food with purrs and affectionate rubs against her legs. Henry guessed that Millie was simply a "cat person" with special powers of attraction that made her and the little feline instant friends.

May at Oak Forest was a beautiful time of year. The freshness and fullness of the vegetation on and surrounding the estate made it seem like a virtual Garden of Eden. The trees were entirely foliated and the grass had filled in completely now into a lush deep green carpet across the grounds. As for literal gardens, Henry's was progressing quite nicely as well. He devoted a good deal of time to its care and on this Wednesday afternoon he found himself ambling along a row of cabbage plants with a hoe, chopping any weeds that had sprung up.

Millie stepped out the back door with a bowl of food for the cat who had been lying in the shade under a tree near the garden watching Henry but now sprang from its position to investigate Millie's offering. She stepped toward Henry to admire his handiwork in the bright sunshine.

"Mmm-mmm! That garden sure looks nice!" she praised him as she halted just at the edge of the grass where the yard stopped and the garden began.

"Well, thank you!" Henry acknowledged with a grin as he paused from battling invading weeds and wiped his brow with his handkerchief. "It's coming along, that's for sure. All the rain this spring has really kicked it in the rear end. I expect it's going to be a good crop."

The two stood for a moment in silence soaking up the pleasant scene and admiring the many types of vegetables in various stages of growth that Henry had neatly ordered in the garden. His attention to detail and their care looked to again this season be well on its way to yielding exceptional results.

"That cat sure can eat," Millie said as she glanced back to the patio where the now not so little cat was voraciously attacking its bowl of food.

Henry, still focused on the garden, hadn't fully processed her words before she spoke again.

"Say Mr. Engel, as long as he is going to be hanging around here and such, seems like he ought to have a name, doesn't it?" This was a topic they had both carefully avoided for some time now. Any references to the animal had been restricted to "he" or "him" or "the cat." Designating an actual name felt to Henry like a major step and he had not as of yet reconciled himself to it.

"Oh. Well, I don't know. I hadn't really thought about it," he responded as he absorbed what she had said and the repercussions it entailed. *A name makes everything real*, he thought. A name meant that he was part of the family and in Henry's world, family left him in one way or another, so it was not a pleasant association and was one he had purposefully and artfully dodged for decades.

"I just thought maybe it'd be nice to have something to call him, that's all. He's such a sweet fella," she continued.

There was no disputing her words. The cat had become a fixture in their daily lives and routines. He spent much of his time following Henry around or watching him work outside from a vantage nearby. He had even begun to regularly appear during Henry's meetings with Jake and the two had shared several conversations. There was little doubt that a name was in order but it wasn't a bridge Henry had resolved to cross just yet.

"Yeah, I don't think so," Henry dismissed the idea and immediately turned his back to her to resume his hoeing. The move was so emphatic that Millie sensed it was best to let the topic lie for now. She didn't know how or what had happened to Henry in his life but any fool could see that he harbored deep pain as it related to family and relationships and was very gun shy to opening himself to either at this stage of his life. She dropped the subject and went inside.

Though he had cut Millie off and stamped out the idea, he continued to think about it as he worked. He wondered to himself, *What truly is the harm in naming the cat?* He pondered why he had often had an issue with declaring affection for something or someone in his life.

It had been this way from childhood. From the moment he had met Mary he had fallen for her. It had been love at first sight. Yet it had been many years later before he had ever declared his affection for her. It was not a quality that he valued in himself. Had he acted sooner, things in his life might have turned out differently.

*　*　*

The thoughts sent him backward in time to the years after he first encountered Mary. She, Bill, George, and Henry had spent a lot of time with one another and had become great pals. As they grew older, in the late 1930s, they went through all of the trials and triumphs that teenagers do and grew even closer. In early 1941, Henry had been quietly devastated when he learned that Bill and Mary had begun to date. He had never told anyone, not even George, of his feelings for Mary but it was a terrible time for him. When his brother first took Mary to the movies, Henry had never seen it coming. Neither she nor Bill had any idea of Henry's feelings at the time and even if either had, how could it have ended well? Henry was younger than Mary and at that age, a couple of years between an older girl and a younger boy felt like a lifetime.

The relationship between Bill and Mary progressed that year as Henry suffered in silence. The courtship was slow and methodical but the assumption was that it was going to develop over time into something more serious. However, the Japanese had other ideas. On December 7, 1941 on what President Franklin Delano Roosevelt would later term as "a date which will live in infamy," the world as everyone knew it changed. With America's entry into World War II, able-bodied men over the age of 18 were called to arms and Bill was off to war.

Before Bill shipped out in early 1942, he and Mary agreed that they would put their relationship on hold until after he returned. No promises were made but a future together was implied. Henry recalled the pride and angst he had felt as he watched his big brother board the train in St. Louis to leave not knowing if they would ever see one another again. He remembered the sting of Bill's last words to him, "Keep an eye on Mary for me." It was a cruel fate to be cast in the role of protector of the woman you loved on behalf of another, let alone your own brother. Nevertheless, Henry was honorable and did exactly that. He, Mary, and George were inseparable. They hung on every radio broadcast for news of the war and gathered together to read Bill's letters which arrived regularly. In the meantime, there was plenty of work to be done on Uncle Ed's farm and Henry occupied himself with it while waiting on his 18th birthday and his chance to serve in the war effort.

The news of 1942 was not good as the Allies faced defeat on many fronts. At least Bill was safe though, as he was in Australia undergoing training and awaiting deployment to fight in the Pacific. August soon came and with it, George's 18th birthday. Rather than wait for induction, the day after his birthday he said his goodbyes and enlisted in the army. He and Henry agreed that Henry would soon follow in October and between he, George, and Bill they would see this thing to a speedy conclusion so they all could get on with their lives.

Henry and Mary were left to hold down the fort at home and spent virtually every free moment together. Even though Henry could not and would not pursue a romantic relationship with her, their close friendship was very important to him. He counted the days until his birthday and was anxious to get into the war while at the same time dreading the thought of leaving Mary behind. Letters from both George and Bill during those months only added to his desire to contribute as they were.

October 17, 1942 arrived and Henry was now 18 years old and eligible for military service. Just as George had done, he had decided to forgo the delay of waiting for the inevitable draft notice and had enlisted into the army. This is where his best-laid plans hit a snag. He failed his physical and was designated as rated 4-F, or unfit for military duty. A second subsequent physical confirmed the fact that Henry had a hole in his left eardrum and was therefore unqualified to join the army. The doctors believed it was the result of a childhood ailment and though Henry only suffered from a very minor loss of hearing that did not hinder him, it was on the list of requirements for a soldier and he was out.

Henry was devastated. The feelings of shame and inadequacy were overwhelming. His bruised ego had been soothed, however, by Mary's expression of joy and relief that he would not be in harm's way as Bill and George were. In addition, she was elated that he would be able to remain in Lewis to look after her. To further relieve his burden, Uncle Ed had correctly pointed out that every able-bodied man could not be devoted to warfare because someone was needed at home to tend the crops that fed the troops. In this fashion, Henry was indeed doing his part and was an invaluable piece of the overall effort for victory.

As time passed, Henry's shame faded and he felt great pride in his work. He had generally enjoyed farming a great deal but now it had even greater purpose for him. With the emphasis on maximizing productivity to support the war effort, Mary had taken on an important role at the farm as well, helping in any way she could. A side benefit of this for Henry was that it allowed them to spend even more time together than they previously had been able to. Their bond to one another grew even stronger in the months that followed.

Henry was not alone in his fondness for Mary. Uncle Ed had always liked her from the outset and as time wore on and he had been able to work alongside her and share meals with her, his fondness for the girl had grown immensely. Even Aunt Mathilda, a notoriously cold woman who showed no special interest in Bill or Henry, seemed to have a mild affinity for her. Aunt Mathilda had been unhappy at the arrival of two small boys on the farm following their father's death and had never warmed to them during the years that followed. Being a mother simply was not in her nature. However, having another female around appealed to her slightly. Whatever the reasons, Mary was as much a fixture around the household as if she had been a member of the family.

Through the winter months, letters from George only trickled in and those from Bill stopped altogether. Henry reasoned that during combat the need for secrecy overruled the desire for communication and assumed that everything was ok with both of them. Uncle Ed had mandated from the beginning that no news would be interpreted as good news and Henry agreed that this was a wise course of action.

The peace of mind provided by this strategy came to an end on June 11, 1943. It was a nondescript Friday and the family was gathered at the kitchen table for lunch when the Western Union boy rapped on the front door. The knock startled them but no one paid it any special attention as Mary was first to get up and went to answer it. When she opened the door, she saw the boy and his bicycle and let out a shriek as she immediately recognized it was the type of message every family in America dreaded to receive in those days. Uncle Ed sprang from his seat and moved past her to take the telegram from the boy before thanking him and closing the door. He and Mary walked back to the kitchen with faces of stone. Henry couldn't breathe as Uncle Ed tore open the envelope and began to read the words aloud: "The Secretary of War regrets to inform you ..." Henry didn't recall the rest of the words. The image of Mary collapsing to the floor and the flood of tears in Uncle Ed's eyes were overwhelming.

The gist of the message was that Bill was "Missing in Action" and presumed dead. His big brother would never be coming home. There was no mention of where or how it had happened. All he could remember of those next moments was Mary sobbing and saying that "There isn't a name! If they don't say the name of where he was killed, it isn't real."

\* \* \*

Henry sliced the dirt with the edge of the hoe as he reached the end of the last row in the garden. He looked at his watch and noticed where the hands were positioned; it was time to walk to the mail box and get the mail.

He took a glance back at the patio where the cat had been eating earlier and recalled Millie's words. *No, no name*, he thought. A name makes it real.

## CHAPTER 13

# No Ordinary Joe

JUNE BROUGHT UNUSUALLY hot and dry weather that year in contrast to the mild and moist spring they had experienced. This would have been a cause for consternation in some parts but in the Midwest the inhabitants were ready for whatever came and took it in stride as cheerfully as possible. Henry actually preferred the hot days of summer to most any other time of year and not only endured the heat but seemed to thrive in it. His upbringing on the farm had conditioned him to love the outdoors and in his later years he had returned to his roots and made the most of any opportunity to get outside and absorb nature. Between caring for his garden and his flowers and tending to the upkeep of Oak Forest, he found a steady source of work to satisfy this urge as there always seemed to be something that needed to be done around the grounds.

One bright Tuesday afternoon, Henry was in the midst of parading across the front yard with a sack of bird seed filling his assorted feeders when he heard the sound of the USPS truck approaching. It could mean only one thing: Lucy had a package for him. It whirred down the driveway past the pond and then up the hill toward his house. He was in the process of filling the last feeder, which hung from a bracket on a large oak in the middle of the island, when she tapped the horn playfully to say "hello" as she passed him on the way around the circle to the front door.

Lucy was a slender woman in her late forties with short brown hair and a face that spoke of a hard life. In her younger years, she had been the victim of physical abuse at the hands of her first husband during an ill-advised and brief marriage following an unplanned pregnancy. However, she had come through it and found happiness with a blue collar man and solid citizen from Lewis named Chester Dawson. He was a decent fellow with a successful plumbing business and had not only adopted her son as his own but had created four more children with her. Their road to make ends meet was hard but they seemed genuinely happy as a family. Lucy was the type that never seemed to have a bad day and always wore a smile every time Henry had ever seen her over the 20 years she had been bringing him his mail.

Henry flashed a grin at her and set the feeder and bag of seed on the ground before walking over to the vehicle, which had come to a stop at the head of the sidewalk. Already knowing the answer he still couldn't help but glance at his watch to verify the obvious. The time was 1:58 p.m. Lucy had done it again. *Her relentless punctuality is almost superhuman*, Henry thought with a chuckle.

"Hi Henry!" she called from her seat behind the wheel on the right side of the little blue and white mail truck. As she sorted through a box of mail to her left, he approached.

"Hey kiddo, what do you know?" he asked enthusiastically as he passed around the front of the truck and stopped next to her door, which was slid wide open.

"I know it's pretty damn hot!" she laughed.

"Yeah, it's a little warm out today for sure, but it's not all that bad up here in the trees," he offered.

"Well this damn thing doesn't have any A/C so it's cookin' in here," she responded with a slight note of aggravation mixed with humor. "It must be in the 90s today! If it's this hot on the 10th of June, I hate to think what July and August are gonna be like."

Henry nodded his head in agreement as she handed him a stack of mail and a small box.

"This one needs your John Hancock," she said as she passed him a ballpoint pen and a small note card related to the package.

"You bet," he agreed. Once he had scribbled his name across the indicated line acknowledging receipt of the item he passed it and the pen back to her.

About that time, Oak Forest's most inquisitive resident leisurely eased around the far corner of the house to investigate who had come for a visit. As Lucy was filing away the document Henry had returned to her she noticed him.

"What an adorable cat! When did you get him?" she asked with a surprised tone as she had never known Henry to have a pet in all the years she had been delivering mail to his home.

"Oh, it's a long story. Let's just say he kind of came along on his own a few months back and was determined to stay," Henry replied with a slight chuckle, amused at the recollection of his failed efforts to run the animal off.

"He's gorgeous. What's his name?" she inquired.

"Name? Umm ... well ... he doesn't have a name," he replied, now instantly flustered by the lack of a proper moniker for the cat.

"Really? Well, how come?"

Now, even more embarrassed by the silliness of his lack of commitment to the creature by having deprived it of a name, all he could muster was raised eyebrows and a mumbled, "I honestly don't know."

*That was a dumb thing to say*, he thought. Here was a man who had handled high-powered business negotiations and had been responsible for deals that at times totaled tens of millions of dollars and he "didn't know" why he hadn't named his stray cat. He suddenly felt foolish and Henry rarely if ever felt like anyone's fool.

Lucy sensed something was amiss by his reaction. She had merely been making small talk with him and moved to relieve the tension she had unwittingly created.

"Aww well, so what? I had an uncle who was just a crazy drunk who had a dog when I was a kid and he used to just call it 'dog.' Never did give the mangy critter a name. It works." The expression on Henry's face was priceless. Though she had intended to alleviate the stress she quickly realized she had only increased it with her anecdote. Deciding it was best to quit while she was behind, she quickly excused herself and shot out of the driveway to continue on her appointed rounds.

Henry stood dumbfounded on the sidewalk holding his mail. He realized that he apparently had not thought this thing through. He was definitely no one's crazy drunk uncle and this little well-groomed cat was anything but some mangy critter. Very well then, the time had come; there would have to be a name given. He looked over at the feline who sat a few feet away looking at him quizzically.

"Hmmm, what are we going to call you?" he asked him.

Not surprisingly, the cat didn't offer a response. He was generally tight-lipped and whenever Henry spoke to him simply looked back and listened as a student might to a teacher. Henry was certain that he knew what he said to him but the cat generally played his cards pretty close to his vest. *I think it's likely you know a lot more than you let on,* Henry thought.

The balance of Henry's afternoon was occupied with rolling names around his head. The list of candidates was seemingly endless. Millie had been especially excited by the prospect and had strongly offered the name of "Hobo" instantly when asked for input. Henry was a little surprised by how quickly she devised the name but she was a clever gal, he thought, and also had been fast to come up with the ideal place to feed the cat so perhaps she was onto something.

Henry was leaning toward "Houdini" himself. He had always thought of the cat as a magician with some sort of mystical powers to appear and disappear. The recent weeks had done nothing to dissuade him of that perception either as it was not unusual for the cat to instantly appear at his feet or nearby in the yard when he was working. Often, just as quickly, he would vanish. Henry liked to joke with the cat that he had a "teleporter," a hypothetical device for instant transportation from one place to another, and if he would only share his secret with him they could patent the idea and retire as a couple of rich old fellows to the Caribbean.

Five o'clock seemed to come quickly that day and before long, Millie was heading to her car and Henry was arranging his meeting with Jake at the kitchen sink. He had just finalized the details of the conference when he heard the side door reopen and the sound of Millie's footsteps coming back through the laundry room to the kitchen.

"What did you forget?" he asked the hurried woman.

"Oh, as usual, my car keys," she laughed as she picked up the set of keys that were lying on the counter next to the answering machine. "You know me."

Henry laughed along with her as it was a well-known fact that Millie had a special talent for forgetting her car keys. Her special gift was the belief that they were in her purse or jacket pocket when in fact each and every time they would be located next to the answering machine. Henry couldn't explain this sort of targeted amnesia but it always provided them both with a good laugh.

"Don't forget now, Hobo is a fine name for a cat," she said with a wink and a smile as she stepped past him and through the kitchen door.

"I know, I know," he acknowledged, wondering if the forgotten set of keys wasn't really just a ruse in order to make a final pitch for her choice for the name of the cat.

"All right then, I'll see you again," she called out as she closed the side door behind her.

He stood for a moment toying with the name. Hobo. Hobo. Hobo. It was a fine and even somewhat appropriate name, but it just did not click for him. It was missing something. He headed outside to the front bench to conduct what was to be an especially important meeting. He hoped that Jake might be able to provide some input.

Per the new norm at Oak Forest, the cat was waiting for him. He was stretched out to the right of the front door in the middle of a lazy afternoon nap. He had developed into quite the companion for Henry whenever he was outdoors. The animal met him in the morning and generally followed him directly or remained in the vicinity throughout the day. When Henry walked to the mail box in the afternoons, the cat went along. While Henry cut the expansive grass on the estate each week, the cat would find a comfortable spot in the shade and watch him. As Henry moved along, so did the cat to a new position always keeping him in sight.

Fred. What about Fred? No, he certainly didn't look like a "Fred." *Houdini? Great name and absolutely appropriate,* he thought. However, names for pets typically start out as elaborate multi-syllabic designations only to ultimately be cut into a shorter, simpler, single syllable out of laziness when addressing the animal. Houdini was destined to become "Hoo" or "Hood" and that was unacceptable.

Fluffy, Hunter, Roosevelt, Paws, Elvis. Dozens of names from the clever to the ridiculous passed through Henry's mind. Jake remained mum on the topic and the cat, apparently not sensing the importance and gravity of the meeting that was to determine his name forever dozed fitfully with complete indifference.

The second highball was nearly gone and no decision had been made. Henry had not realized that selecting a name was going to be so agonizing. He felt as if he carried the weight of the world on his shoulders. For a man who had made a living making critical decisions, he was choking on this one. Though he felt frustrated, it really should have come as no surprise to him because he had no experience of any kind in this regard. He had never named anyone before. He had never had children and his only childhood pet, Socks, had been named by his father. The closest he had come was to selecting the name of Oak Forest for his estate but that had come easy for him and didn't really seem to matter as much as picking a label by which someone would be known for the rest of his life.

Socks? What about Socks? That would be the perfect name for a cat that bore the same distinguishing leggings that his previous pet by the same name possessed. No, he decided that was not an option. There could be only one Socks in his life. His beloved dog who had seen him through the loss of both of his parents and his brother deserved that respect.

The names all seemed to blur together into a mix of frustration and confusion. He began to think that he might not be able to solve this riddle in the short term and naming his friend would have to wait. It was then that he remembered something that George's grandfather Joseph had told the boys one night at the dining room table in George's home back in St. Louis. He had said that when you are faced with a difficult decision and you have exhausted all options, settle on the two best choices and simply flip a coin. His experience had taught him that even if one made a less than perfect choice, indecision and inaction were worse outcomes.

He reached into his pocket and pulled out the large silver coin he carried with him everywhere. It was a 1921 Morgan Silver Dollar and Joseph Schuetz had given it to him the very same night he had offered the advice on decision making, presumably to drive home the point. As the elder man spoke that evening, he had reached into the breast pocket of his suit coat and pulled out two matching brand new dollar coins and handed one to Henry and the other to George. Henry had carried it with him every day since as a sort of good luck piece and as a result it now was quite worn and retained very little of its original detail.

Henry fondly remembered the words of Joe Schuetz. He was a sage and savvy person who along with his son George Sr. had played a large role in helping Henry become the man he was today. *All right then*, he wondered, *what two names would Joe pick as finalists?* He flipped the coin in his hand a couple of times before it hit him. *Wait a second*, he thought as he sat forward on the bench and looked at the cat.

"By God, that's it! Hello Joe!" he exclaimed with excitement.

The little cat, now named Joe, was startled from his slumber by Henry's voice and jerked to look back at him.

"You know your name, don't you, Joe?"

Joe wasn't sure what the hell Henry was saying but he looked happy enough so it was all right by him. He appraised the situation briefly and then after determining there was no cause for alarm carefully repositioned his body on the cool concrete to resume his nap.

Henry was utterly tickled with himself. This called for celebration. Today's meeting ran longer than expected and a third highball was employed. He loved the name. It was so obvious he hadn't seen it at first. It was simple, one syllable, and perfect for the handsome cat. He "looked" like a Joe, Henry thought with complete satisfaction. Furthermore, if Millie wanted to call him "Hobo Joe" that would be just fine too. He hadn't wanted to offend her by discarding her idea for a name that frankly had merit. He simply had not been entirely wowed by it. However, "Joe" or "Hobo Joe" was the perfect compromise. He was quite sure she would see the genius he had channeled to come up with it and they would all be satisfied that it was the optimal choice, no coin flip needed.

Henry's belief that Millie would like the name was understated. She did not simply like it, she *loved* it. He interpreted her exuberance to mean that she appreciated the brilliance of it, which of course she did, but he could not have known the deeper reason for her joy. She had watched this man, a person she had worked for and grown to care for greatly over the past 23 years open his heart to a little stray Siamese cat who simply wouldn't take no for an answer. Millie had always been able to sense the tender side of Henry that she believed existed within him but to finally see it firsthand was very moving to her. She had gambled that time and patience might melt his heart and she had won. In addition, she had grown extremely fond of the furry fellow as well so the fact that he was going to be a part of the family on a permanent basis was a reason for joy.

"Well, hello Joe? What do you know?" became the catch-phrase she used to greet the cat each day when she saw him for the first time. Though his official name was Hobo Joe Engel, Millie thought that just plain Joe fit him perfectly.

# CHAPTER 14

## The Perfect Woman

HENRY PULLED AT a few scraggly strands of nut grass that had sprung up in one of the flower beds in the back yard as the late morning sunshine began to gather strength. He crept along on his hands and knees following the perimeter of the circular bed while weaving his hands between the marigold plants to pull out anything that did not belong there. All offending vegetation was tossed into a bushel basket that he kept in tow for the casualties of his war on the weeds.

The back yard with its flower beds and vegetable garden, which Henry watered on a near daily basis, was an oasis compared to the rest of the area. The heat wave that had begun in late May had continued throughout June with no measurable rainfall. Combined with above average temperatures and day after day of unabated baking sun, conditions in and around Lewis bordered on serious drought. Things had become so dry and dangerous in fact, that with the July 4th celebration just under one week away, the use of fireworks, which was typically allowed in and around the city limits, was being discouraged as a dangerous fire hazard. Talks at City Hall had even begun as to whether or not they would have to be forcibly banned altogether and the town's annual display canceled as the potential for brush fires was a real and ominous threat.

Somehow, despite this desperate lack of rain, the weeds that intermingled with the grass across the pasture still managed to grow enough to annoy Henry. He had thought that perhaps one side benefit to the drought would be that the grass-cutting hiatus usually provided by the hot and dry conditions of late July and August would come early this year but as of yet, no such luck. He had set aside that afternoon to run the big International tractor over the open ground below the house and would mow the yard around the residence with the smaller John Deere tractor and push mower that evening.

Henry had just completed his circuit of the flower bed in front of him when he heard the French door on the rear of the house close. He looked up to see Millie approaching with a tall clear glass of ice-cold lemonade for him. He stood up and brushed his hands together with a wide smile to greet her.

"You are a sight for sore eyes, young lady," he said gratefully. His dark tan brow was beaded with sweat and the droplets ran down his face onto his already soaked light yellow cotton shirt.

"I figured by now you could use a cool drink," she said as she handed over the glass to him.

"Yes ma'am. Thank you!"

"It sure reminds me of Georgia when it gets hot like this," she said, referring to her birthplace. "So where's your partner in crime?" She scanned the area but didn't see Joe who typically was attached to Henry's hip.

Henry did not immediately answer as he was in the process of drinking the entire glass of lemonade with a single series of large uninterrupted gulps. He hadn't realized how parched he had become but when offered the chance to quench his thirst he acted like a man who had been crossing the desert and guzzled the refreshment.

"Delicious! Thanks again," he said as he handed the empty glass back to her.

"You want another?"

"No thanks, I'm good," he replied while wiping his face off with a white handkerchief he had pulled from the back pocket of his tan trousers. Now regaining his wits he recalled she had asked about Joe but he had not answered her.

"I'm pretty sure Joe is in his hole staying cool." Henry was referring to the crawl space below the bay window where Joe had made his living quarters.

"That's where I'd be if I was him. Poor guy has to wear a coat all the time. It's got to be miserable hot for him during the day." Millie had begun a subtle campaign to add Joe to the roster of inhabitants *inside* the walls of the house but Henry was not having any of it. Though he cared a lot about the cat he was not interested in taking things any further than they had gone. Joe had a place to live, food to eat, and a name. Henry figured that was good enough. Millie knew it was a long shot but occasionally she still slyly put it out there just to keep the idea in his head. *All things come to those who wait*, she thought to herself.

After a fine lunch of fried ham sandwiches and potato salad, Henry walked down the hill with his water jug in hand to the stable where the tractor and brush hog were garaged. His companion, who had been a no-show for the weed-pulling party in the a.m., had emerged from his hiding place and was playfully along for this adventure. Joe seemed to enjoy the weekly trip to the stable when Henry would cut the meadow. Henry figured his interest was more than likely driven by the fact that while Henry used the tractor it gave Joe an opportunity to venture inside the stable and hunt for any mice that might be lurking about.

The two reached the bottom of the hill and after coming to the paddock fence, which Henry climbed over and Joe scooted under, cut across the grassy field toward the building. Henry grumbled each time he hobbled over that fence rather than make the walk around to the gate nearer the driveway. It was an aggravation, as was the trimming required around the fence posts where the mower deck couldn't reach, but it was outweighed by his appreciation of the appearance of it all and he just could not bring himself to tear it down. He never intended to own even a single horse but that really wasn't the point. He liked it, and since he did, it didn't have to make sense to anyone else. That was another lesson Uncle Ed had taught him.

The pair arrived at the stable and Henry unlocked the large hanging door and slid it open along its rails to his right to reveal the aged 1967 International Harvester model 424 tractor that was waiting within. Its red and white paint job was faded and it showed the rust patches and grease stains one might expect to find on a 30-year-old piece of equipment, but the motor ran like a well-tuned clock and it started on the first attempt every single time.

Joe shot past Henry through the open doorway and deep into the bowels of the stash of assorted old farm implements and various other pieces of junk stored off to the right side. Meanwhile, Henry stepped to his immediate left inside the door to a bench where he kept the things necessary to operate a large tractor. On the top, he had a jug of motor oil and a small funnel that rested in the mouth of an old glass milk bottle to keep it from dripping leftover oil on the counter when not in use. To the side, a small selection of wrenches and tools of various sizes sat in front of a green multi-drawer tool box. Next to that, he kept a pile of soiled oily shop rags, which showed evidence of repeated use over the years. Beneath the bench, a larger funnel reserved for fuel and a pair of 5-gallon gas cans were neatly stowed.

Henry placed his small blue jug of water onto the black vinyl seat of the tractor. He then took a few moments to check both the gas and oil levels and added the necessary amounts to each. After completing a couple of additional steps on his pre-flight checklist he was satisfied that all was in order and he climbed aboard the tractor like a fighter pilot preparing for takeoff. He placed the jug in the mounted tool compartment that was welded to the right fender and then settled comfortably into the seat. Satisfied that all was finally ready, he depressed the brake pedal with his right foot and the clutch with his left before moving the gear shift between his legs into the neutral position. He then inserted the key and turned it to the right, which activated a red light on the weathered dashboard and a whirring and clicking sound from under the hood. He took his right hand and pushed the throttle lever upward before placing his thumb on the black rubber push button starter switch and igniting the beast.

With one great explosion of energy the motor fired and a puff of black smoke ejected from the gray vertical muffler that rose through the hood in front of him. After the initial burst, the motor settled calmly into its typical rhythmic pattern, which resembled a sewing machine running at high speed. Henry took his right hand and placed it over the knob of the lever that was next to his seat and eased it back toward him. As he did, the three-point hitch of the brush hog, which was mounted to his rear, began to lift and the large mower deck raised off the ground. All systems were now go, and with both hands Henry shifted the machine into second gear. After a final adjustment of the throttle, he released the brake and then the clutch and the iron workhorse eased forward and out of its shelter.

* * *

Something about sitting high atop a tractor felt good to Henry. It was a place where he had spent thousands of hours of his life and he felt comfortable there. Often, when using the International, he was reminded of his days on the farm and how Uncle Ed had first taught him to drive a tractor by letting him steer through the farm fields while sitting on his lap. He recalled how Uncle Ed first teased him that he drove "like a snake." However, when he had grown both in years and experience, his uncle had relinquished control to him and he had felt like a man as he operated the massive contraption alone.

He had wanted to follow in his uncle's footsteps and make agriculture his life's pursuit. He and Bill had both discussed it on many occasions. After the news of Bill's death in June of 1943, Henry had become even more devoted to the idea as a way to honor his own dream as well as that of his lost brother. Uncle Ed often spoke of the day when he would retire and turn the farm over to Henry and the two men worked side by side with great pride that they were maintaining and building a family empire that perhaps Henry's children might one day own.

The weeks following the notification from the War Department were sad indeed as everyone grieved the loss and came to grips with the new reality of things. Mary's friendship with Henry and romance with Bill had caused her to spend increasing amounts of time on the Engel farm to the point where she now felt as if she was one of the family and belonged there. Likewise, the Engels' saw her the same way, each from their own unique point of view. Uncle Ed had come to care for her like a daughter and Aunt Mathilda even occasionally spoke to her, which was in and of itself high praise. Henry, as always, remained head over heels for her, but now more than ever was resolved to a life without her. He could never pursue the girl that was destined to have been with his brother who had been killed in the war.

That was, at least, until one afternoon in late September of 1943 when he and Uncle Ed were mending a fence for Old Man Janson. Uncle Ed had always known that Henry was crazy about Mary from early on. His youngest nephew lit up like a firefly whenever she was around and he suspected that although Mary had a brief romance with Bill prior to his departure, she had developed feelings for Henry as well. Uncle Ed could see the obvious road block that sat between them and decided to take measures into his own hands before allowing this sweet girl to get away from Henry and from all of them.

"Henry, we need to talk," Uncle Ed opened the discussion.

"Yeah, ok, what about?" Henry replied.

"You, your brother, and Mary," responded the elder man, not prone to beating around a bush.

Henry was shocked and unprepared for the discussion so he exhibited some of the good common sense Engels were known for and stayed quiet.

"Son, I know what's going on. Anybody with a pair of eyes can see that you are in love with that girl and you have been since you were a kid."

Henry knew that Uncle Ed was a sharp man but he found it almost impossible that he could know this after the measures

Henry had taken over the years to conceal his feelings. Uncle Ed continued on.

"Look, I know how you feel. I do. Remember, I lost a brother too once. It hurts like hell and nothing can take that away but the Good Lord and a calendar. But son, time will pass and this will get easier to live with. Problem is, right now you don't have time to wait on that. With Mary, I'm afraid if you don't speak up soon, she's going to slip away from you."

Henry could see from the look in his Uncle's eyes that he was dead serious and he knew that as usual, he was right. It was not a thought that Henry hadn't considered a hundred times. However, how does one even broach a topic like this with someone?

"What the devil should I say?" he asked sarcastically. "'Hey, now that my brother is dead would you like to be *my girl?*' You know, I'm an Engel too."

Uncle Ed had managed a weak chuckle before replying.

"Nah, that might be a tad too harsh," he jokingly advised. "How about you take her aside and tell her what's in your heart? Just tell her the plain truth of the matter; who knows where it might lead. Look, of course she was sweet on Bill but everybody needs to understand that life goes on. It always has, and it always will. It must. I suspect you might be surprised at what she has to say, Henry. If it were me, I'd hate like hell to live life not ever knowing what *she* feels anyway."

That was the last they spoke of it but it caused Henry to reevaluate everything about his relationship with Mary. Neither had ever so much as flirted with the other out of propriety and duty to Bill but they had a very special closeness to one another and shared a stronger bond than many married people. What Henry couldn't tell on his own was if that bond was that of a sister or something more. Was it possible that Mary had developed feelings for him? By then, he and Mary had spent considerably more time together than she and Bill ever had by a factor of 20. Was it reasonable to even consider that she might actually have come to love him too?

He pondered the possibilities and weighed his options carefully again and again. His uncle's advice continued to haunt him for a few days afterward. What if Mary left? She had made no indication of any kind that she intended to alter her daily routine of coming out to the farm but if Bill had been the attraction, why was she still coming? He tried to make sense of things but it left him confused and frustrated to the point where he decided he would rather get it over with and settle the matter one way or the other before it drove him crazy.

On a cool early October evening just after supper, he and Mary were sitting on the front porch of the house swaying on the swing together and listening to the frogs in Old Man Janson's pond. He finally mustered the courage to tell her what had been a secret to everyone, except for Uncle Ed apparently, since he was 11 years old. He braced for a crushing rejection or even a scathing rebuke for suggesting such a notion on the heels of his brother's death but instead he had been shocked and elated when Mary burst into tears and hugged him. If he tried hard enough, he could still hear her words.

"Oh Henry! Of course I LOVE YOU! I've known it for over a year. Why on earth do you think I've practically moved in over here? I didn't know what to do. I couldn't tell Bill in a letter, that wouldn't be fair, and I didn't know how to tell you so I was stuck. Bill and I fancied each other but we NEVER said 'I love you' or made any promises other than we would wait and see and I honestly don't know where things would have gone. It felt like it was my duty to wait and see when he came home but then the more time we spent together the more I knew I was falling for you. I couldn't help it. The day the telegram came ... I cried for Bill because of course I cared about what happened to him, but I also cried because I thought it meant I would never get the chance to be with *you*. How could it all work out now? It would look like I was chasing whatever brother would have me. It felt wrong even though it wasn't. I never dreamed you loved me too."

The words had been like fresh air in a stale room wiping out all of his anxiety and concern about the future in an instant. *The woman sure can keep a secret*, he had thought.

Shortly thereafter, they shared the news of their romance with Uncle Ed and Aunt Mathilda who were thrilled. Uncle Ed seemed almost as excited as Henry and he gave them both giant bear hugs to express it. He loved both of them and expressed that he hoped that they would make this into a permanent arrangement.

Aunt Mathilda was equally as giddy as she gave Mary a small peck on the cheek and even went so far as to pat Henry on the shoulder. Much to his surprise, they all survived the excitement generated by her outpouring of affection.

Immediately, a full-blown courtship erupted. To outsiders the relationship didn't look a whole lot different as Henry and Mary were already inseparable long before that time. In fact, many of their friends were surprised at the news because they had already assumed the couple to be an item based on their constant companionship. Nevertheless, the pair was not completely without detractors as a few people in town found the romance to be a tad untoward due to Mary's previous affection for Bill.

On one occasion, Henry and Mary had been leaving a dance held at the high school gym when they had overheard a drunken childhood rival of Bill's, named John Everett, tell a group he was standing with "there goes Mary Winters ... she'll grab onto anything named Engel that will have her. I guess the uncle is next!" Though the comment was not made directly to them, it was still loud enough that they had been able to hear it and Henry was enraged and wanted to go back and confront the "jackass" who had said it. However, Mary had diffused the situation when she reminded Henry what Uncle Ed had told the two of them. He had told them to follow their hearts and "don't give a damn" about any idle talk that might come about. "Gossip is for the weak," he always used to say.

By Christmas Eve, an engagement was proposed and accepted much to the delight of everyone involved. Uncle Ed had given Mary a congratulatory kiss under the mistletoe with a little more gusto than Henry preferred but that could be owed to the quantity of hot buttered rum he had celebrated with and not any nefarious intentions he held. He genuinely adored this young couple as if they were his own son and daughter and tearfully made certain that they and all in their company knew that he intended for them to live on the farm in a house he would build for them. He also declared that they would someday inherit everything in order to assure the Engel family legacy would live on.

* * *

Henry's daydream was interrupted by a rumble from the brush hog as it leveled the uneven mounds of earth left behind by an industrious mole. The meadow was more than half mowed now and the sun was beating down with full force. He made the long slow turn around the far end of the pond and directed the wheels to make another trek back toward the stable following the edge of the remaining uncut turf. Even with a large deck such as the brush hog had, it was a time-consuming and mind-numbing process. It was a lot like NASCAR, he liked to joke with the gang at The Beaver, just a LOT slower and without the crashes.

Henry didn't mind any of it though. He often found the hum of the tractor and the ability to think quietly on his own without distraction therapeutic. In fact, even on a smoking hot day like this one, he looked forward to the task and made the most of it.

As he approached the driveway and the end of this pass he prepared to turn to head back for another. Just then, the familiar sight of Lucy's truck appeared above him at the mail box. A hand shot out of the window to greet him and he responded in kind. She filled the box with a stack of mail and sped down the road. Henry was sorry she hadn't brought a package because he could hardly wait to announce to her that his cat now had a name. He would have to order something, he thought, so he could clear up that fiasco about pet names from their last conversation. He checked his watch just for fun. It read 1:57 p.m. How could anyone not admire Lucy Dawson?

## CHAPTER 15

# Home Is Where the Heart Is

H ENRY PULLED THE stable door to rest back in its original position before securing it with the rusty padlock that had hung from the latch for years. He was hot, dusty, and sweaty but satisfied that things looked sharp again so he felt that the effort and short-term discomfort had been worth it. It was a few minutes past five and he paused briefly to take a few swigs from the little blue jug before walking the short distance from the building to the mailbox. He was eager to get to his meeting with Jake, but recalled the mail Lucy had left hours before and retrieved it from the box before he headed back to the house.

Joe sat dutifully waiting for him halfway up the hill. He was casually watching from the shade of an oak he had retreated to earlier after completely inspecting the stable for prey and coming up empty. For today, his consolation prize would be a bowl of cat food supplied by Millie and he wouldn't even have to chase it. It was hot and he was tired so it sounded like a good option to him at that point.

Henry closed the door to the mailbox and began the march

home as he sorted through the various correspondence and periodicals included in the day's delivery. The first thing that caught his eye was the July 1997 issue of *Coin Universe* magazine featuring a stunning 1799 Draped Bust Dollar on the cover. Scanning the new edition would be an enticing option for tonight's entertainment. He was sifting through the other items for anything else of importance when his eyes landed on the one thing he always dreaded to see. In his hands was another plain gray business envelope with only Henry's name and address on it. It was just like the one he had received back in March and discarded despite Millie's protests. The handwriting was unmistakable to him and it always elicited an emotional response whenever he saw it. Though these letters had been randomly appearing several times per year in his mailbox for the past decade or so, he still had not been able to completely steel himself against the memories they dredged up within him each time one appeared.

\* \* \*

Henry was reminded of a former life he had led and the demons that he had not yet made his peace with that still caused him pain when he allowed it. On this occasion, he was reminded of a chilling day in March of 1944. He and Mary had set their wedding date for the fourth Saturday in April and everything had felt as if it was falling into place for the young couple. Though World War II raged on with no end in sight, Henry had felt insulated from it on the farm. Letters from George, who was now stationed in England, continued to arrive with news of the conflict but it all seemed very far away from Lewis. Uncle Ed had contracted with a man from town to help him design and construct their home just to the west of the main house and buildings and every day seemed to bring about new excitement at the prospects for their future. He was young and in love. It just felt as though all was going to work out after all.

When Henry found Uncle Ed's lifeless body in the barn, the world he had known was shattered and a chain of events that would alter his life forever was set in motion. A massive stroke had taken the patriarch of the family from him at the age of 62 and left him without the father figure and wise counsel he had so heavily relied upon. It was yet another close member of his family tragically and abruptly lost and it devastated him. If that was not enough to bear, an additional gut punch was on the way to test his mettle even further. Only days after his uncle's funeral and burial in the cemetery at Calvary Lutheran Church, Aunt Mathilda had dropped the bombshell that she intended to sell the farm and move east to live with her sister. There would be no inheritance, no farming, and no future for Henry and Mary in Lewis as Uncle Ed had so proudly professed and deeply desired.

With nowhere else to turn, Henry had gone to St. Louis to see George's father to seek advice. He was the only man Henry could think of who might know how to pursue the matter legally and see Uncle Ed's intentions, and Henry's dreams, somehow still become a reality. George Sr. had listened intently at the dining room table to Henry's plight and after appraising the situation had delivered the somber news that there was nothing Henry could do to stop Aunt Mathilda from proceeding as she desired. Unfortunately, his uncle was not a lawyer or a businessman and hadn't put his intentions onto paper or set up any legal instruments that might have prevented Aunt Mathilda from shattering her husband's plan for the family. As things stood, it was all hers to do with as she wished and her cold heart had no room whatsoever in it for Henry and Mary. She had always been a dutiful wife but had never accepted her role as a mother nor shared in Uncle Ed's passion for an Engel family legacy. She had resented that Henry and Bill had been forced upon her and in a final stroke was taking her revenge and making her escape from the life that she hated. That would be the last that Henry would ever see or have contact with her.

On a more promising note, George Sr. immediately recognized that this was his chance to pry Henry from a life on the farm and offered him a position with the Schuetz Shoe Co., which Henry gratefully accepted. The older man had always been very fond of Henry and on any occasion he could, he had attempted to infuse him with as much knowledge of the business as Henry was willing to absorb. All of the evenings spent at the dining room table with George, his father, and grandfather were now going to pay off handsomely for both the boy and the company. George Sr. had just signed a deal with the U.S. Army that called for his firm to supply the military with tens of thousands of pairs of boots and other assorted footwear and he installed Henry as an assistant to the president within the newly created division that had been formed to fill the order. He was charged with learning the business and seeking out ways to improve the bottom line results for the company. Henry was in the right place at the right time and was being given a golden opportunity to get his foot in the door at a successful and rising company that men twice his age and experience would have killed for.

Henry and Mary were wed back in Lewis at Calvary Lutheran Church before a small gathering on April 22, 1944. They loaded their sparse belongings into a car borrowed from Doc Winters and left that evening to begin their new life together in St. Louis. George Sr. had rented a house for them in Black Jack, MO, a little suburb north of downtown, and the young newlyweds set up their first household there. The adjustment was very difficult for Henry in the beginning. Most everything in his life had been turned upside down in a matter of weeks, shaking him to his core. However, Mary had smoothed the way with ever present encouragement and unwavering faith in her husband's ability to learn quickly and excel at his new profession. He did both.

By May of 1945, Henry had performed his duties so well that George Sr. had rewarded him with a generous cash bonus and a promotion to vice president in the company's military footwear division. When the previous occupant of the title had fallen ill and been forced to miss nearly two months of work, Henry had assumed the role and handled it with such skill that George Sr. had decided to make the position permanent and re-assign the other fellow within the company upon his return to health. Times were good and the money rolled in.

At home, everything was also going along extremely well. He and Mary were very happy and had begun discussions of starting a family. The war in Europe had come to an end and everyone hoped that the conflict in the Pacific would soon cease as well. The price of victory thus far had been terribly high with the loss of Bill, but at least as of yet George had come through it unscathed. Henry hoped that it would not be necessary for his friend to have to now participate in the invasion of Japan after having run the beaches of Normandy and defeating the Nazis.

\* \* \*

Millie's white sedan appeared above him and met him a moment later at the base of the hill. She brought the car to a halt next to him and lowered the driver's side window to address him.

"It's just after five Mr. Engel and I'm on my way home. I left a fresh bowl out for Joe and you've got fried chicken and mashed potatoes for your dinner tonight." Millie knew he was going to be hot and tired and she made a special effort to prepare one of his favorite meals for him.

The news brought a broad smile to his face and elicited his favorite catchphrase as related to Millie's choice of entrée.

"What's better than fried chicken?" he asked.

"More fried chicken," she answered with a laugh.

Looking him over she then added, "You aren't going to still run over the yard up top are you?" She was referring to his stated plan from the morning whereby he intended to mow and trim the yard around the house in the evening after the day's chores were complete.

He could tell by her tone that she thought it was a bad idea in light of the extreme heat of the day and the fact that the yard wasn't looking all that rough to begin with.

"Nah, I'm going to let that go until tomorrow. It'll be there."

"Well good, you get yourself to your meeting and have a nice long talk with Jake and Joe and cool off some."

"That is the plan," he agreed emphatically.

"All right then, I'll let you get to it. I'll see you again."

"Good deal; be careful driving home," he replied.

Millie eased the car past him and headed up the driveway as he resumed his trek to the house. Just a bit ahead, Joe still sat patiently watching and waiting for him in the shade so they could go and see Jake together. Henry looked at his pal and recalled something Millie had just said. She was right. His meetings, which had for so many years been held in strict privacy with his longest and most enduring friend, had now taken on another participant. Meetings with Jake had morphed into meetings with Jake and Joe. It had transitioned naturally over time but now Joe never missed a meeting and seemed to almost look forward to the event as he often arrived on the front porch before Jake and Henry got there. This sense of timing that Joe possessed always impressed Henry because as far as he knew the feline didn't own a watch and likely was not able to tell time anyway.

He reached the cat and without breaking stride continued past as the smaller Engel stood, stretched, and then joined him.

"What do you say, buddy?" he greeted his companion.

As usual, Joe didn't have much to say but the sound of Henry's voice was pleasing to him and he trotted alongside the man with a spring in his step. In short order they reached the front porch and Joe took up his post sprawling to the side of the door while Henry went inside and fetched Jake. The house was filled with the aroma of Millie's freshly fried chicken and Henry was looking forward to digging into it, but for him, business always came first.

He returned to the porch and assumed his position on the throne as the King of Oak Forest and called the meeting to order.

"It's been a damn good day, fellas," he announced to the boys while bringing the glass to his lips. After a long slow swallow, he let out a heavy sigh and allowed the muscles in his body to release. No matter what was happening in his world good or bad, he had conditioned himself over his lifetime to put it on hold for an hour a day and decompress.

\* \* \*

It was a tactic first revealed to him by his business mentor, George Sr., shortly after Henry went to work for him at the shoe company. He had taught the young man that taking an hour out of one's hectic day to relax, reflect, and strategize was an invaluable tool that provided many benefits. It was an opportunity to reduce stress and quiet one's mind and it often yielded sound decisions made calmly and prudently rather than flawed knee-jerk reactions that others made in the heat of the moment.

Henry and Jake hadn't gotten along too well at first but became much better acquainted when George returned from the war. His best friend's homecoming was a cause for great celebration as not only was he safe and sound but he would be joining Henry at the Schuetz Shoe Co. The two pals would be able to pick up where they had left off prior to the conflict. With the loss of Bill from his life, George now was the closest thing to a brother Henry had. Those were heady times indeed and Henry quickly realized that either he could control Jake or Jake would control him.

After a particularly raucous night on the town with George and several of his war buddies celebrating the recently announced victory over Japan, Henry had made a thorough ass of himself and Mary hadn't spoken to him for a week. He decided that enough was enough. From that day forward, his only interactions with Jake were his highballs at meeting time. Beyond that, he rarely ever drank any alcohol except for an occasional glass of wine or bottle of beer at a dinner or party.

It was not so hard to understand how Henry had gotten carried away by it all. He and Mary had been pushed from their nest and rather than plummet to earth had found their wings. Henry had thrived at his new career and the money was rolling in. Likewise, Mary was the perfect wife and their house had truly become a home, which they had arranged to purchase from the landlord. They were more in love now than ever and made the decision it was time to start a family. The icing on the cake was George's safe return. For once, all the pieces seemed to be in place.

However, for Henry, the calm often preceded the storm. In

yet another life-altering twist he would soon be tested in ways he could not have possibly imagined or prepared himself for.

It was just after dinner on a rainy Wednesday evening in October of 1945 when the telephone mounted on the kitchen wall rang. Mary was washing dishes and Henry was doing the drying so he dropped his towel on the counter and proceeded across the room to answer it. He had been expecting a call from George related to some matters at the office that they needed to discuss. He figured that at least for now, he was off the hook with the dish drying and answered the phone with a playful tone.

"He-e-ello," he said after picking up the handset.

There was silence.

"Hello?" he repeated. Still nothing. He wondered if perhaps he and the other party had a bad connection but before he could speak again he heard a voice come through timidly from the other end.

"Is that you, Henry?" said the voice. Henry's face turned pale and a chill ran down his spine. He couldn't speak.

"Henry?" repeated the ghost with more confidence this time. It was impossible. It simply could not be. The voice was one he knew extremely well but had never expected to hear again.

Shocked and bewildered, he could only manage a whisper, "Who is this?"

"The last person you expected. It's me kid. I'm back." The words were surreal to Henry but the voice was unmistakably that of his big brother.

"Oh, my God!" Henry exclaimed as he sank into a chair at the kitchen table.

At first, Mary was preoccupied with her dishes and had not really paid attention to what Henry was doing, but now hearing the alarm in his voice she turned to her husband and saw a man in a total stupor.

"What is it, Henry?" she asked deeply concerned about what was happening.

Henry couldn't hear her. His mind was racing and his heart was pounding wildly. The room started to spin as he tried to breathe.

"Jesus, Bill! How can this be? Where are you? We were told you were dead over two years ago!" The stunned silence had given way to a flood of emotions and questions that poured forth with no regard for Mary who was standing a few steps away and processing the things he had just said.

"Oh ... my ... God!" she declared once it had sunk in and fell into the chair opposite Henry as her legs suddenly were unable to support her.

"I'm in Lewis," answered his brother. "I thought I was coming home. Only now I found out I don't have one anymore ..."

"Bill, honest to God we got a telegram that said you were missing and presumed dead back in '43!" Henry interrupted. "Where the hell have you been?"

"I've spent the last two plus years of my life scratching it out in a Japanese prison camp. Let me tell you, it was a real hellhole. When the army liberated us I was in pretty bad shape so I spent some time on a hospital ship getting my strength back before they shipped me home. A guy in records told me they had notified my family I was dead so I figured I'd better come home and surprise everyone in person rather than send some damn telegram and give Uncle Ed a heart attack. Sounds like that wouldn't have mattered, huh?"

"Wait, what do you know? Who told you about Uncle Ed?"

Henry inquired, now quickly recovering his wits and realizing that Bill likely had even more questions than he did about what had happened over the last couple of years.

"I talked to Old Man Janson. He said Uncle Ed dropped dead in the barn back in '44. I asked about you and he said you had moved to St. Louis and had taken a job with the Schuetz Shoe Co. He also told me what that old bitch did to all of us." He was now referring to the cold and heartless sale of the farm, which had ended their family legacy and left them both without any inheritance or a place to live in Lewis.

He then continued, "I gotta tell you kid, it tears me up to see everything the way it is. I can't believe it, I just can't believe it."

The last statement was referring to the actions of the Allied Gas Co., which had purchased the farm on the cheap from a woman in a hurry to sell. Their interest was in the ground and not the buildings so they promptly leveled and removed all of them. Henry had never returned to Lewis to see it but he had read about it in the *Lewis Gazette*, which he still received on a regular basis. Uncle Ed's final humiliation had been authorized by someone in a boardroom and his only monument from then on was the modest headstone that adorned his grave.

"Bill, what else do you know?" Henry asked with trepidation. His brother sounded upset and distressed but based on the world as it now was and the ordeal he had survived only to come home and find all lost, it was a reasonable reaction.

Mary sat with tears streaming down her face and her hands over her mouth as she stared off past Henry into the abyss. She could not even fathom all that was happening and what it might mean.

"Oh, you mean your wife?" Bill answered casually. His cavalier response floored Henry who guessed that either Bill was in complete shock by all that had transpired or he was sarcastically toying with him. It turned out to be both.

"Yeah, you son-of-a-bitch, I know about your wife," he declared with the cold hard tone of a judge sending a prisoner to the gallows. There it was. The elephant in the room was out of its cage.

"Bill …" Henry had wanted to say something, anything, to explain and make his resurrected brother understand that no one was to blame but Bill cut him off almost before he could get started.

"Not a word, Henry, not a word. How could you? I've been living on her memory and the hope of getting home to my family for two years while every horrible thing imaginable was happening around me. Now, I come back to find out that I have no home, no gal, and no family."

"Bill, we're still brothers. We've got to talk this thing out," Henry implored.

"Nope Henry, I'm out of here. I've got friends in New York and I'm heading there to try and make some sort of life for myself. I don't have a brother anymore. Now you're the one who's dead." Before Henry could say another word he heard a click and then the dial tone on the line.

He dropped the handset onto his lap and stared at the ceiling in disbelief. How could all of this have happened? How could things be such a mess when the discovery that Bill was alive should be cause for incredible celebration? He was losing his brother all over again.

Mary rushed out of the kitchen in tears. Every twinge of guilt she had ever felt about Bill now came at her all at once and she was overwhelmed. Henry, on the other hand, just felt numb.

He was in total shock and couldn't think of what to do next so he called an emergency meeting with Jake. Unlike the current meeting he was involved in with Jake and Joe on this hot summer's day, the meeting on the night Bill rose from the dead was considerably longer and less enjoyable.

## Chapter 16

# Uncle Sam's Day

FRIDAY, JULY 4, 1997, was a clear and scalding hot day. The thermometer had already crashed the 90s by mid-morning and the forecast called for a high of 105 degrees in Lewis for the celebration of America's independence. As Henry rolled down County Road 27 toward town the hot wind generated by his speed whipped through the cab of the 1930 Ford Model A truck. It was a far cry from modern air conditioning but it was good enough to help keep him cool, if only just a little. The corn fields along the road looked stressed but were still shoulder high despite the drought that had held a firm grip on the area since late May.

One unfortunate byproduct of the unusually dry weather had been the cancellation of the annual town fireworks display. The mayor and city council had been reluctantly forced by Mother Nature to pass an ordinance banning any and all pyrotechnics within the city limits due to the arid conditions and the risk of fire. Everyone was saddened by the move but agreed it was the necessary and prudent thing to do.

For this year, the parade would have to suffice as the highlight of the event and Henry, as usual, was prepared to do his part.

He had spent the better part of the previous day washing, waxing, and polishing his prized truck for its prominent role as the carriage that annually transported the parade's grand marshal. Each year, the citizens of the town nominated candidates and elected a worthy honoree who then would have the privilege of leading the procession down Hughes Avenue while greeting the throng from the bed of the classic vehicle.

He slowed the old Ford and eased it into the turnoff of the county road and onto Main Street. The adornments of the holiday were immediately visible as nearly every building in Old Town featured an American flag or some other form of patriotic bunting on its exterior. The flagpole in the town square near the founder's monument, which typically displayed a modern day version of the Stars & Stripes, now featured a large Betsy Ross flag with its oval of 13 white stars against a field of blue. It was a special tribute to the nation's birth that the city fathers ordained for one week each year.

There was a feeling of electricity in the air as Henry neared the parking lot of Calvary Lutheran Church. Each year it served as the staging area for the parade and the surrounding streets were lined with the cars and trucks of those who would be participating in the grand procession. People of all ages were scattered about and migrating slowly toward the gathering place. Henry neared the entrance of the lot and checked his watch, which read 11:20 a.m., before slowly navigating through the crowd to his place at the head of the line.

The scene was an impressive sight to behold. Besides Henry's Model A, there were several other antique vehicles and vintage tractors in addition to a total of nine floats of varying sizes and quality being staged for the noon kickoff. The marching band from Lewis High School was practicing a rousing rendition of "You're a Grand Old Flag" and dozens of bicycles with red, white, and blue crepe paper were lined in rows awaiting their riders from the local elementary school. At the rear end, Louis Benhardt and some of his fellow firemen readied the town's hook-and-ladder truck for its role as the tail end of the dog.

The mayor of Lewis, a portly man in his late fifties named Richard Ross, donned a somewhat comical Uncle Sam costume complete with top hat and vigorously passed out 5" x 7" American flags on wooden sticks to seemingly anyone he could get to take one. Independence Day was his Super Bowl and he expended great energy before, during, and after the proceedings to assure that the town's signature event was a success. Henry felt badly for the man as he surmised it was miserably hot for him in the outfit but still found the sight entertaining.

No sooner had Henry shut off the motor than a gang of teens from the local youth group descended upon the truck with various decorations. A group of three large boys, looking more to Henry like lumberjacks than kids, carefully hoisted the grand marshal's throne onto the bed of the truck. An older gentleman in a hideous Hawaiian shirt directed the action and implored them to be careful not to scratch either the Model A or the antique chair. For his part, Henry paid little attention as he had been through this drill many times before and had always found the truck to survive it just fine. He suspected that the other man's true concern was the safety of the piece of furniture as it was the pastor's seat taken from the altar of the church. Regardless, Henry truly enjoyed soaking up the scene and the enthusiasm of the younger generation. *Whoever believes that the youth of America are going to hell in a hand basket has never been to Lewis,* he thought.

The time for launch neared and this year's grand marshal, Charlie Heinz, approached the truck flanked by a very sweaty and red-faced Uncle Sam. As the only member of the starting five from Lewis High School's 1976 championship basketball team to have made his home in Lewis, even at the age of 39, Charlie was seen as something of a rock star by the local populace. Henry remembered him as a shifty and swift guard with a deadly shot. He had been the hero whose buzzer beater had cemented that team forever into the hearts and history of the town. Children who weren't even born yet when he played to old timers who barely recalled his heroics uniformly shook his hand or "high fived" him at any encounter. However, Henry figured at his present weight, which was no doubt bolstered by regular meals at The Eager Beaver, he would have to rely on the shot because the speed and agility were most likely gone.

Charlie reached the truck and immediately extended his hand to Henry with a large smile on his face. It was easy to see why he was the most successful car salesman in town.

"Hey, Mr. Engel!" he greeted him enthusiastically.

"How you doing, Charlie?" Henry responded just as warmly.

"What a day! It sure is a hot one, huh?" the younger man said as he climbed into the back of the truck and took his seat in the large, ornately carved wood chair.

Before Henry could comment, the half-melted mayor of Lewis stepped alongside and lifted something up to Charlie. Henry practically fell over when he figured out what the mayor had.

Someone had removed Charlie's letterman's jacket from its place on the wall at The Eager Beaver and the mayor, in an incredibly ridiculous act, was petitioning Charlie to wear it in the sweltering heat. Prior to this moment, Henry had always considered

Richard Ross to be a fairly level-headed guy who made sound decisions. The townspeople apparently agreed as he was currently serving his third consecutive term in office. However, this act of foolishness had Henry, who was only wearing a light blue short-sleeved cotton shirt and khaki shorts yet still sweating profusely, scratching his head. He made a move to intervene but when he saw Charlie relent and stand to slip on the jacket he decided that perhaps he was the only sane one there and had better just get into the truck and let them work things out. As he climbed into the cab, he just so happened to take a quick glance back and found it rather amusing that his assessment of Charlie's physique jived with the memory the jacket had of him too. After some failed pro wrestling moves attempting to get the coat on, the executive decision was made that it would look just as good hanging from the back of the chair. Henry couldn't help but laugh to himself and think that it had all worked out for the best for Charlie for more than one reason.

The quick burst of an air horn was the appointed signal for everyone to take their places and those driving in the parade to start their engines. A moment later, a second burst of the horn and a hand wave from Mayor Ross officially started the procession on its way. A trio of uniformed boy scouts who took turns carrying aloft an apparently heavy large American flag and pole led the way with Henry right behind. The parade route was a straight shot from the outskirts of Old Town through the heart of Lewis and concluded just at the far side of New Town at the high school. They were moving now and they headed out of the parking lot and to the left down Hughes Avenue.

The first group of parade watchers was camped out along the front of the Lewis Bank & Trust parking lot. From there, the entire route was manned by a throng that everyone agreed easily exceeded 5,000 in number. Henry marveled at the figure. Considering that the stated population of the town was only 3,753, this was an impressive total and a testament to the drawing power of the event. Each year it not only captivated every living soul in town but it also brought in folks from places further away such as Troy and St. Louis.

The extensive cavalcade crawled slowly along the parade route to the sheer delight of all present. Henry steered with his right hand while waving one of Mayor Ross's tiny flags out the window with his left. He saw countless familiar and friendly faces along the way and felt gratified by the endless calls of "Hi Henry" and "Hello Mr. Engel!" he received. It was humbling to him get this attention despite the fact that the town's most famous citizen was riding in back. He was the one who felt like a rock star today.

For his part, Charlie seemed to be having a great time as well. He was tossing handfuls of bubble gum and candy from a box at his feet to the crowd on either side and greeting everyone he saw. Always the consummate professional, he also mixed in the occasional "Come see me" or "I've got a car for you" to prospective customers he identified amongst the multitude.

Though the whole endeavor took nearly 45 minutes to complete, it went by quickly and before he knew it Henry was parking the truck in the lot at the high school. His duty was successfully fulfilled for another year. As the remainder of the procession arrived it was flanked by what looked like the whole town who had filled in behind it with many coming on foot to the site of the picnic.

The annual gathering was centered on the football field behind the school gymnasium. An assortment of carnival rides and a Ferris wheel were set up on one end as well as games and attractions to entertain the attendees. At mid-field, booths hawking food and drink offerings from several local businesses were stationed. On the other side, a large seating area consisting of eight-foot square tables and scores of chairs was located beneath a large tent that had been erected to give the patrons a respite from the scorching sun. Large stand fans were posted on each corner providing a constant slow breeze underneath the canopy. The high school's portable stage had been set up strategically nearby leaving ample room for a dance floor in between. Typically the platform was used for the fall concert and the spring musical held in the gym, but during the summer it became the main stage for the picnic.

Throughout the day, several events were held there including what was typically a very entertaining rendition of the Gettysburg Address performed by the town's kindergarteners, clad in patriotic dress of course. The culmination of the activities would be a country music act, which would provide the evening's entertainment. This year, a five-person local band called "Four Roosters & a Hen" was the headliner. Henry hadn't heard them yet but their reputation around town was that they were a solid cover band with some equally good original material.

As the crowd poured in, the picnic grounds came to life and the area became a smorgasbord of sight and sound. Rarely could one find this sort of diversity in a single place and Henry always found the people watching to be perhaps the most entertaining part of the event. From refined older ladies in sundresses to obese tattooed rednecks, it was all here. People that would not normally mix together, on this day found each other's company tolerable and even desirable. It was one of the most endearing aspects of

Lewis, Henry thought to himself. Regardless of appearances, he believed Lewis to have the highest percentage of decent citizens per capita of any place in the world he had ever been during his extensive business travels. Lewis wasn't like Paris or Munich or Barcelona. It was better. They might not have the Eiffel Tower or the Vegas Strip but they had something more. They had home-baked apple pie, Midwestern values, and the secret to happiness. In short, the people of this town found their pleasure in simple things, which in turn provided the deep and real satisfaction that the rest of the world seemed to constantly be chasing.

Henry worked his way through the masses shaking hands and greeting old friends and acquaintances as he proceeded to the lemonade booth. After standing in line for what seemed to be an eternity, he gratefully acquired an extra-large cup of the cold drink and headed for a table under the tent to find some small relief from the heat.

"Over here, Henry!" came a call from his left. He turned to see a now much-cooler version of Uncle Sam seated alone at a table near one of the large fans. It looked to be a good spot and Henry accepted the invitation and joined him.

"Well, Dick, I think you've pulled it off again," Henry declared in praise of the efforts by the man to skillfully coordinate the event.

"Thank you, Henry. It's all worked out pretty well, all but the drought I guess," he commented with a bit of disappointment.

"Yeah, I agree, but you know what? It's good enough. You can't always have everything in life now, can you?" the elder man advised while taking a sip from his sweating cup.

The mayor knew that Henry was a "glass half full" kind of

fellow and appreciated the comment. He knew Henry was right and moved on to more pressing business.

"Say Henry, I've been needing to call on you," he began.

"Uh-oh, here it comes," Henry replied playfully.

The mayor smiled knowing that Henry was usually one step ahead of him and generally made these types of requests easier for him than anyone else in the same position would.

"Yeah, you know me, always got a hand out," he replied with a laugh.

Leaning toward him, so that they could speak more privately, Henry nodded for him to continue.

"Well, we've got a problem over at the community center. The roof is shot and there's no money to replace it."

"What about Johnny? What does he say?" asked Henry, knowing that the man who had donated the funds to originally build the center was a multi-millionaire in his own right from profits made from his Allied Gas Co. ties.

"That's the kicker, Henry. Johnny is down in a nursing home in St. Louis and apparently has lost his faculties. I guess it's Alzheimer's. Anyway, his only child, a daughter who lives in Florida says she has the power of attorney on everything now and they have done enough for Lewis over the years," explained the mayor in a hushed tone.

"Hmm. Yeah I had heard he wasn't doing well. So, Ann has the money now and told you to stick it in your ear?"

"Oh, you know her? Yeah, that's basically it," Dick agreed, shaking his head. "I'll confess, I'm at a loss as to what to do. It's going to be a big bill and the town is flat broke. We spent our wad fixing up this place last year and upgrading the fire house. We haven't had a chance to build up any savings yet. You know the economy; folks around here are scraping by as it is so I can't see going to them for more of what they don't have. On the other hand, that community center is a key place around here. Most of the kids in town use it along with everybody else." The mayor had laid the situation out succinctly and accurately. Henry thought he was showing considerably more sense now than he had done earlier with the letterman's jacket.

Henry understood the dilemma. In a town the size of Lewis, the economy was a sensitive issue. There was only so much money to go around and so many jobs to be had. Raising taxes or acquiring more town debt through the sale of bonds could easily upset that balance and send things spiraling in a negative direction. Just as important, the community center was an integral asset that was universally used by all. Closing it would be a devastating blow to the community and a lost selling point for prospective new businesses and residents considering relocation to Lewis.

"I was hoping somehow we could possibly raise the funds through donations from some of our more affluent citizens. Folks such as yourself, Gus Grainger, Hank Fitzgerald and John Everett ..."

The last name struck a chord with Henry. He would have no involvement in any venture that included that man.

"Nope," Henry answered staring off into space and considering the options.

The shoulders of the mayor sagged in response to Henry's reaction. He had been counting on him for help based on his previous willingness to be of assistance whenever he had approached him with a civic issue.

"No, that's not necessary. You can send me the bill for it on one condition," Henry declared.

Mayor Ross was floored and it took him a few seconds to realize what Henry had just said.

"My God, of course Henry, of course. What's the condition?" he asked excitedly.

"This has to be 100% anonymous. It's just between you and me. I really mean it," he firmly cautioned the town's leader. "If anyone ever finds out, don't ever come to me for help again."

The mayor knew Henry to be a generous but private man and didn't question his motives. Without hesitation, he offered Henry his hand and a firm promise that he would take the secret to his grave.

Both men were eminently happy with the arrangement. The mayor had solved what was the number one problem he currently faced in an instant and the invaluable community center could remain open. For Henry, it was a win on several fronts. It was a chance to help out the mayor who was a great leader and truly had the town's best interests at heart. It was also an opportunity to guarantee that an important resource used by so many in the town he loved would remain available. Finally, it was a chance to deprive John Everett the stage he so desperately craved. There was no doubt in Henry's mind that if they had followed through on the mayor's idea and gathered a consortium of benefactors together, Everett would have made a token donation and then spent the rest of his days declaring himself the savior of the town. For all of these reasons, it was worth every penny to Henry to buy a roof.

"Now that we've got that settled, tell me, what the hell were you thinking trying to get Charlie to wear a letterman's jacket?" Both men burst into laughter at the thought of it.

"It was a weak moment for sure," the mayor agreed after he had composed himself.

Over the next hour, the two men sat and shared lively and animated conversation on a broad variety of topics while occasionally being interrupted by a passerby saying hello. When the mayor finally recognized that he needed to circulate, he vigorously thanked Henry again for his extreme generosity and politely excused himself to go make the rounds. He walked away as the happiest Uncle Sam in America that day.

## CHAPTER 17

# "It's All about the Timing"

EXACTLY ONE WEEK too late for the fireworks display, the skies mercifully opened and drenched the parched earth in and around Lewis, MO. After a nearly six-week hiatus, the heat and drought were finally broken bringing much-needed relief to all concerned. It was a case of feast or famine. After having no measurable precipitation for such an extended period of time, it now seemed as though the sun might never shine again. It rained all day and all through the night with varying degrees of intensity for three straight days. All Henry could do during this soggy weekend was stand at his window and watch the river that had formed across the back yard cut deep swaths through his vegetable garden.

One unforeseen consequence of the continuous showers was the realization that Joe's food bowl needed to be moved somewhere under cover because its usual place on the patio was exposed to the weather. Henry selected a new location for it near the side door on the porch. Joe quickly gave the change his approval by emptying the bowl's contents on the first day it was there.

Sometime during the third night after the arrival of the unexpected monsoon, the downpours ceased. The following morning, Henry was grateful to finally get out of his house and be able to stroll through his waterlogged yard for a change of pace. With his morning coffee in hand, he assessed the condition of his garden and was relieved to find that the damage done to it was primarily cosmetic. Joe appeared to also have been afflicted by a bit of cabin fever as he ventured beyond his normal range and made a wide circuit along the very outskirts of Oak Forest stretching his legs and checking things out.

Right on schedule, Millie's white sedan made its slow approach up the hill before coming to a halt in its customary place beside the house. Henry heard her pull up and made his way across the yard to greet her.

"Well good morning, Noah!" she quipped as she exited the car. "Where's your ark?"

Henry laughed at the remark and shook his head. "Thought maybe I was going to need one for a moment there. It looks like we got every bit of seven inches since Friday according to the rain gauge."

"My word, sure seems like it's all or nothing this summer, don't it? Well, at least it broke the heat; they're calling for mid-80s all week."

"We'll take that," Henry agreed as he followed her inside to get a refill. The cooler temps would be a welcomed change to the streak of triple-digit readings they had suffered through in recent days.

"Say Millie, how'd you like some barbecue today for lunch?" he asked while pouring himself another cup of coffee.

"Barbecue?" she echoed back from the front hall where she was organizing a few things in her purse before placing it in its usual post by the hall tree. "Oh you know me, I can always eat barbecue. But are you sure you feel like cooking out today?"

"No, I was thinking about getting some from Big Jake's. I want to run by the bank and it kind of sounds good to me," he explained. Henry had broken from form over the weekend and skipped his normal jaunt into town due to the lousy weather. Truthfully, the need for a change of scenery was a greater motivator for his trip today than his desire for barbecue or the visit to the bank.

"Well that sounds just fine to me. I'll have the pulled pork sandwich and some coleslaw please."

"You got it," Henry acknowledged. He went into his office with his coffee and spent some time at his desk endorsing the week's checks and completing the deposit slip. After he was finished, he opened the safe and removed two narrow boxes of coins, which he put into his briefcase to take with him. Once at the bank, he would swap them out with other coins from his extensive collection and bring a new group home for a visit.

In short order, all was ready and Henry was headed down the road toward Lewis. He had everything timed so that he would arrive back home, with food in hand, around noon and just in time for lunch. It was a pleasant diversion to drive to town and he was in a good mood when he arrived at the Lewis Bank & Trust. Upon going inside, everyone who worked there took note and made commentary in regard to how rare a sighting of Henry inside the bank on any day other than Saturday truly was. It was nearly a hotter topic than the recent weather, which seemed to only slightly trump the stir created by Henry's weekday visit.

After he concluded his business and was back in his Explorer, he recognized that he now knew what it felt like to be a unicorn or Big Foot due to the attention he received. With a laugh he decided he might need to make an effort to vary his trips to Lewis, if only just a little, to prevent inciting mass hysteria in the future.

A few moments later, Henry pulled the SUV off of Hughes Avenue and into a parking spot in front of a small white cinder block building. Across the front windows, a flowing red cursive moniker, "Big Jake's BBQ," and a telephone number were painted and outlined in bright yellow. J.P. Jasterson wasn't the only "Jake" Henry called a friend.

Even before he opened the door of the vehicle, Henry could smell the sweet hickory smoke from the massive grills that were out back and already loaded to full capacity with the day's fare. It was a simple place with a handful of tables arranged in rows before a counter with six stools lined across the front of it. The walls were relatively bare, save for a few old framed photos, which seemed to have no particular correlation to each other, and a small television, which had been mounted near the ceiling in the far corner. No one ever noticed or cared about the décor because it wasn't the atmosphere that kept people packing the place anyway. It was the quality of the food that drove the business. Even before the Walmart had been erected behind Jake's place, it had become a destination all on its own. Of course, the additional traffic provided by the extremely popular retail giant was welcomed and assured that Jake's would remain a thriving establishment.

Henry opened the door and was greeted by the voice of a man on the television hawking fitness equipment. There wasn't a soul in sight but it was quite early as it was just moments past the 10:30 a.m. opening time posted in the window.

Henry knew the proprietor was likely out back tending to his grills. Therefore, he walked behind the counter and through the kitchen toward the open rear door where the smoke he had smelled was originating. As he passed through the threshold, he could see a dark black hand attached to a large muscular forearm vigorously flipping slabs of ribs with a set of oversized steel tongs.

"There he is!" called Henry warmly.

"Well hello, Henry!" boomed the voice of the owner of the arm as a broad smile stretched across his face.

A warm and engaging fellow in his late forties, Jake Le Detour was a huge man. At 6'6" and 270 lbs., he dwarfed Henry, who was no pipsqueak himself. Jake was born in New Orleans to a Creole father and Jamaican mother and possessed one of the more interesting accents Henry had ever encountered. Shortly after his return to Lewis in 1974, Henry had met the younger man at The Eager Beaver. Jake had just finished a stint as a cook in the U.S. Army and had won a bus ticket in a poker game that led him to Lewis. He had no particular plans for his future at the time so the trip to a place he had never heard of seemed like an adventure. After his arrival in Lewis, he had liked the looks of the town and had seen a "Cook Wanted" sign in the window of The Beaver. He immediately applied for and got the advertised job working in their kitchen.

Gus Grainger, then owner of the diner, had liked the kid right away and hired him on the spot. Henry also was fond of him from the first time the two met and dubbed him "Big Jake." It seemed everyone else in town had a similar reaction to the young man as the name stuck with him to the degree that later on when he opened this, his own restaurant, he appropriately named it after himself.

"How's business these days?" Henry greeted his friend who was clad in chef's whites and covered in a mixture of sauce and sweat.

"Outstanding! Yeah buddy, we're selling it as fast as we can cook it these days!" exclaimed the delighted man as sheets of smoke rolled up from the grill where he toiled. "Ya hungry? I got a deal on ribs today!"

Jake's enthusiasm and passion for his work was obvious. It was the same today as it had been 15 years before when Henry had first pulled him aside at The Beaver and suggested he might do well to start his own business in town. Henry knew that no man ever got rich working for another, and after having seen the skill and work ethic that Jake possessed had encouraged him to try his hand out on his own. A year later, it was Henry who extended a loan to Jake to start his restaurant. It had also been Henry, who along with Gus, had advised and taught the emerging entrepreneur what he needed to know to succeed in business. Henry's faith in the young man had been well placed. His establishment did so well, in fact, that he was able to pay Henry back in full three years prior to the original terms of the agreement.

"Of course I'm hungry you big ox! I didn't swing by just to see your pretty face!" Henry joked.

The larger man let out a sonic boom of a laugh at his mentor's teasing.

"But I'm so handsome!" he laughed. "All right then Henry, let's get you fixed up!"

"I think I'm going to have to take you up on those ribs. Yours are the very best I've ever had."

"Well, I thank you! But ribs aren't tougher to make than any other barbecue. Just slower is all. With ribs, it's all about the timing."

Henry thought to himself how true those words were for most things in life. The two men walked inside and Henry moved around to the front of the counter where he took the seat closest to the cash register.

Jake took pen in hand and scribbled Henry's order onto the pad in front of him. After Henry had finished making his requests, Jake tore the ticket from the book and carried it with him into the kitchen to gather Henry's food.

"So how have you been, man?" he inquired while preparing Millie's sandwich.

"I'm good, buddy. No complaints here. How about you? How's Jessie?" Henry inquired about Jake's wife.

"Aww man, she's mean as ever," he answered with another of his signature booming laughs. Henry had to chuckle as well at the obvious joke as both men knew that Jake's bride was likely one of the sweetest women to have ever walked the face of the earth.

"Hey, Millie says you got a cat out at your place now?"

"Well, as a matter of fact, we do," Henry responded, remembering that Millie often frequented Big Jake's and had known him almost as long as he had. "He's got a face like you."

"Handsome?" Jake interjected referring to his earlier joke.

"Black!" Henry ribbed playfully.

"Well then like I said, handsome!" Jake shot right back as both men laughed.

"Yeah, I tell you what, he's a dandy, Jake. He's about the

best-looking cat I think I've ever seen. He's a Siamese with a black face and black socks and tail. Just really marked nice, you know? And he's just a good soul. He follows me around the place and keeps an eye on things. I confess, half the time I swear he knows what I'm thinking. And when I talk to him, he always looks at me like he can understand. I know it's dumb, but it really seems like it. I tell you … he's something."

This was a softer side of Henry than Jake had seen before. They had shared many meals and conversations over the years but the younger man had never known Henry to directly open up that way about his personal feelings for something or someone else. He saw Henry as a dear friend and mentor and the tenderness expressed touched him.

"That's a great thing," he congratulated as he placed a large brown grocery sack containing Henry's order on the counter. His voice was more hushed now and the joking that was ever present was now replaced by sincere happiness for the man who had been so instrumental in helping him over the years. Many was the time that he and Millie had discussed Henry and lamented the fact that he had no wife or family to provide him companionship on his large estate in the countryside. Jake was happy to hear that now Henry had finally found someone to share his home with.

After their typical friendly debate about whether the food should be free or not, Henry won out as always and forced his protégé to accept full payment. Jake had been trying for years, to no avail, to provide Henry with even one free meal, but Henry would have none of it. Business was business, he always said, and the bills must be paid.

They said their farewells and Henry walked out just after

11:00 as the first car pulled in. As was the norm, it was going to be a busy day at Big Jake's BBQ.

On the drive home the aroma of the delicious feast sitting in the passenger's seat filled the cabin and taunted Henry. *No one can match Jake when it comes to barbecue*, he thought. For Henry's part, it was the sweet and smoky sauce, made from Jake's secret recipe, that put it in a class all of its own. His earlier urge to get out of the house and head to town was now replaced by the anticipation of getting back home and sampling the chef's special of the day.

As he rounded the last bend before home, he disturbed a small group of doves who were bathing leisurely in a puddle that the rains had left in a depression in the asphalt. He slowed but as he passed they panicked and flew up in front of him and then over his Explorer to safety. The sight triggered memories of Mary as always was the case anytime Henry encountered the graceful birds.

\* \* \*

His wife had been especially fond of doves. She liked to refer to them as "God Birds" because of their significance in the Bible. It was a fancy from her youth that had endured into adulthood. Henry recalled the difficult days he and Mary had shared after the reappearance of his once-lost brother Bill. It was a hard time as the two struggled to sort out their own feelings about what had happened, what to do, and what it all really meant for the future. In the weeks that followed the revelation, their once warm and passionate relationship had remained polite but had turned cooler and more distant.

It had remained that way, with no end in sight, until Mary broke the ice and brought clarity to the situation. She had been praying regularly for guidance as to what to do and was doing so again while walking home one day. It was a particularly moderate afternoon in November, and she had opted to stretch her legs and go on foot to the corner market for a few items she desired. On her way back, as she asked God for a sign that all was ok and that she and Henry were in the right with him, a dove had flown down and landed briefly on the sidewalk in front of her before hurrying away. A moment sooner or later, and she might have passed without seeing it but she had been in the right place at just the right time.

She believed the sighting to be an unmistakable sign that everything was going to be ok for the young couple. Her mood soared and by the time Henry arrived home from work, all within the household had returned to normal. She met him at the door with a loving embrace and kiss, and quickly explained to him all that had occurred. For his part, Henry was not so religious and was less impressed by the "miracle." However, Mary's passion and sound reasoning about the truth of things swayed him. Everyone had acted in accordance with the facts as they knew them to be and without malice toward another. It was time for them to continue their lives. Henry agreed and hoped at some point to reconcile with Bill, but if that day never came, that's just the way it was meant to be.

The next few years were some of the happiest of Henry's life. He and George excelled professionally and ascended together to the highest ranks within the Schuetz Shoe Co. Henry's abilities had advanced to the point that Schuetz's top rival, an aggressive manufacturer based in Chicago, had made inquiries attempting to lure him to their side. Along the way, the money poured in and he made numerous investments that were doing equally as well. Aside from his business pursuits, life at home with Mary was splendid. They had not succeeded yet in conceiving a child but Henry was having a wonderful time trying. Mary was adamant that she wished to give birth to a family and dismissed Henry's overtures that adoption might be a viable option if their efforts failed to produce children. She redoubled her efforts to get pregnant and Henry, with a smile on his face, gladly complied. Once again, it felt as though everything had fallen into place and was going to work out. Based on previous events from throughout his life, that alone should have been enough to alarm Henry. However, as usual the coming storm Henry would be forced to weather was still over the horizon and concealed from view.

* * *

He steered the Ford past the mailbox and down the driveway eagerly anticipating his lunch. The barbecue stop had originally been more of a lark than a mission, but now he was famished and ready to sample Jake's handiwork. Bringing the SUV to rest beside Millie's car he climbed out with the large bag, not even thinking to bring in the briefcase underneath it, and proceeded inside through the side door.

"Hey Millie! Soup's on!" he called out as he stepped through the laundry room and into the kitchen before setting the bag on the counter of the island.

"Soup? I thought we were eating barbecue," she teased as she came down the staircase carrying a basket of dirty laundry.

"Ohh, yes ma'am! Can you smell that? We are absolutely eating barbecue today!" he declared gleefully.

# CHAPTER 18

# Betrayal

"FOR MY MONEY, Stan 'The Man' is the greatest Cardinal ever and one of the top five players the game has ever seen. Good Lord, it should be obvious to anyone with a third grade education. The guy had 3,630 hits for Pete's sake, that's 4th all time! And I tell you what, he had to be the most consistently great player the game has ever seen too. He played in 24 straight All-Star games so that tells you all you need to know right there. Three-time NL MVP, won seven batting titles ... I bet you didn't know that."

It was true, Joe had no idea about the exploits of someone named Stan "The Man" Musial. In fact, he had no idea whatsoever about what had gotten Henry so excited or even what he was saying, but he could tell from the animated gestures and excited tones that he was angry about something. In any event, Joe was a skilled listener and let Henry vent without interrupting as they made their daily march to the street to collect the mail.

The source of Henry's agitation was a sports talk show he had been listening to moments earlier on the radio while cleaning his garage. A caller, clearly an idiot in Henry's estimation, had the audacity to suggest that not only was Musial not worthy of consideration as one of the game's greatest players ever, but that he might not even be the best to have ever worn the birds on the bat. Being a life-long St. Louis Cardinals and Musial fan, the affront was sacrilege and had sent Henry into an incredulous rant against the strange voice on the radio. Steve from St. Louis had unwittingly made the blood of Henry from Lewis boil.

"And I'll tell you another thing ..." Henry continued as they neared their destination. "He's one of the nicest men I've ever had the pleasure to meet. You'd never know he was anybody special. Real down to earth, quality guy, you know what I mean?"

Joe sensed that Henry desired something from him but since he still was in the dark about the meaning of all of this, he passed on the chance to acknowledge Henry's words and instead became distracted by a butterfly that was flitting nearby.

Realizing he had lost his audience for the moment, Henry suspended the campaign and reached inside the box to retrieve the day's mail. The yield was typically light on Thursdays and on this one in early September, that was indeed again the case. Three envelopes and a postcard were all that had come but he wasn't disappointed as it was such a pretty day and the walk had allowed him to clear the air about Mr. Musial. The heavy three-day rain in mid-July not only broke the drought and extreme heat of May and June, but signaled a shift to more moderate temperatures over the duration of the summer. In fact, no one could remember a more tolerable August than the one that had just passed.

"I'm heading home, Joe," Henry called to his cohort as he strolled back down the slope on his return trip. Joe heard his voice and decided that since the butterfly had ruined the game by flying high and out of reach, he might as well go back too.

Walking along, Henry read the postcard, which was printed on both sides with information about a coin show in October in St. Louis. It was being organized by the same group that hosted the numismatic expo in the Gateway City in April each year. The card explained that due to the success of the spring event, they would be holding an additional show in the fall. The goal was that it too might become an annual gathering that would complement the other. As he read through the details, he assumed that it would be held at the convention center, which was the place he had been going to each spring for as long as he cared to remember. However, he stopped in his tracks momentarily when he read the name of the venue. This show would be at the Clairmont, one of St. Louis' oldest and most historic hotels. The name literally halted Henry as he had a history there too. *What a shame*, he thought. *It might have been fun to attend.*

Joe had walked a few steps past him by then but stopped and looked quizzically back trying to understand what was going on. Henry recovered and looked up to see Joe waiting for him. Suspecting his friend was confused by his actions he felt the need to explain why there had been a delay.

"Sorry pal, I'm coming. I had a moment there. I haven't thought of this place in a long time," he said as the held up the postcard. "I don't think I ever finished telling you about Mary, did I, Joe?" Without waiting for a reply he continued, "Well, the last time I ever laid eyes on her was on Christmas Eve, 1953, at this very hotel."

Though they had gotten past the startling return of Bill and had thrived for a time, things changed as Mary became increasingly frustrated by her inability to become pregnant. Henry was fully engrossed in his career by then and was less concerned by family matters than she preferred. His distraction was seen as insensitivity by his wife and, over time, the stress and arguing about the lack of progress on the home front drove a wedge between the two of them and became a breaking point. By late 1952, things had gone from bad to worse. Blaming Henry for their plight, Mary had insisted she would not share a bed with him any longer. Deciding he would win the war of attrition, rather than sleep elsewhere, for the next year Henry slept on the floor next to the bed becoming more agitated and suspicious of his spouse with each passing day.

Mary had become consumed with her desire to bear children and pursued any and every option she could find, from the routine to the outlandish. She had become ultra-religious, seeking counsel from priests and help from God, while at the same time seeking advice from palm readers and quacks who advertised in magazines. Her obsession had taken on a life of its own and had been largely responsible for the discord between them. Henry was not a religious man and was extremely practical so much of what she was doing at the time grated on his nerves and he chafed at talk of it. In turn, Mary became more secretive about her actions to avoid conflict and the whole state of affairs had driven Henry from their bed, guaranteeing that no resolution or pregnancy would come any time soon.

"That last year was rough. She was acting really strange all of the time. Lots of whispered phone calls and time unaccounted for so I started paying closer attention to what was going on. One day she loved me like crazy and the next she wouldn't talk to me or it felt really forced and awkward. It was like living with two different people. Sometimes you can just 'feel' that things aren't right, you know?" Henry asked.

Joe sauntered along up the hill in silence hanging on Henry's every word.

"So, finally I have to tell somebody or I'm going to go crazy because even though it's been bad, she was my wife. You never want to believe that your wife is doing something so awful. So, I tell George all about what's been going on. You remember him? He was my best friend at the time. Anyway, George says I'm crazy. No way is Mary cheating on me, she's too good of a gal for that. I guess it was what I wanted to believe because after that I felt better and things at home even seemed to improve. That was ... until Christmas."

Henry's voice trailed off and his eyes raised to the sunny sky as he let out a deep sigh. He had never told anyone this story before. It was ground he hadn't retraced in 44 years and it had bite. He stopped near the point of the island to pull a couple of weeds that had sprung up along the edge of the asphalt as he continued his tale.

"So, the day before Christmas Eve I come home and Mary is whispering with someone on the phone. She doesn't see me come in and she's writing on a note pad. About the time she hangs up, I make a noise and she jumps, all nervous, and races out of the room. Weird. Later on, after she was asleep, I couldn't get that out of my head so I went into the kitchen and did a little detective work." Henry remembered how he had taken a pencil out of the drawer and then by flashlight, rubbed it over the next page on the pad to reveal the impression made on it by Mary's pen earlier. The information it revealed sent a chill down his back and cost him a night of sleep. It read "Clairmont Hotel, Market Street, 11:30 a.m."

"On Christmas Eve I told her I had to run over to the office for a bit in the morning and Mary said she had to run a couple of errands too. I left first but waited down the street to follow her and sure enough she headed right to the Clairmont. I was sick. I knew what was going on but I didn't want to really believe it. It's the worst feeling in the world to be betrayed by someone you love."

Henry gave her time to get inside before following across the street and into the hotel. The spacious and luxurious lobby was filled with an assortment of holiday travelers and bustling with activity. Some were resting on large couches and chairs while reading newspapers or smoking cigarettes. Others were at the counter checking in or waiting in line to do so. Henry made a quick scan of the room but did not see her. He stepped over to a man getting his shoes shined in the corner and asked him if he had seen Mary come in. The man politely indicated that he had and that she had walked into the hotel restaurant off to their left. As he stepped across the marble floor toward the dining room, Henry knew what he was facing, yet still wasn't truly prepared for it.

He paused for a moment just outside the doorway to gather strength and with a deep breath, opened the door and walked in. Immediately he was greeted by the maitre d' who inquired if Henry would be dining alone or meeting someone? Before Henry could answer, his eyes, which had been scanning the room over the man's shoulder, had raced across the crowd and landed on Mary who was seated at a table on the far side. His worst nightmares had been confirmed. Seated at the table beside her, holding her hand no less, was none other than the ghost of Christmas past, his brother Bill. Just then, Bill leaned over and kissed her on the cheek, unaware that they were being watched.

It was all a blur after that. Henry's initial impulse to fire across the room and deck the son-of-a-bitch had quickly been overwhelmed by a wave of nausea and flush of heat that made his head spin. He stuttered some sort of excuse to the maitre d' and turned and hurriedly left. He didn't know what to do or where to go so he did the first thing that came to mind and retreated to his office.

"So, after I see my wife kissing my brother I just lost it. I didn't know where to go or what to do. So, I went to my office to try and figure out my next move. I decided to call George. Figured I'd lean on my best friend. Seems reasonable right?" The pair walked back to the big garage as Henry kept speaking.

"Well here's the real kicker; I'm telling George what I just saw and my BEST friend in the world tells me *he knows all about it* and it isn't what I think. He claims Mary says she's trying to get me and Bill back together. How the hell could George be so gullible? To this day, I don't know what the worst part of it was Joe ... Mary, Bill, or George."

The betrayal, in Henry's mind had been comprehensive and complete. His wife was having an affair with his brother and his best friend had known of it and concealed it from him. It was more than any one man could be expected to bear and Henry erupted.

In a total fit of rage, he shouted a resignation at George before slamming down the telephone, storming out of the office, and jumping into his car. He steered toward the highway and with only the clothes on his back and his briefcase beside him, left St. Louis for Chicago. During the next five hours on the road, he planned out the rest of his life. He vowed to never speak again to any of the "assassins," as he labeled them. He intended to seek the job so frequently offered to him by Schuetz's competition and divorce Mary as quickly as a judge would approve the paperwork. He resolved to make a new life for himself devoid of intimate relationships or love. He would never again endure the tragic losses his life had seemingly always centered on. He would devote himself to business and make millions. He would show the world that he could be happy alone. True to his word, in time, Henry made good on every promise he made that day on the road.

During the months that followed, George made repeated attempts at contact, which Henry brushed aside. He hired the best lawyer in St. Louis to represent him and offered Mary generous terms in exchange for a swift and painless dissolution of their marriage, stipulating that any and all future communication with Mary must be handled by his attorney. He compiled a list of items that he wanted and sent a moving company to the house to retrieve them, never setting foot on the property again.

"So, I did the only thing a man can do in a spot like that. I left as fast as I could and started over. It wasn't easy," he declared while looking around at Oak Forest, "but I guess it worked out in the end, huh buddy?"

Henry spent the balance of the afternoon completing his task of cleaning the garage. From time to time, his mind drifted back to the conversation with Joe and the memories from so long ago that he had revisited. It was painful for him to relive those days but he realized that after telling Joe the story, he actually felt a little bit better. *Maybe the time spent avoiding such reminiscences is actually worse than facing the demons*, he thought to himself. At any rate, it was made ok because he had someone who was willing to listen and not judge him. He had someone who was there for him. Who needed a wife or a best friend or even a brother anyway? They were just cold-blooded "assassins." Henry had a true friend; it was a cat named Joe.

# CHAPTER 19

# A Shocking Morning

THE FOLLOWING MORNING, Henry got a later start than usual due to a few impromptu hits on the "snooze button" of his alarm clock. He had stayed up into the wee hours the night before devouring a new book on George Washington that he had become engrossed in. In wasn't often that he was fortunate enough to find a text that compelling so he had given in to the desire to keep reading even though he knew he would pay for it the next day.

He had just set foot on the bottom step when he heard Millie unlocking the side door. He hurried to help her but she had gained entry before he could be of assistance.

"Good morning Ms. James!"

"Why good morning to you, Mr. Engel," she replied as she walked through the kitchen. "I don't see your paper; you getting a late start at the office today?"

"Yeah, I was out late dancing again so I slept in," he responded playfully while pouring himself a cup of coffee. Once upon a time he and Mary had often gone dancing and Henry was actually quite good, but it had been decades since he had cut a rug and the reference amused him.

"Let me guess, up late studying coins again?" she asked returning from the hallway.

"Wrong. George Washington!" he declared with a smile as he passed her. He was headed toward the front door on his way to retrieve the morning's newspapers, which typically by now had been completely read and discarded.

"Ahhh, I see. Finally got into that new book you've been wanting to read."

Henry unlocked the dead bolt and turned the knob to open the front door. Through the storm door he could see the two newspapers, the *St. Louis Post-Dispatch* and the *Lewis Gazette*, stacked neatly by the front porch rail waiting for him. Something was smeared along the front sidewalk and across the porch toward him but he couldn't quite make out yet what it was. He opened the storm door to get his newspapers and investigate the strange substance.

As he did, his eyes followed the brownish red smears to their cause, which was lying motionless under the bench. It was Joe.

"Oh my God!" exclaimed Henry as he rushed out the door. "No, no, no, no! Joe!" he shouted as he dove to the side of his injured friend. The wounded cat did not move or respond to the sound of Henry's voice. "Millie! Millie come quickly!"

"What's the matter out here?" Millie asked as she pushed open the storm door alarmed by the sound of Henry's cries for help.

Before Henry could reply, she brought her hand to her mouth and muttered, "Oh dear Lord! What's happened to our Joe?"

"I don't know," Henry answered frantically. "It sure looks like something tore the hell out him."

Instantly Henry remembered the words of Louis Benhardt spoken in his kitchen months before. He pointed out that a cat like Joe would never survive in the wild. Louis had predicted that it was only a matter of time before one of the perils of the forest would catch up with Joe and it looked as if that time had come. Henry was comfortable with the concept then but now he was devastated. How could he have been so stupid? How could he have not seen this coming and provided some better shelter for Joe than just allowing him to fend for himself against coyotes, stray dogs, and the like? What on earth had he been thinking? There would be time for guilt later; right now, the need was for action. It appeared that Joe was still breathing.

"Millie, quick run and get a bath towel," he implored.

"Is he still alive?"

"Yeah, I think so but we've got to get him to town."

If there was any chance to save Joe's life it rested in the hands of the veterinarian clinic located in Lewis. He was critically injured and had by all appearances lost a lot of blood. There was no telling how long he had lain there but somehow he had managed to drag himself home and now there wasn't a moment to lose.

Millie returned with a large towel and Henry carefully picked Joe up and placed him onto it before wrapping it loosely around him. He was surprised by how soft Joe's fur felt as this was the first time he had ever touched the cat. He could see that his rear right leg was badly mangled and he had various gashes around his neck and head. Much of his fur was bloodied so it was difficult to tell what other damage there was to him. Joe did not move or react in any way to being handled and Henry feared the worst. He could only hope that the rotten scoundrel who had done this to Joe had gotten as good as he gave and was licking his wounds somewhere himself.

To expedite matters, they raced to Millie's car and she held Joe as Henry drove. Henry accelerated like a driver leaving the pit at Daytona as he shot out of the driveway and onto the county road. He knew what was at stake and headed toward Lewis with all possible dispatch.

For her part, Millie seemed the calmer of the pair. She held Joe against her chest and gently swayed him like a mother rocking a baby. Henry couldn't help but notice how comfortable she looked and in the panic of the moment did something he had not done in 23 years.

"Millie, look at you. How on earth is it you don't have children? You're a natural." Were it not for the adrenaline pulsing through him he would have never broached the topic but now that it was out there, he was curious to finally learn the answer to a question he had often privately wondered about.

A long pause followed before Millie responded to the inquiry. "Well Mr. Engel, I do have a child."

Her words seemed to just hang in the air for a while as Henry absorbed them. They had always intentionally avoided such personal topics but Henry was aware that Millie had a life beyond the confines of Oak Forest and was prepared, or so he thought, for whatever she had to say.

"You do?" Henry was shocked by the revelation.

"Yep, I'm a mama. A long time ago when I was just a girl back in Georgia I was fixing to get married to a man who I had known my whole life. Well, it turned out he was no good. Of course I didn't know that then, but along came our wedding day and he disappeared. Never saw him or heard from him again. Something mean like that does terrible things to a 17-year-old girl and I went wild for a time. I ran with a fast and rough crowd. Looking back, I suppose I was really just running from myself but I ended up in trouble. You know what I mean?"

Henry nodded.

"Well, my folks knew how hard it was going to be for me and that little baby so it was decided I would go to my grandmother's house in Atlanta until it was born. After that, the baby would be put up for adoption. I cried and cried and cried but it was the only thing to do," she said as she stared out the window.

"I didn't have no money and the baby's daddy was no good so the only chance for my little one was to find some nice people to raise him. So, that's what we did. I have a son, Mr. Engel. His name is Edward, after my daddy, and I haven't seen him in 35 years. He's all grown and probably got himself a family somewhere by now. After he was born, I couldn't go back home to live so I came up to St. Louis and stayed there until my Auntie Bess took ill here in Lewis and needed my help."

"That must have been awful for you. Have you ever tried to find him?" Henry asked while processing it all.

Millie wiped a single tear from her left cheek that was streaking downward. "No. I've thought about it a million times but then I always stop myself. I mean what on earth would I say? 'I'm the woman who abandoned you, want some pie?'" she said with a forced laugh. "How could he ever forgive me for what I've done? It's unforgivable and it's too late to make it right."

Henry didn't know what to say. He was most certainly no hypocrite. How could he offer her advice based on his own experiences? Somewhere out in the universe he had an ex-wife, brother, and former best friend all of whom he was estranged from. It wasn't exactly a ringing endorsement of his ability to judge people or his life skills, so he stayed quiet and let the matter drop. The rest of the drive they rode in silence as each pondered the past.

In record time, the white Ford sedan was pulling into the lot of the veterinarian clinic, which was located a couple blocks east of Hughes Avenue in New Town. Once parked, Henry raced around to the passenger's side to open Millie's door and help her and Joe safely exit the car. The clinic was housed in a ranch house that used to be a residence but had been converted into a commercial property. The main entrance was once upon a time someone's back door.

"Hi, can we help you?" greeted a receptionist as they pushed through the door with Millie carrying Joe.

"Yes," Henry answered. "It's our cat; he's been attacked."

"Oh dear! Let me get Dr. Miller right away," she exclaimed as she stood from the desk and rushed through a door and out of sight. Within seconds the receptionist reappeared trailing what was presumably the doctor.

"Hi folks, I'm Dr. Cheryl Miller. What do we have here?" the tall slender woman asked as she began to pull the towel back slightly from Joe's head. Dr. Miller looked to be in her early thirties and had light brown hair pulled back into a ponytail. Her blue eyes were framed by black wire-rimmed glasses that when combined with her white lab coat made for an impressive professional appearance of someone who knew their field.

"Hello, I'm Henry Engel and this is Millie James. My cat was attacked by something. I'm guessing maybe a coyote? Not sure. He hasn't moved and there was a lot of blood on the porch. I know his back leg is all mangled and he's really gashed up," Henry unloaded in a single breath.

Dr. Miller could clearly see how shaken Henry was and calmly listened and noted everything he said before springing into action.

"Ok, June, buzz Katie and tell her to meet me in exam room 2 please," she directed the receptionist to summon the vet tech for assistance. "All right folks, let me take him and we'll see what we can do."

As she took the bundle from Millie, Joe let out a low guttural groan. It was the first sound he had made since they found him.

"Well that's a good sign," the doctor offered in a baby talk voice directed toward the patient. "At least he can still tell us he's hanging in there."

Redirecting her attention to Henry and Millie she then asked, "Has he had his shots?"

"No, not that I am aware of, doctor. He's a stray that showed up a few months back and honestly I never thought about it until now. I'm not a big animal person," Henry explained sheepishly.

"That's ok, I just needed to know what we are dealing with. Does he have a name?"

"Yes ma'am, his name is Joe."

"All right then, how about you make yourselves comfortable and we're going to take a look at Joe for you. It'll be just a bit."

"Thank you, doctor," Henry said gratefully.

"You're very welcome." Dr. Miller then disappeared behind the door with Joe, and Henry and Millie made their way to seats in the reception area.

It wasn't until he sat down in the chair that Henry realized how upset he was. Everything had been happening so fast since he opened the front door that he hadn't taken time to consider what it all meant. However, now there suddenly was only time and nothing more to do and the voices in his head began to work on him.

They said it was all his fault. If he had given Joe a proper home he would never have been hurt. What kind of man lets a living creature sleep under a window at night and doesn't take him in? He threw this poor lost cat a few bowls of food a week and thought that he was some sort of saint. Hell, he didn't even know enough to get the poor thing vaccinated. It was ridiculous. What's more, most likely now the little guy would die and it would be on Henry's head.

He felt horrible. It felt like the other times in his life that someone he loved had suddenly and tragically been taken from him … his mother, his father, his uncle … even Bill when the telegram came. He felt helpless. He was so deep in thought that he hadn't even noticed the shaking of his hands or the tears welling up in his eyes. That was, at least, not until Millie placed her hand on top of his and brought him out of the depths of despair.

"Mr. Engel, it's gonna be alright. Don't you worry yourself none about that little ole cat. He's tough. Remember how you always said he was a Houdini? Well, he's playing one of his tricks right now. You'll see. He'll fool everybody. Soon enough he'll be getting the mail with you again. You'll see."

Her words made Henry feel considerably better. Her touch did as well. He was glad he wasn't facing this alone and that it was Millie who was with him. He had for years thought of her as an outstanding employee but now realized that she too, like Joe, was considerably more important than what he had been admitting to himself.

The time passed slowly as they waited in silence for a report from the examination room. Finally, after about 45 minutes, a somber and serious Dr. Miller emerged through the door. She motioned for them to stay seated as she took a chair from across the room and pulled it in front of them and sat down.

"Well, the good news is that Joe is still alive. That's one tough cat in there. The bad news is that the damage is very extensive. That rear right leg is a real mess; it will probably have to come off. There are a lot of cuts and bruises and several need stitches. Worst of all, Joe's got a punctured lung and has lost a ton of blood. Taken as a whole, I'd say there is only maybe a 5% chance for recovery, if that. I'm really sorry. Honestly, Mr. Engel, we're talking about an incredibly expensive recovery involving a complicated surgery I'm not qualified to perform that has almost no chance for success. Personally, I understand you love your cat but professionally I am duty bound to recommend a humane euthanasia. Joe won't feel a thing. It's really the only reasonable choice at this point."

The doctor's words outlined the worst-case scenario Henry had been bracing for. He stared at the floor and listened intently to everything she had to say and then took a moment before responding. He had never faced death with even a "5% chance" to beat it. In every other experience, when he lost someone he cared about, it had been abrupt and decisive with no choice, *no chance at all* for life. He was determined to make a difference this time.

"Ok doctor, thank you for your advice. Now, how do we proceed?" he asked resolutely.

"Well, we make the animal comfortable and then administer an injection. They don't feel a thing. You can certainly go and see Joe first if you like ..."

"No," he interrupted while shaking his head. "You don't understand. How do we proceed in trying to *save* his life?"

"Mr. Engel, there is nearly a zero chance of recovery and we're talking about thousands and thousands of dollars to even attempt it. In a case like this ..."

"Dr. Miller, with all due respect that's *my* cat in there. Money is no object here. I want Joe to have the very best state-of-the-art care there is," he proclaimed.

"Mr. Engel, I don't think you are hearing what I am saying ..."

"Doc, are you hearing what I am saying? I don't care about the cost, we have got to at least try."

"But Mr. Engel, it doesn't make any sense to ..."

Henry's German temper and the stress of the morning got the better of him and there would be no further debate. "God dammit Doc, enough! Now, your job is to save lives, right? I mean this is a business you're running here, isn't it? I want that cat to have every chance at survival there is. If there's a better place for him to get care then get on the phone and let's fly him there but he WILL NOT be put to sleep. If he needs a procedure you can't do, find someone who can and let's get after this. We're wasting time. Are you or are you not going to help us and try to save Joe's life?"

Dr. Miller was accustomed to dealing with passionate pet owners but had never met anyone who had given her a mandate like this. In a town like Lewis, her practice survived by balancing budgets vs. practical care. To encounter a pet owner of Henry's resolve and financial means was a rare occurrence and she suddenly threw aside her pragmatic caution and felt like a high school football player who had just received a rousing pep talk right before game time. Seeing the look in Henry's eyes, she knew that the discussion was over and there was only one course of action to take.

"Well, ok then Mr. Engel. Let's give it our best shot," she declared as she stood with a smile on her face.

Henry and Millie stood with her. "And Doc, whatever it takes, no matter the cost, he keeps that leg. Do you hear me? He keeps it." If ever Henry was to have a John Wayne moment, this was it. The Duke couldn't have made the point more emphatically.

"Yes sir, we'll do everything humanly possible for Joe. If you folks want to leave your information with June, I'll call you later on tonight with an update and to go over a plan of action with you. For now, why don't you head on home," she said as she turned to go back behind the door. As she reached for the knob, she paused for just a second and turned back to them. "By the way, you might want to rethink the Joe thing unless it's short for Josephine ... because your cat is a girl," she quipped with a wink and smile before exiting the room.

After Henry and Millie picked their jaws up off the floor they had a much-needed laugh at themselves. Somehow they both had just assumed that Joe was a male cat. The revelation was startling but brought some levity to a difficult morning and helped to diffuse some of their anxiety about Joe's prognosis for the future. They took seats in front of the receptionist so that Henry could fill out the necessary paperwork to establish his financial responsibility for all of Joe's treatment. *She* would receive the best care money could buy.

While they waited a moment for the receptionist to make a photocopy in the back, Henry whispered to Millie in a very hushed tone.

"Psssst."

"What do you want?" she asked.

"You're not a man are you?" Henry teased.

"Stop your fooling," she replied, surprised by his uncharacteristic quip.

"Well, you never know ..." he joked.

With a giggle Millie fired right back, "I sure don't think so, but all the same I'm going to check just as soon as I get home."

# CHAPTER 20

## *Family*

T HE DAYS IMMEDIATELY following Joe's brutal beating were some of the most agonizing Henry could recall. The ups and downs intermingled with ever-present worry were exhausting. He stayed in constant contact with the clinic throughout the weekend and his mood swung with each report. On more than one occasion Joe had lost ground in her battle for recovery but each time when it looked as though all might be lost, she rallied and fought back. On Monday, much to Henry's relief, there was finally some solid good news delivered to Oak Forest. That afternoon, Dr. Miller called and informed him that the transfusions of blood had worked and that Joe had stabilized, hopefully for good this time. In light of her improved condition, a specialist from St. Louis was coming to perform the complex surgery needed on Joe's badly damaged leg. She went over the plan with Henry who listened intently and asked questions along the way. He was encouraged by Dr. Miller's confidence that there was a very good chance for success. After consulting with the specialist, she now believed that not only would Joe be able to keep her leg but there was a high probability she might regain the use of it as well. She was adamant that Joe could make a 100% recovery in time and seemed genuinely excited at the prospect. It was a complete reversal from Friday for the woman who was now backed by unlimited resources. *What a difference a couple days and a few thousand dollars makes*, Henry thought to himself.

"Well, what do you know about that?" Henry said aloud with a smile as he put the handset onto its base on the kitchen counter.

When the phone rang, Millie had been engrossed in the deep cleaning that had never taken place on Friday but she immediately took a break and came into the room to eavesdrop. She was seated at the island near the refrigerator and hanging on every word. Now that Henry had concluded the phone call, she was looking for the rest of the story.

"So what'd she say? How's our Joe?" she quizzed him impatiently.

Henry spun around and placed his hands on the counter top opposite her. After he let out a huge sigh, he repeated nearly every word from his conversation with the doctor for Millie's benefit. The news was almost better than anyone could have imagined and euphoria quickly swept over the room.

As she often did on cleaning days, Millie had turned the radio on in the family room earlier that morning to the "Oldies" station and a classic Beatles song was just beginning to play. Henry's ear caught the familiar sound of the harmonica and the drum beat and sailed into the other room. Millie was too caught up in the excitement about Joe to notice. Henry, not known to Millie as an avid music aficionado, turned the dial on the radio to full blast. The first line of the #1 hit from 1964, "Love Me Do," blew through the house with Henry skipping along right behind. The shock of sight and sound nearly knocked her off of her chair.

"Do you dance, Millie?" he asked as he approached her.

"Do I, do I what?" she replied in utter disbelief.

"Well, you do today!" he exclaimed as he grabbed her left hand and pulled her from her chair.

The youthful voice of Paul McCartney and the perfect harmonies of the Fab Four filled the air.

Henry led and Millie followed as they swayed and twirled in perfect synchronicity around the kitchen table and into the family room. Millie giggled as Henry gave her a spin for good measure and he sang along emphatically to the lyrics in a surprisingly well-done impersonation of the Mop Tops.

Perhaps it was the elation about Joe or something more that had prompted the spontaneous and jubilant eruption, but the brief dance held a deeper meaning. It was an acknowledgement in the open of what had been happening underneath the surface for months. Their distant relationship as employer and employee had warmed and walls had come down. They were beginning to feel comfortable seeing each other in a new way. It was like trying on a new pair of shoes and then celebrating when they fit perfectly. After all of the years, they had become friends and it called for dancing.

In just a moment, the song was over. They laughed at the spectacle they had just created as Henry returned the volume on the radio to its previous position.

"You're quite a dancer! I had no idea you could move like that," Millie complimented him, clearly impressed.

"I wasn't sure I still could," Henry laughed. "It's been years for me, but that was fun. I thank you for the dance." He strolled from the room a little bit embarrassed at his outburst but pleased with both his dancing prowess and Millie's obvious admiration of it.

Millie shook her head and smiled as she went back to her cleaning. She had seen a remarkable change in this man over the past few months and though she had always liked him before, this version of Henry was, hands down, her favorite so far. He was a more sensitive and caring person than he let the outside world see and she wondered again about what events had caused him to seal off the big heart that she always had suspected that he possessed. She didn't know what had happened before but she was certain what had touched off the metamorphosis she was witnessing. It was a little stray Siamese cat named Joe.

For the next few days their conversations often centered on how they would transition Joe into the household after her release from the clinic. Henry did not want to chance a repeat performance of the latest episode for fear Joe may be getting short on spare lives at this point. So, he had made the decision to bring her indoors, at least at night if not full time. It was not a move to be taken lightly though because there were several considerations to be addressed and changes that would have to be made. Joe was an outside cat now; how would she adapt to living inside the home? What happens if she decides to turn the house into a jungle gym? How much does she shed and how would they deal with it? How would they keep her off of counters and out of trouble?

One little detail Henry neglected to think about was how the cat would relieve herself indoors. Fortunately for Joe, Millie was on the job.

"What in God's name do you have there?" Henry asked as

Millie came into the kitchen toting a large plastic lid and tray one morning.

"It's a litter box for Joe," she replied casually.

"A what? For who?"

"You know, a litter box … for your cat," she explained.

"Not in here," Henry protested.

"Of course not. I just want to get the tags off of it. I was thinking it could go in the laundry room," she suggested as she placed the brand new box onto the island in the kitchen and went to work on the tags affixed to it.

"Oh no, I don't want a stinky box of cat crap in my house. That's craziness," he dissented.

"Well, now what exactly do you expect Joe to do now that she's going to be living inside, jump up on the toilet or just cross her legs until you let her out to go?" Millie fired back, annoyed by his reaction.

"I don't know, I guess I hadn't really thought about it," he answered.

"Mm-mm, typical men's nonsense," she mumbled, becoming aggravated.

"What? What did you say?" Henry retorted defensively, sensing she was sassing him.

"I said this is typical nonsense. Some fat man in some office somewhere decides that you need a big old sticker on your box and some other fat man at a factory in China uses super glue to put it on here so that even after you pay for it you still have to see what it is that they are trying to sell you even though you already own it." She rattled off the whole stream of consciousness on a single breath while tearing at the stubborn label with her finger nails.

Henry was relieved to discover he was off the hook for the clearly idiotic stance he had taken on feline restroom arrangements. However, he had barely followed Millie's line of thinking about what one fat man had done to another or how she knew they were obese. It left him wondering if perhaps he was the sane one and the crazy people were those that thought cats relieving themselves in boxes in houses all over America was truly a civilized thing for an advanced society to embrace. He was about to leave the room when he noticed a pair of silver bowls sitting inside the tray of the litter box.

"What are these for?" he asked as he picked one up.

"Those are Joe's food and water bowls I bought her," Millie responded, looking up briefly from her challenge to note the frown on Henry's face. "Let me guess, you just figured she'd eat at the table with you or were you planning on her eating outside and just fasting the rest of the time?"

Sensing defeat and now certain that the fat guy at the factory routine had been Millie covering her tracks after taking a shot at him, he rolled his eyes and retreated into his office with his cup of coffee.

Not impressed with the lack of appreciation he had shown for her efforts to acquire the items for Joe, and becoming increasingly angry at the stubborn label, she couldn't resist taking a parting shot.

"If we don't feed her, how's she ever going to fill up this box with crap?" she called after him.

In silence Henry took it like a man. *Sass*, he thought to himself, *definitely sass.*

* * *

A week later, the day Henry had been waiting for finally arrived.

It was time for Joe to come home. He had missed their conversations immensely, and the meetings with Jake, which had for most of his adult life been pleasing diversions, now suddenly felt empty without Joe also in attendance. As for Joe, she was sick and tired of hospital life and was overjoyed at the sight of her people when they came to pick her up. Despite her somewhat rough appearance, which was augmented by scores of shaved patches to accommodate her stitches, she was in good spirits and purred during the entire drive home while resting on Millie's lap.

Dr. Miller's instructions called for restricted space and movement while her surgically repaired leg healed and the downstairs bathroom was selected as the infirmary for the foreseeable future. It was furnished with a small box containing a blanket for Joe to sleep on, the new food and water bowls, and the much-maligned litter box, which was now free from the influence of advertisements authorized by oversized men.

Millie and Henry were unsure about what to expect but Joe acted as if she had lived there her whole life. After a cursory inspection of the amenities, she limped to her new bed and curled up into a ball on the blanket. Henry sat on the toilet for a while and just watched her as she eased off to sleep. He marveled at how far she had come since the morning he found her injured and lamented how far she still had to go to fully recover. Finally, after he had become quite uncomfortable sitting on the hard toilet lid, he stood and left the room pulling the door closed behind him.

By mid-October, Joe had made remarkable progress. With each passing day, her limp seemed to improve slightly and with her stitches gone and wounds healed, much of her fur had grown back to the extent that she looked very much like her old self again. It would be a while yet but there was still great optimism that someday she might be able to run and jump once more. In the interim, Jake had been happy to celebrate the return of Joe and the trio had enjoyed many lively meetings on the front porch. Though Henry had cleaned it several times with peroxide, a faint brown stain in the concrete served as an ever-present reminder of the horrible experience Joe had survived. Whether it was due to her limited range of movement or fear of the predator that had done her harm, Joe never set foot beyond the edge of the porch and often gazed wistfully at her former domain. The adjustment to house life had been more natural for her than anyone could have reasonably expected and Henry was certain now that in her former life she had been a house cat.

By November, Joe was nearing complete recovery but the limp she possessed appeared to be permanent and despite any coaxing she refused to jump up on anything. The latter issue was acceptable to Henry as he did not want her jumping up on his furniture and countertops anyway but it represented a limitation and signaled that perhaps Joe had come as far as she was going to on her journey toward complete health. However, both Henry and Joe were about to get a surprise.

The week before Thanksgiving, Henry was clearing leaves out of the front yard with his leaf blower. It was a big job that took constant effort over the course of a couple weeks to accomplish as the numerous giant trees lost their dense foliage in stages providing a daily harvest for Henry to battle. He was near the front porch when he noticed Joe sitting behind the storm door and observing him. It made him smile as it reminded him of how all summer she had followed him around the yard and watched him work. He swung the blower back and forth scattering the leaves before him and pushing a growing pile toward the side of the house.

A few stragglers flew up and onto the porch and Joe seemed very interested as she watched them float down to earth right in front of her. Henry noticed this and decided she might like to feel the air so he directed the blower toward the base of the door, which was now just a few feet away. Neither he nor Joe was ready for what happened next.

The burst of air Henry directed toward the cat shot beneath the door with force and startled her so severely that she jumped two feet vertically with hair standing on end. In midair, she seemed to turn and landed with feet scrambling for safety.

"Oh shit!" Henry exclaimed feeling badly about the prank gone awry but amused by the spectacle. In an instant Joe was gone.

A moment later, Millie stood at the door with a bewildered expression on her face. Sensing she wanted to speak with him, Henry shut off the blower and approached the door as Millie opened it and began to speak.

"I think our cat is healed," she declared.

"Oh yeah?"

"Well, a minute ago she came flying through the house and shot straight up on top of the bookcase in the family room! She's settled down now but I sure don't see no limp," she announced.

"I'll be damned. Yeah, I think that's my fault. I didn't mean to but I scared her with the blower and she lit out like a rocket down the hall."

They both laughed and shook their heads and went about their business. Whatever limitations Joe had previously displayed, whether self-imposed or not, now seemed to have vanished. She jumped up on top of the bookcase? It was going to be a whole new ballgame, Henry concluded.

For the first time since he bought Oak Forest, Henry decided to spend Thanksgiving in Lewis. Every other year, he traveled somewhere that week and ate his turkey in a restaurant surrounded by strangers. He would never admit it, and maybe didn't even recognize it himself, but it was a defense mechanism. It was easier to spend the holiday on the road in a hotel than it was to be at home and acknowledge his lack of a family. Besides, he enjoyed sightseeing so he would go to historic sites such as Mount Vernon or Independence Hall and indulge himself in history. This Thanksgiving, however, was going to be different.

As usual for this time of year, Millie was off to Georgia for a two-week visit with her family so Henry was left to fend for himself. The fact he wasn't leaving as well threw her a curve ball and sent her into a fit of anxiety about how he would care for himself for two weeks rather than the one that had been the norm before this. She offered to reduce the duration of her trip but Henry was having none of it. He assured her he could survive until she returned and urged her to enjoy her well – deserved time away with her family. "We'll see you on the 8th," he said and reluctantly she agreed.

The Monday before the holiday Millie was off to Atlanta and Henry made plans for the preparation of his Thanksgiving dinner. He shopped for the required groceries and spent the night before and the morning of the big day preparing his feast. It was a fairly elaborate and well-done meal featuring a roasted turkey with all of the traditional side dishes. His years after Mary and before Millie had forced him to learn how to cook and he was relatively accomplished at it. Joe certainly seemed to agree anyway as she devoured two generous pieces of moist turkey from a saucer at the chef's feet during the meal. With stomachs full, the pair retired to the family room and Henry nodded off in his chair while watching football as Joe dozed on his lap.

The days that followed went more quickly than Henry had expected they would without Millie's presence. The only discord had been the receipt of another letter from his favorite "assassin," which received the same treatment as every other that arrived in his mailbox. As usual, it triggered a walk down memory lane but Henry shook it off quickly and moved on with his life.

He wrapped up his outdoor preparations for winter and spent the balance of his time reading or studying his coins with an occasional John Wayne movie sprinkled in for good measure. Joe made for a great companion as she tended to stay in whatever room he was in and always slept at the foot of his bed each night. Henry often laughed as she demonstrated time and again her ability for teleportation while silently moving around the house without being detected. She would magically appear and in the next moment vanish only to reappear somewhere else. Houdini still had her skills.

In addition, she had revealed a stunning ability for contortion as she sprawled and twisted into various outlandish positions while she slept, which always brought a smile to Henry's face. Perhaps most impressive of all of her talents though, was her ability to play "fetch." Joe liked for Henry to throw a wadded-up piece of paper across the room, which she would then bat around the floor for a few moments before grabbing it in her mouth and bringing it to him for another round. It was an aptitude they had accidentally stumbled upon one day in his office when an errant throw across the room at his waste basket resulted in Joe hunting the paper ball down and returning it to Henry's feet. Now, it had become daily sport and it was impossible for Henry to crumple papers without a reaction from Joe.

Millie's return from the South was a cause for celebration at Oak Forest and both Henry and Joe were glad to see her. They had enjoyed their exclusive time together but it didn't feel the same without her there. The 8th of December that year was to be remembered for more than just a homecoming though. It was to be the first day that Mother Nature reminded the residents of Lewis that winter had arrived.

# CHAPTER 21

## Melting Ice

THE SKIES OVERHEAD were a dark and ominous gray as Henry returned from the mailbox. There had been no indication of any precipitation in the forecast but just as he reached the crest of the hill, the first ice pellets plunked his head and dotted the asphalt around him. Things quickly intensified and by the time he reached the sidewalk, the increasing volume of ice was mixed with splashes from raindrops that froze almost on impact with the cold ground.

"Idiots," Henry said aloud, referring to the meteorological fraternity as he stepped under the cover of the porch and surveyed his yard, which was quickly turning white.

Disgusted, he entered the home and closed the door tightly before taking off his coat and hanging it on the hall tree. Joe, who had come to investigate, could feel the cold coming off of Henry's clothing and tested the air with a series of sniffs loud enough for Henry to hear.

"It's cold out there, babe," he told her as he walked past and into the kitchen looking for Millie. Through the back doors and kitchen window he could see a steady barrage of ice falling.

"Hey Millie, where are you?" he called out.

"I'm scrubbing the floor in the upstairs bathroom. What do you need?"

"Have you looked out a window lately?" he asked while wondering why on earth she was cleaning the floor of a room no one had used in years.

"No, why?" she replied with a much calmer demeanor than he anticipated she would have if she knew what was happening outside.

"I hope you brought some pajamas."

"What is that supposed to mean?" came a suddenly more concerned tone this time.

"Just take a look; you'll see what I mean," Henry called back setting her up for the surprise.

He heard some fairly inaudible muttering as she got off of her knees and walked down the hall to his bedroom to see what the commotion was about. However, the diatribe she unleashed next on the weatherman was loud and clear and made even Henry blush a little. She stormed down the stairs continuing to rail against the fates as if the storm were a personal vendetta against her.

Henry stood silently as she reached the bottom step and made eye contact with him, which caused her to realize everything she had just said was out loud for him to hear.

"I confess, Miss James, I wasn't aware you knew language like that," he needled her.

"Uh-umm, sorry 'bout that. I guess I lost my temper," she said in a now considerably softer voice.

"I just can't understand how modern science couldn't predict this ... ," she pleaded while pointing outside to what had turned into an all-out winter storm.

For years, their standard plan during the winter months had always been to watch the forecasts closely and at any sign of possible inclement weather, declare a holiday. It was a system that had worked for 23 years and never failed them until now.

"Well, it's safe to say that you aren't going anywhere in this. I'd take you back in the Explorer but this is mainly ice falling and four-wheel drive or not, we'd never make it. We'll just have to wait it out," he stated with a matter-of-fact tone as he stared through the window.

"Yep, I suppose that's all there is to do at this point. I've got a bag out in the car I carry with some sweats and things in it. I guess I'll grab it now before my doors freeze over."

"Here, let me get it for you," Henry offered as he walked to get his coat. Millie was already one step ahead of him though and passed by him with her coat already on.

"Oh thanks, but I've got it. It'll give me a chance to cool off," she chuckled, now feeling a little bit ashamed of the words she had used a moment ago.

The onslaught continued throughout the afternoon and evening. The weatherman on television expressed great shock at the day's events and presented a litany of excuses as to why he hadn't seen it coming. Millie, in the meantime, set up camp in the upstairs guest room. She had cleaned it countless times over the years but now as a guest saw it from a different point of view and truly appreciated what a pretty room with a wonderful view that it was.

Henry spent most of the afternoon and early evening in his office catching up on paperwork. Millie occupied her time with the preparation and cleanup from dinner and by baking a coffee cake that they could share in the morning. Joe was perhaps the busiest one of all. She split her time moving between the two of them and supervising their activities with an occasional break thrown in for a little play time with a paper ball.

Mid-evening Henry emerged from the office and decided they should have a fire on such a wintery night. He gathered some logs from the ample supply he had stockpiled under the cover of the side porch and started the blaze, which drew both Joe and Millie into the family room to join him.

He took his usual seat in the recliner, while Millie sat on the couch and Joe stretched out in front of the fireplace.

"So, what should we watch?" Henry asked them as he picked up the television's remote control.

"Considering it's Monday night, I figured we'd watch football," Millie declared.

Henry spun his head toward her with a quizzical smile on his face. "Really? You like football?"

"Oh yeah, my Daddy was a BIG football fan when I was coming up. He loved the Georgia Bulldogs. Me? I'm a Niners fan. I love Jerry Rice."

The stunned expression on Henry's face was priceless. Somehow over more than two decades this morsel of information about Millie had eluded him. He realized at that moment, just as he had the day they drove Joe to the hospital, there was a LOT about Millie he didn't know.

"Well all right then! Carolina is at Dallas so let's see how that's ..." At that exact instant everything went dark. The only light in the room was that which was provided by the fledgling fire in the fireplace.

"Aww damn, that's not good!" Henry announced. They sat in silence for a moment digesting what had happened and what it meant.

"Guess the ice must have brought down the power lines somewhere. Looks like no Monday Night Football for us," Millie stated while watching the flames flicker in the fireplace. "That's alright, I hate the Cowboys," she laughed.

"I'm sure you're right about the lines. We're probably going to be out of commission for a while around here and the worst part is it's going to get cold. I better throw another log on this fire," he said as he stood and moved toward the fireplace.

Millie stood as well. "I'll go call and report the outage so they at least know about it anyway."

"Good idea," he agreed. It was hard telling how widespread the issue was and ordinarily in a remote location such as theirs it might be days before anyone addressed it. Of course, being a man of Henry's means had its privileges and if the power company didn't resolve the issue on their own in a day or so he was a man who knew how to go up a ladder and get action quickly.

For now, it seemed the only thing to do was bundle up and sit by the fire. Henry retrieved a flashlight from his office and used it to light the way for more firewood to add to the reserve in the family room. Millie completed the phone call reporting the outage and returned with a blanket from upstairs for each of them and an oil lamp from the guest room.

"Shoot, at the rate it's coming down I might not make my doctor's appointment on Friday. We're really socked in. Hey, I forgot that was in there," Henry remarked upon seeing the lamp.

"I've been dusting this thing for years, about time somebody finally got to use it," she laughed in response. "Why do you need to go to the doctor?"

"Just my annual checkup is all, nothing else."

The light given off by the lamp illuminated the room well enough to read by and it suddenly took on the feel of an old homestead on the prairie.

"I've always loved this house," Millie stated. "It's got such a warmth to it, you know what I mean? Just the way that man designed it. He took such care about every detail so it'd be just so."

Henry nodded in agreement. She was spot on. The original builder had been meticulous in the design and construction of the house and it exuded a real sense of "home" that was often absent in other domiciles.

"You are right about that. That was one of the reasons I had to have it. Between this house and the grounds, I was hooked from the first moment I saw it. You might not believe this, but I honestly wonder sometimes if it wasn't all really built just for me. It fits me like a glove. It's my favorite place on earth."

They sat for a while in silence just watching the fire and listening to the tick of the wall clock. Joe was less taken with the scene and rolled over onto her back with paws stretched to soak up the heat provided from the fire.

"Millie, I'm going to have a talk with Jake. Have you ever met him?" Henry asked as he rose from his chair.

"Well, I can't say that I have Mr. Engel, but I do know some of his friends. I think I might like to meet him."

"Good! I'll see if I can't arrange an introduction for you," he said as he left the room with his flashlight in hand.

"Sounds good to me. I'm gonna blow out this lamp to save

the oil for when we need it," she called after him before extinguishing the flame.

A moment later he returned with a near full bottle of whiskey, two tumblers, and a pitcher of water and sat them down on the coffee table in front of the couch. "Too damn cold out for ice," he laughed as he took a seat next to her. She watched as he removed the cap from the whiskey bottle and poured a precise three count into each glass. Next he added a splash of water to each before handing one glass to Millie and taking the other in his hand.

"Millie, meet J.P. Jasterson. His close friends call him Jake," he said with a smile as he sat back into the corner of the couch opposite her.

"Well, hello sir," she said to the glass, "I've heard a lot about you."

She was no big drinker but she settled back into her end of the couch and gladly took a sip from the glass.

"Well?" he asked waiting for a critique.

"Hmmm … I like this guy. He's all right," she reported before taking a second much larger sampling from her glass. Henry smiled in approval. His friend Jake had always been popular and most everyone who met him, liked him.

"Mr. Engel, I might be speaking out of turn but I want to ask you something that has been on my mind for over 23 years."

Henry braced for what had to be the most obvious question she would have for him and he wasn't sure he was prepared to answer it. Finally, after a long delay, he took a swallow from his drink and then nodded for her to continue. "Ok, fire away."

"What on earth is your middle name?"

They both laughed at what was clearly a joke well played by

the female representative at this special meeting with Jake and Joe.

"Ha ha ha. It's William. My middle name is William, named after my father. My brother got it for a first name and I got it for my middle, but both of his sons got his name."

Silence followed for a time as Millie considered the words just spoken. She didn't know Henry had a brother; she didn't know much of anything about him from before their first meeting in 1974. That was the real mystery she wanted to ask him about.

"William. That's a real nice name, Mr. Engel," she finally replied.

Henry sat for a moment looking at the flames dancing in the fireplace and then said, "How about we try Henry from now on; I think that would be ok."

Millie was speechless. Another wall had come down right before her eyes. First Jake, then this; it was a lot to digest in a short period of time after so many years of formality between them.

Before she could speak again, Henry began to talk about his childhood in St. Louis. He poured them each another drink and walked her blow by blow through the stages of his life as she sat on the edge of her seat. Millie marveled at what he had endured and come through and later achieved in his life. She compared the true story she was now learning about to the fantasy she had concocted in her mind over the years about him. She quickly concluded that in real life he was much more interesting and appealing than any fiction might have been. He was a sensitive, thoughtful man who had grown up with tremendous tragedy and pain in his life only to find even more of it as an adult. It was no surprise to her, based on these revelations, why he had lived the way he did for so long or why he guarded himself from everyone and everything, even her.

*Our stories are not so dissimilar,* she thought to herself. They both had endured pain and loss and had run away from it. He into in his own world, and she into his. She could have started over and tried for love again with someone else or attempted to raise her son alone, but instead she hid inside the security of Henry's life. Caring for him had been the safer path and she had devoted herself to it. He needed to be alone. She needed to be needed by someone.

Their meeting lasted for hours until they both were exhausted and Millie was beginning to nod off. Henry covered her and added some more logs to the fire before retreating to his recliner and pulling a blanket over himself. Joe looked up at him briefly but then put her head back down and resumed her slumber.

"Good night, Millie," he said softly.

"Good night, Henry."

The next morning Henry woke to an ice-cold house and found Joe burrowed into his armpit. At some point in the night she had abandoned her position of leisure in front of the fireplace and opted instead to take advantage of his body heat. Millie was entirely covered with only her mouth showing and based on the snoring he heard coming from her direction, he was sure she was still asleep. The fire had burned itself out overnight so Henry got up from his chair and quickly started another. When he was satisfied that the fire was well established, he took the matches and went into the kitchen. He quietly removed several pots from the cabinet beneath the island and filled them with water before placing them onto the stove. After he had lit a match, he proceeded one by one to turn the knobs on the front of the unit and held the match next to the corresponding burner until the gas emerged from it and it ignited. It was a trick anyone with a gas stove knew and it was a fool-proof solution to generate some heat during a power outage.

While he waited for the water to boil and help remove the chill from the room, he looked out the window over the sink at the winter wonderland Mother Nature had left behind. Everywhere he looked a glaze of crystal ice glistened in the morning sunshine. He noticed that the icicles hanging down from the gutter were dripping, indicating that the air was warmer than 32 degrees Fahrenheit. It was typical of the Midwest, and in this case the sudden change was a welcome sight. Within hours the temperature climbed into the upper 30s and the ice on the asphalt was melting away. In just a day or so, the entire event would be a memory as the mercury rose into the 40s on Wednesday and melted the evidence of winter's fury.

The news on the power outage was equally encouraging. By noon a truck from the electric company was stationed on the road just past the mailboxes. A pleasant young man appeared at the front door and informed Henry that they would have the power restored as quickly as possible. Just before sunset, the man proved to be as good as his word and the lights at Oak Forest came back on.

By week's end, as Henry drove to St. Louis for his doctor's appointment, proof that it was December was hard to find as the high for the day was expected to be in the mid-50s and icicles were nowhere to be seen.

Henry's appointment went smoothly and he received a

clean bill of health. Doctor Ames asked if Henry was still speaking daily with Jake and when informed that he was, suggested he might have to prescribe a similar protocol for his other patients as it clearly seemed to be working for him. After leaving the medical center, Henry decided he would make a stop at his favorite coin shop before heading back to Lewis. He didn't expect to find any coins he needed there but he always enjoyed chatting about numismatics with the owners and wanted to pick up some supplies.

Just past 11:00 a.m., he pulled up to the coin shop, which was located in a strip mall on Olive Blvd. It was bracketed on either side by a hair salon and a real estate office and the parking lot was bustling with activity. Through the front windows Henry could see several customers milling about and one of the owners, a delightful woman named Jean Goins, standing behind the counter and conversing with a silver-haired man. He exited the Explorer and pulled the door open activating a small chime to alert the staff that someone had entered or left the premises.

Hearing the alarm, Henry wondered if the sound of that chime all day every day was pleasing as it represented the prospects of commerce or the most annoying sound ever. A moment after he had arrived, a young lady left the store and activated the alert again. After only two instances of hearing it, Henry was convinced that if he owned the establishment it would have to go.

"Hi Henry!" greeted the woman, interrupting her conversation to acknowledge his entrance.

"Hi Jean! Where's your worse half?" he asked with a smile referring to her husband and the shop's co-owner, Al Goins.

"He just ran across the street to grab us some coffee," she answered. "He'll be back in a minute."

Henry nodded and winked as he allowed her to return her attention to the man who apparently was buying a stack of proof sets from her. Henry couldn't see his face but based on his view of him from the rear, he looked to be about the same age as Henry and he guessed based on the time of year and the type of purchase that they were Christmas gifts of some sort. He couldn't put a finger on it but the man's voice seemed familiar to him. He suspected he had bumped into him before at the annual St. Louis coin show. Coin collecting was a small universe and many of the same faces appeared in it time and again.

Henry moved across the showroom floor to the far wall where Al and Jean kept several shelves stocked with coin flips, storage boxes, and various other supplies that collectors might need. He spent a few moments surveying the offerings and then began to select several stacks of flips of varying denominations for purchase. He intended over the weekend to re-holder some of his coins from their seller's holders into new clean ones he could then make his own notations on.

He turned to ask Jean if she had more nickel-sized coin flips in back and was startled by the face before him. It was the man from the counter. Now with his purchase complete and a brown paper sack of 1997 United States Mint proof sets in hand, he had walked over to Henry to confirm what he himself already had suspected. He too had recognized Henry.

"My God, Henry Engel!" the man said in utter disbelief.

It was the voice of the past. It was a face that, though weathered and aged as his own had become, he recognized in an instant. It was George Schuetz. Beneath the thinning silver hair and behind the wrinkles earned over a lifetime were the eyes of the younger man he once knew so very well. He was heavier now and looked rather tired and haggard, but his expressions and mannerisms were unmistakable.

Henry's breath left him for a moment as he processed what was happening and before he could regain his senses George took his hand and shook it vigorously as one would do with a long-lost friend.

"Wow, George?" was the best Henry could muster for the moment.

"What's it been, Henry? Forty years?" George asked with tears forming in his eyes.

*It'll be 44 years on Christmas Eve since we have seen one another or spoken but who's counting, right?* Henry thought to himself.

"You look great! How are you?" George asked.

Overwhelmed, Henry was somehow able to set aside the flood of emotions suddenly washing over him and make the small talk typical of people who had not seen each other for a long time.

"I'm doing really well, thanks. Say, how's your dad these days?" he asked.

"Oh, well, we lost Dad back in '90 right after we sold the business. He always said that when it went, he'd go too. I guess he was right."

"I'm very sorry to hear that," Henry offered. "I always had a lot of respect for him." Henry genuinely meant that. He had known of the sale of the business but he had not known of the death of George Sr. It was unwelcome news.

"I appreciate that. You know he thought a lot of you too. It was hard for him to understand when things happened the way they did and you left us." George's comment created an awkward silence between them. Henry's attempt at a benign question had only landed him right where he had no intention of going. He then made a last ditch attempt to avoid the elephant in the room with what had to be a no-risk topic, or so he thought.

"So, I see you bought some proof sets today?" Henry asked, already knowing the answer.

"Yes, I have seven grandkids and each year Claire and I give them proof sets. Kind of hoping at least one of them takes up the hobby someday," he laughed.

"Claire? So you're married?"

"Forty-three years last June," George responded in a decidedly darker tone indicating trouble.

"What?" Henry asked sensing his pain.

"She's sick. Cancer. Over at St. John's right now. I just left there and was headed home for a bit but decided to stop here and pick these up. Gotta keep going, right?" he said with a weak smile ineffectively attempting to disguise his worry.

Though he had not seen this man in over half of his life and had ample reason in his mind to despise him, he couldn't help but feel empathy for George. He was clearly in crisis and facing an incredibly difficult journey. Perhaps it was this compassion for another human being in pain or maybe it was curiosity after all of these years but when George suddenly asked Henry if he'd like to grab a cup of coffee, he accepted. It turned out to be a wise decision; without question, the men had plenty to talk about.

# CHAPTER 22

# "By George, He's a Good Man!"

GEORGE AND HENRY decided to head across the street to a donut shop where they purchased coffee and took seats at a table in the corner. Settled into their chairs and with no one close by they picked up the conversation exactly where it had left off.

"What type of cancer does she have?" Henry asked.

"Inoperable brain tumor. Last spring she had a couple dizzy spells so we went to the doctor. That's what you do when something isn't just right. So, he says maybe she has an inner ear infection but thinks that just in case she should have some tests done. Ok, of course. No big deal, right? She's never sick. Claire doesn't even catch a cold ..." His voice cracked and he paused for a moment to compose himself. "Anyway, they found something ..."

"So what's the prognosis, George? What are they doing about it?" Henry inquired, now suddenly invested in the outcome.

"What they can. Radiation and chemo. It's in a bad spot."

"How about another opinion?" Henry offered.

"We've had four from the best in the business; our next move after this is an experimental program offered by Duke University." George stared out the window and Henry drank from his cup as they just let things simmer for a bit. It was a brutal situation at best.

Henry realized in that moment that although much of his life had been impacted by sudden tragedy, he now felt like the lucky one. He had never had to sit bedside and watch someone he loved dearly die right before his eyes. He had never known the help-lessness of watching his wife suffer and wither while powerless to alter the future. The closest he had come to this was when Joe was injured and he had not liked the experience one bit. Everyone gets dealt a hand in life and is left to make the best of it. Perhaps he had gotten off easy.

"Henry, there is something I've wanted to get off of my chest for 40 years ..."

"No George," Henry tried to interrupt.

"Please Henry, now more than ever I need to say this to you. I know what you think. I know how it all looked, but I never ever betrayed you. I had no idea whatsoever about anything going on between Bill and Mary. I swear it. Before God Almighty I swear it. If I had, I would have come to you immediately. We were like brothers. You saved my life for Christ's sake! I could never do such a thing to you. But Henry, there is a lot more to the story ..."

"George, I don't want to relive it. What's done is done. The past is past. We can't go back now. It's too late for that. I don't know what to say. Let's just see if there's somewhere we can go from here, ok?"

Sensing the resolve in Henry's voice, George realized there was nothing to be gained today by pushing the issue further. Dozens of unreturned phone calls and unanswered letters over the years had been trumped by a chance encounter in a coin shop and for now it was time to consolidate the gains made without greed for more.

"Fair enough," George agreed. He sat for a moment just looking out the window and then a thought occurred to him. Reaching into his pocket he pulled out a well-worn silver dollar and placed it onto the table in front of Henry. "Do you remember that?" he asked.

Henry looked down at the gray smooth coin and smiled broadly. He reached into his pocket and pulled its twin brother out and placed it beside George's.

"Sure do," he chuckled. The men were amazed that the other had been carrying around the silver dollar he was given so many years before by George's grandfather. It was a nice surprise and reminded them of the bond they had once shared.

"So, tell me, what are you collecting these days?" George asked, pivoting the conversation to lighter topics.

The two men sat for over an hour and entertained one another with stories of hobby glories and failures. They realized that on more than one occasion, they had bid against each other in auctions for the very same coins. George teased that since he had introduced Henry to numismatics he should have let him win a bit more often. They lamented the amount of money they had wasted unknowingly competing for lots and laughed at the thought. In addition to anecdotes, they exchanged useful information about hobby happenings the other wasn't privy to and planted the seeds for several potential trades down the road.

George was not surprised when Henry told him he had moved back to Lewis in 1974. Apparently, Henry was not the only one who read the *Lewis Gazette*. Henry suggested that perhaps when Claire was feeling better they might like to drive out and visit. George was enthusiastic about the concept and agreed to bring along his collection when the time came.

The two men exchanged current telephone numbers and addresses and agreed to stay in touch. It was a good conversation and even though the events of the past could not be reversed, it was enough for them at this stage of their lives to be able to set it aside and move forward. They parted company both feeling very good about what had just occurred.

When Henry arrived home, the reception from Joe was both warm and vigorous as she rubbed happily against his legs until he bent down and picked her up.

"Well, there's your Daddy," Millie said to Joe while rinsing some dishes at the sink. "We've been waiting on you. So, what did the doctor say? You were gone a long time," she asked in a concerned tone.

It hadn't occurred to Henry that he had given her cause to worry with his tardiness. He wasn't accustomed to anyone tracking his movements but it felt kind of nice to know that someone cared about him and his whereabouts.

"Oh, I'm sorry. The doctor said I am fit as a fiddle. That isn't why I took so long. I made a stop at the coin shop and I ran into George," he explained as matter-of-factly as someone might relay a grocery list.

"George? You mean George from the other night George? George? Mr.-I-haven't-talked-to-you-in-40-years George?" Millie responded to the bombshell statement. She was so surprised at the news that she let a cup slip from her hands and it made a splash as it fell back into the sink in front of her.

"The one and the same," he answered.

"So? C'mon on now, you can't just leave a girl hanging. What happened?"

"We talked. It was pretty awkward at first but we talked and it was actually really good. I had forgotten how much I liked talking to George," he said as he put Joe down on the floor and took his usual seat at the island.

"Well? What did you talk about?" she pressed forward impatiently.

"Coins," Henry answered, knowing that his response would drive her nuts.

"Coins? Coins. The last time you see your best friend you quit your job at his daddy's company, have a blowout, move to Chicago, and divorce your wife. Then some 40-odd years later when you two finally run into each other you talk about coins? Men!" she exclaimed in disgust, disappointed by the lack of juicy details she had hoped to hear.

Pleased with himself, Henry laughed at her reaction and went back to work on her.

"Well, I guess maybe it wasn't *all* just coins," he offered, slyly trying to bait her.

"And?" She quickly switched back into curiosity mode, anticipating the *real* story.

"Yeah, we did talk about something pretty serious."

"And?"

"I told him I slept with a whiskey drinkin' girl named Millie the other night!!"

"Ohhhhh, you crazy fool! Get on out of here with your silliness. Trying to find out something about a man and all he gives me is a headache. Take your nonsense somewhere else!" she declared not remotely amused by his feigned innuendo.

Henry roared. As he headed up the stairs to go change his clothes, he laughed so hard that he cried. In fact, he could not remember a time in recent memory when he had become so giddy and it made him happy inside. He felt lighter these days. Weight that had held him down silently and undetected for decades seemed to be lifting off more all of the time and it felt like fresh air rushing into his lungs. His spirits soared.

Once he and Millie had both calmed down, he told her all about the chance encounter and conversation with George. Though they were complete strangers, she was equally as saddened as he had been to learn of his wife's illness. As good people do, she felt empathy for George and Claire's struggle and told Henry that anytime he wanted her to, she would be happy to cook or bake something for him to take to them.

Over the next few weeks, Henry and George exchanged several phone calls and shared lengthy conversations on a vast array of topics. Henry filled George in on the details of his life and vice versa. The exchanges were good for both of them. It was therapeutic for George to have someone from his past, with no ties to his present, to be able to talk with and vent to without prejudice or bias. Also, it was enjoyable for him to revisit happier times from their youth and it provided a much-needed respite from the drudgery of doctors, needles, and cancer.

For Henry, their phone calls became the highlights of his day as he had someone to talk coins with who knew as much or more than he did. Also, it was good to finally be able to make some sort of peace with a part of his past and his feelings about George's role in the whole affair softened dramatically. Henry came to realize that put into the same position, he likely would have handled it the same way that his friend had.

Christmas came and went at Oak Forest with little fanfare as usual. Henry had lost interest in the holiday long ago and each year just tried to outlast it and get on with his life. His lone nod to the season was a small two-foot artificial tree with a single strand of lights placed on a table in the family room. Henry allowed this one expression of Christmas cheer because of his love and admiration for his father who always said that "a home without a Christmas tree just isn't a home."

His feelings about Christmas were not due to an obsession with hoarding his money as was the case with Charles Dickens' cold-hearted character. He was no "Ebenezer Scrooge." In fact, he was quite the opposite. Despite his own feelings, he understood the fascination others had for the season and also the need for those well off to be charitable. Each year at this time, he wrote sizable checks to charities he believed in and made anonymous donations to several local causes that needed his support. He sometimes liked to stop at local retailers and secretly pay off a few layaway accounts for others less fortunate than he was. Closer to home, he always presented Millie with a sizable expression of his gratitude for her efforts throughout the year.

No, his disdain for Christmas was not financially motivated. Henry's personal aversion to the holiday was a product of something entirely different. It stemmed from unresolved feelings about a Christmas Eve in St. Louis in 1953 that had forever left him scarred.

On New Year's Day Henry called to wish George well for the coming year but was met with somber news. Overnight, Claire had taken a turn for the worse and had slipped into a coma. It was only a matter of time now. Though he was shaken, Henry thought George was handling it all remarkably well. In recent days he had sensed his friend's acceptance that there would be no trip to Duke and that all that could be done had been attempted without success. Claire's condition had been rapidly deteriorating and her pain increasing so this latest development was in fact merciful and a relief to George. At least now, her suffering was at an end as her life's journey neared its conclusion.

The next two weeks brought little change. Henry and George spoke almost daily as George maintained a bedside vigil with his wife and the hours dragged on for him. Henry enjoyed the chats immensely from the comfort of his recliner as they always were about happy topics relating to their coin collections or childhood or sports, never about Claire or the future. George needed a diversion from all of that and Henry was happy to supply it.

Then, in the third week of January, the phone calls suddenly stopped and those made by Henry to St. Louis went unanswered and unreturned. Henry knew what that meant, and though part of him felt the need to be involved to support George, he realized that this was a time for their family and friends to gather and he was an echo from the past. Rather than entangle himself in their mourning and distract George, he would stay away and wait for George to contact him when he was ready.

Around 11:00 p.m. on Friday night the call came. George explained that Claire had passed away peacefully on Tuesday, the 14th of January, and had been laid to rest that morning. This phone call was unlike any other they had shared. They spoke into the wee hours of the morning about Claire and George's family and what he would do now. There was no talk of coins or anecdotes about the past. This time they discussed all of the fears and uncertainties George was grappling with and what life alone would look like. The man who had seemed so strong recently now was very fragile and lost. Reality had set in and he was grappling mightily with it. Fortunately for George, there was no better person on planet earth more suited to offer advice about what lay ahead and living with loss. Time and distance evaporated and it was as if they were two boys once again at Old Man Janson's pond. For the second time, Henry was there exactly when George needed rescuing.

After the initial shock waves passed, George rebounded fairly quickly, all things considered, thanks in large part to the shoulder provided by Henry. Claire's lengthy illness had at least given him some time to prepare for life without her and in the following weeks he seemed to be coming to terms with it as well as anyone could under the circumstances. He felt at peace. He and Claire had shared a long and glorious life together, produced three children who in turn provided seven grandchildren and had left nothing undone or unsaid between them. He felt blessed and grateful for a life so different from Henry's.

Early February was particularly cold and snowy but unlike years past, Henry didn't seem to mind as much about the winter weather. He enjoyed his books and coins and Joe provided a daily diversion with countless games of "fetch" and antics that were always amusing. On several occasions, Millie had made use of the guest room as well due to the inclement weather and pestering her was always good sport to chase the winter blues away. His telephone calls with George continued and he longed to see his friend again. They agreed that as soon as the weather got nicer, George and his coin collection would make the trip to Lewis to pay Oak Forest a visit.

Typical of the Midwest, that day came sooner than expected as warm air and showers moved in before month's end and cleared the snow from the landscape. By the first week of March, it seemed as though spring intended to come early again as it had done the year before. The weather was cooperating but now George had become ill and the get-together had to be postponed until the following week after he had recovered. Finally, the date was set and they agreed to meet on Sunday, March 8th at Henry's home for an afternoon of coin conversation and show and tell.

Just after noon on the appointed day, George's silver Mercedes pulled up to the front porch. Henry saw the reflection of the sun off the windshield through the storm door and rose from his seat at the kitchen table to go and greet his guest. As he reached the door, George was pulling a large plastic tub from the trunk of the car.

"There he is!" Henry bellowed as he opened the door and stepped onto the porch.

"Hey Henry!" George responded as he balanced the tub against his leg with one hand and closed the lid to the trunk with the other.

"It'd be easier if we were stamp collectors!" he joked in reference to the large heavy container of coins he had carried with him.

"Wouldn't it though?" Henry agreed. "How you feeling?" he asked.

"Oh, just a little cough left. A lot better, thanks," he replied as Henry held the door open so that he could carry the container inside.

"Man, this place is beautiful!" George complimented him. "The stable and pond, this house—what a treasure!"

"Thanks. I was damned lucky to find it, that's for sure. You can just set your box anywhere," Henry directed, motioning toward the kitchen table. He had a stack of his own coin boxes arranged at one end and George placed the tub on the floor next to the closest chair.

"Before we look at coins, you want the nickel tour?" Henry asked his friend.

"Sure, absolutely! Lead on," George replied enthusiastically.

Henry led George around the property and through the buildings for nearly an hour as they chatted and laughed. George was impressed by everything he saw but the highlight of the excursion had to be Uncle Ed's 1930 Model A. He simply couldn't believe it and commented that it looked better today than when Uncle Ed had taught them to drive it when they were just teens and wet behind the ears. George beamed from ear to ear when he sat behind the wheel again after all of the decades.

With the trip down memory lane accomplished, the men headed back to the house and settled down to the business at hand at the kitchen table. George removed the lid from his tub to reveal at least a dozen double-rowed boxes of coins that he had brought along. Before he removed any of the coins though, he reached alongside the boxes and retrieved a book and handed it to Henry.

"I want to give you this," he said as he passed the thick hard cover volume across the table to his host.

It was an antique book from the early 1800s written about the life of George Washington. Henry had mentioned in passing his deep admiration for the nation's first president and George had made note of it.

"Oh George, this is amazing!" Henry exclaimed as he took it in hand. "I've never even seen this one."

"It was my grandfather's," George stated, referring to Joseph Schuetz. "He was a fan of Washington too. How come you think my dad and I got the name George?" he explained.

Henry's eyes shot up at him. "Really? I never knew that. George, I can't take this," he said as he started to hand it back.

"No Henry, it's yours. I insist. I even autographed it on the inside."

Henry opened the front cover and on inside of it George had written an inscription:

"To my long lost best friend and brother, thank you for saving my life … twice. Your friend, George"

Henry became choked up. It was a thoughtful and touching gift and he had little experience with such things. George could tell that it was awkward for Henry, and that he didn't know what to say, so he diffused the situation by reaching into his stash for a box of silver dollars for them to look at.

The men enjoyed an afternoon of haggling and laughter as they swapped coins and stories and truly just enjoyed one another's company. In all, 15 coins changed hands and there was no possible way to account for the total number of jabs and chuckles that flew back and forth across the table that day.

As things wound down, Henry brought out Jake to join in the fun. It was the first time in over 40 years that the three of them had been together and the first drink was a toast to the elder Schuetzes who had been so important to both of them.

George knew Henry was in an especially good mood and he had hoped that the gift of the book might soften him for a conversation that was decades overdue on a topic that weighed heavily on him.

"Henry, would you do me a favor?" he asked his friend.

"Are you kidding? Sure, name it," he replied, unwittingly playing into George's hands.

"Will you please hear me out about Mary?"

With whiskey flowing, coins all over the kitchen table, and a brand new George Washington book for his collection staring him in the face, Henry knew he had been had. George proved once again why he was always the more cunning of the two and Henry could only reluctantly nod for him to proceed.

"Henry, you couldn't have been more wrong. Mary wasn't having an affair, she was having a nervous breakdown. She was so twisted in knots about not being able to have a baby that at last, I guess it kind of drove her crazy. She got this idea in her head that she couldn't get pregnant because of what had happened with Bill. She felt personally responsible for breaking up two brothers and it was eating at her. Some damn fortune teller told her she'd never have a baby unless you guys made peace with Bill," he explained.

"What? That's insanity," Henry said while staring off into space.

"That's what I told her when she came to my office asking for help to find him. I told her she needed to talk to you but she cried and said that you two were barely hanging on and you'd say she was out of her head and leave her. She was a mess. I don't know why, maybe it was how upset she was or that I loved you both and didn't want to see you split up. But somehow, in some weird way, I bought into the idea that getting Bill back here to straighten things out might fix it all the way around."

"Jesus, George. Why didn't you tell me?" Henry asked while running his right hand over his forehead and through his hair nervously.

"Of course I know now I should have, Henry, but back then I didn't know what to do. I never dreamed things could go so wrong," he lamented.

"Yeah, George but I know what I saw, he was holding her hand and he kissed her!" Henry countered.

"Henry, what you saw was two old friends making peace with their past. He was already married to a gal in New York and had a baby at home by then. He wasn't trying to steal Mary away from you."

"Married? Baby? Are you sure?" Henry was startled by the revelation.

"They were with him, Henry, staying in the hotel for Christmas. The plan was to show up at your house Christmas Day and you guys could work it all out. Mary had set it all up and finally talked Bill into it. For some reason, he felt guilty too; I don't know why but he did."

Henry immediately knew why Bill would have felt guilty but was too taken by the rest of George's story to get into it with him at that point.

"Oh my God," Henry muttered starting to see the bigger picture. "But George, there were phone calls and whispers and times she was gone and it didn't add up," Henry countered again.

"Probably the phone calls you heard were her talking to me. I'm the one who found Bill for her. As far as I know, they didn't even talk until Christmas Eve at the hotel. Once I set it all up I called her the day before and gave her the details about when and where Bill and his family would meet her. She was really nervous about it all. She wasn't sure what she was going to say to him. She felt really guilty about everything even though I kept telling her nobody was in the wrong. She just couldn't let it go. As for the other stuff, I know she was running around seeing fortune tellers and palm readers and priests looking for answers but didn't want you to know. I guess that's what you were picking up on."

Henry was completely floored. He could see now what he had done and it was devastating. His hands trembled and the ice in his otherwise empty glass made a light noise as it shook.

George could see the despair in Henry's face. He had always believed that if he was just given the chance he could make Henry understand the truth of what had happened. He knew the character of the man and was certain that Henry would do the right thing if given the opportunity.

"Henry, I know where Mary is. You need to go and talk to her and set things right. You still have a chance to fix this. Don't wait until it's too late. Don't carry this around the rest of your life. I beg you to go make your peace," George implored him.

Tears welled in Henry's eyes as he listened while George relayed the story of Mary's life to him. After Henry's abrupt exit in 1953, they had stayed in touch and survived his departure together. For all of these years Henry had blamed them for his pain but now he realized it had really been he who was in the wrong. George told Henry that Mary was in St. Louis and how to find her, but now the rest was up to him.

George knew the peace that he felt from having been able to clear all accounts with Claire. He had said everything he wanted and needed to her before she passed. He had no regrets and he knew that if Henry would just go and speak to Mary that he would feel great relief.

After a long embrace, they parted company and George headed back home leaving Henry with much to consider. The better part of his life had been impacted by wrong actions based on false assumptions and information, and decisions had to be made about what he reasonably could and would now do about it.

## CHAPTER 23

# Truth and Consequences

HENRY DIDN'T SLEEP a wink that night. George's words echoed in his ears again and again. He had unknowingly wronged Mary unforgivably and now that he knew it, he grappled with what to do next. He had ended a marriage and broken a heart over a misunderstanding, for God's sake. How does one ever atone for such a transgression? After all of these years is it even possible? Certainly there were extreme circumstances at the time to be sure but the simple fact remained that *he* was wrong. The hours crawled by as he stared at the ceiling and pondered what he had done, all the while desperately seeking a comfortable position that might produce sleep and relieve his mind.

For her part, Joe seemed unburdened by the dilemma as she snoozed fitfully at his feet. She was occasionally awakened by his tossing and turning but each time rolled over and went back to sleep.

Henry was reminded of the days leading up to his profession of love for Mary. He had been mentally tortured to the point where no matter the outcome, it was better to get it over with than to live with the anxiety created by his indecision. He could see the writing on the wall and knew that it would be no different this time. If anything, the longer he put it off the worse it was bound to get. He wondered what his father and Uncle Ed would advise him to do. He imagined the words of George Washington or John Wayne if they were counseling him on a course of action to take.

Around sunrise, he concluded that he must go to St. Louis and speak to Mary. It would be difficult and wouldn't change the past, but a real man would own his mistakes and even if he were nothing else, Henry was at the very least a real man.

He rose from bed and went into the bathroom with purpose. He started the water in the shower and while he waited for it to warm, went into his walk-in closet to select clothes to wear.

"What do you wear to a hanging?" he said aloud with a sigh as he ran his hands over the shirts hanging on the left. He glanced back into the bathroom and could see the sun already gleaming through the back window and illuminating the room. He reasoned that it was going to be a nice day weather wise with temps near the 50s, as had been the trend over the last week, so his attire needed to be appropriate for the day and he decided to go with clothing more slanted toward spring than winter. Mary's favorite color had always been yellow so he chose a long – sleeved, collared cotton shirt of that color with tan slacks as a complement. Joe wearily wobbled into the room to see what the commotion was and stretched her mouth to the breaking point with an enormous yawn as she saw Henry.

"Well good morning sleepy head!" he laughed as he saw his bleary-eyed buddy. "Did you have a rough night?" he questioned as he realized he felt exhilarated and not a bit tired himself despite his own lack of sleep. Joe looked up at him with an expression that seemed to indicate that she wanted to strangle him for all of the disturbances caused by his flopping in bed overnight. Henry didn't pick up on it though as he was running on pure adrenaline at this point and focused entirely on the task at hand.

He took a brief shower before taking great care to meticulously shave his face. He hadn't seen Mary for over 44 years and he was determined to make the best impression he possibly could. As he combed his hair he wondered what she would think of his salt and pepper color but guessed that based on her affinity for Cary Grant, whom he recalled used to be her favorite actor, she likely would approve. It occurred to him that it was not only he who would have changed over the years. He imagined what she would look like as an older woman and predicted she would be as stunning as ever. He remembered her classic cheek bones and sparkling eyes and concluded that time would only enhance such assets as those.

He dressed with the precision of a United States Marine officer preparing for parade. After his shoes were tied and his belt cinched, he stood before his dresser looking into the mirror as he fastened his best gold wrist watch. *I can do this*, he told himself.

Joe was fully awake now and sat on the bed watching Henry's every move with keen interest. She had seen him get up from bed many times but had never known him to do much of anything before going downstairs to get a cup of coffee. She felt slightly indignant as he seemed very preoccupied this morning and had shown only passing interest in her thus far. She felt better, however, when he turned and addressed her.

"So, how do I look babe?" he asked. "Today's a big day for me. I've got to go see Mary so I'm going to be gone for a while but I'll tell you and Jake all about it tonight, ok?" Henry stroked Joe's head and back a few times before giving her a gentle scruff under her chin. This was more like it, she thought. It was short lived though, because a moment later Henry was heading down the stairs toward the kitchen.

He looked at the clock and observed the time to be 8:20 a.m. He walked over to the counter and withdrew his travel mug from the cabinet before filling it with freshly brewed coffee from the pot. As he sealed the lid, he decided he better write a note for Millie explaining where he was or she would be concerned about him as she had been the day he ran into George at the coin shop. The thought made him smile.

Joe trotted down the steps expecting to see her customary saucer of milk waiting for her but there was only Henry writing something at the counter. She assumed he must just be a little off today and figured while she waited for him to get her morning treat, she would scout the house for a paper ball they could use for their typical early game of fetch as he drank his coffee. She wandered around the family room but didn't see anything so next she headed for Henry's office, which was always fertile ground for hunting paper balls. Before she could find one though, she heard the side door close and ran into the kitchen to see if Millie had arrived. She was surprised to see that it was just the opposite. There was no Millie and no Henry either. He had left without so much as a goodbye and there was no saucer of milk in sight anywhere. This was clearly a serious breach of etiquette and complaints would have to be lodged with the management. She took up a post near the refrigerator and dutifully waited for someone to give a piece of her mind to.

Henry's Lincoln Continental was rolling down the county road before Joe had even settled into her seat. He was a man on a mission and wanted to get to St. Louis before he lost his nerve. The drive was a blur as his mind was fixed on Mary and what he needed to say to her. He was determined to speak to her in person. He needed to face the truth and there would be consequences but what if it didn't go well? What if, after all of these years, there was only anger and pain? How could he ever make her understand? How could she ever forgive him? Thoughts flooded his mind from every angle. He had given presentations in board rooms with millions of dollars on the line and spoken in front of hundreds at seminars before, but had never felt so nervous about an upcoming conversation in his life.

At the same moment, Millie was entering the house and was greeted by Joe who talked to her as she came into the kitchen.

"Well good morning, little lady!" Millie sat her purse on the island and bent down to pick Joe up. She noticed that she was especially affectionate and by her reaction she realized that Joe was alone and longing for company.

"Where did your daddy run off to and leave you?" she asked the cat who was squinting her eyes with pleasure at the attention she was receiving. If only she could speak human, Joe thought, she would tell Millie about her difficult night and the neglect Henry had shown this morning. Joe knew that Millie would be shocked to hear that she hadn't gotten a saucer of milk and that Henry didn't throw a single paper ball her way.

Millie scanned the room and noticed the note lying next to

the telephone. She walked over to it, still snuggling with Joe, and was surprised to see Henry's handwriting. Maybe an old dog can learn new tricks, she thought. The presence of the note was a surprise, but the content written on it shocked her.

"Gone to St. Louis to see Mary. I'll be back later and will explain everything. Please stay for dinner tonight – Henry"

"Oh my Lord!" she exclaimed to Joe, "Hell done froze over!"

Henry exited from the highway and proceeded on the off-ramp until he reached an intersection and a red traffic signal. He looked at himself in the rear view mirror and adjusted his glasses before taking another sip of coffee from the near-empty mug. As he did, he realized he needed to relieve himself due to the combination of coffee and nerves and scanned the distance for a suitable option. A block away on the right-hand side was a fast-food restaurant and he determined that would be his destination.

Once the signal turned green, Henry headed for the restroom of the establishment and found relief. Before leaving, he purchased another cup of coffee and promptly poured it into his travel mug. While he was doing so, he noticed a florist located just across the parking lot and had an idea.

"Flowers are always a good idea," he muttered to himself. He pulled over to the building and walked inside without knowing exactly what he wanted.

"Good morning sir," a delightful young lady greeted him. "May I help you?"

"Good morning. I certainly hope so," he replied as he looked around the showroom. The air was thick and fragrant, crowded with the aroma of dozens of competing scents.

"I need something special," he said.

"Of course, is this for your wife or daughter or?"

"No, I don't have any of those. They are for my ex-wife," he answered tentatively while looking through the glass windows of the refrigerated case.

"Oh, ok, I see. Umm, well, we don't get a lot of requests for flowers for ex-wives; did you have something in mind? I'm guessing you aren't looking for roses."

Henry laughed. "No, not roses, but I do want something nice."

"Does she have a favorite color?" the girl asked.

"Yes, yellow," he responded.

"Good. Well, since you are wearing a yellow shirt I'm going to guess we are trying to impress her so how about a nice bouquet of mixed spring flowers, heavy on the yellow daisies?"

Henry had never realized that going to a florist was so personal and felt a little uncomfortable about her appraisal of him. However, he liked her idea and was impressed by her initiative. He had no doubts that this person would make for a successful psychologist were she so inclined.

"Sounds perfect," he agreed.

"Very good! It'll be just a moment."

Henry strolled through the store as the clerk carefully selected a large assortment of various flowers from the cases. She then walked to a counter where she arranged them into a gorgeous bouquet, which she then wrapped with a large piece of clear cellophane. Finally, she slid the entire ensemble inside a triangular plastic sleeve to keep the stems from dripping water as Henry carried them.

Once he had paid for the flowers, they said their goodbyes and Henry went on his way feeling slightly more confident now about the coming encounter. Henry placed the bouquet onto the seat beside him and took a long drink from his mug before starting the car. It was getting closer.

He took a deep breath and then started the automobile, resolved to face whatever lay ahead. The streets were familiar to him as he had lived here for several years with Mary but the area had changed. Progress and urban sprawl had brought development and increased population to the sleepy suburb of Black Jack, MO and it felt surreal to him as he mixed the remainders of what used to be and his memories with the reality he could now see before him.

Henry wondered what life might have been like if he had only stayed in St. Louis on that fateful day and given Mary a chance to explain things to him. Would he and Bill have made peace with each other? Might he and Mary have adopted children after all or produced some of their own? Would George's family have still been forced to sell the shoe company due to overseas pressures or would Henry have been able to help steer them back to profitability? They were questions without answers.

Henry's truth was that he had run away from all of them and left collateral damage behind him. Much pain and suffering might have been averted had he made different decisions but that was in the past. The truth of his life was what it was and he had made the best he could out of the consequences that followed. All that was left for him now was to get himself righted with Mary.

He followed the streets until he finally made his last turn onto Parker Road. The house he and Mary had shared and she had kept after the divorce, was only a block away. Henry sensed a tightening in his throat and his palms began to sweat as he closed in on the address. His head began to swim a bit as well as he suddenly wondered if he should stop at the home or simply pass it by. It came into sight as a chill ran down his back and his feet suddenly felt cold. He would not stop, he decided. He couldn't. Mary was waiting for him.

He drove past the house and other than the fact that it had been painted an ugly light green color he thought it looked exactly the same as he remembered it. He drove down a small hill past a few more homes and an apartment complex that now stood in what he remembered as a farm field. Up another hill he passed Salem Lutheran Church, a gorgeous old classic structure built in 1849 that towered over the area. Mary had been a devout attendee there during their marriage and Henry wondered if that had continued after the divorce.

It was just after 9:30 a.m. when Henry pulled off of Parker Road and into the entrance of the Salem Lutheran Church Cemetery. He gazed across the grounds, which were crowded with hundreds of headstones, some dating back as far as the Civil War. Off to his right, he saw a small frame house and deduced that the caretaker lived there so he pulled over to it.

Henry exited the vehicle and approached the front door. After he had rung the bell, and then upon getting no response knocked loudly, an older man answered.

"Good morning. Can I help you?" asked the man who appeared to be roughly the same age as Henry.

"Good morning, yes, can you tell me where the Winters' family plots are?" he asked. George had told Henry that Mary's dying wish had been to be buried next to her father and mother. Doc Winters and his wife had moved from Lewis to Black Jack in the mid-1950s to be closer to Mary and both been laid to rest here.

"Winters you say? Yes, you see that large cottonwood tree near the back, the one with the stone bench underneath it?"

"Yes, I see it," Henry nodded as his eyes were trained to the spot the man was describing.

"That's them."

"Thank you very much. I appreciate your help," Henry said gratefully as he returned to his car.

He pulled along the single-lane drive that split through the middle of the grounds until he was as close to the appointed destination as possible. From here, he would have to go it on foot. He removed the flowers from their wrappings and took a long deep breath before getting out of the car. The sunshine was bright but the air felt cool on his face and he was glad to have brought his jacket along.

Henry walked in the direction of the tree and bench, which were some 20 yards away. As he did, he glanced at the neatly ordered headstones that stood as monuments to the lives of those they watched over. Buenger, Lampe, Wolff, Snyder. *It's a German "Who's Who"*, Henry thought to himself as he passed. The area had once been dominated by German immigrants and their descendants and the deceased were a tangible representation of that history.

Finally, Henry reached his moment of truth. Three headstones stood in alignment before him beneath the cottonwood tree. They belonged to Doctor Albert Johnston Winters, Martha Louise Winters, and Mary Elizabeth Anderson. Seeing a last name other than Winters or Engel associated with Mary's for the first time felt as surreal as the trip through Black Jack just had. It was a combination of what he remembered and the reality of her life after his departure.

He had been forewarned to expect this. George had told Henry that she remarried in 1959 to a good man named David Anderson. The couple lived in a home in Florissant, MO, which was next door to Black Jack, and had three children together. Mary had given birth to two sons, one in 1960 and a second in 1962, followed by a daughter in 1965. By all accounts she had led a happy life until 1984 when she was diagnosed with advanced breast cancer. After a short but difficult battle, in late 1985 at just 62 years of age, Mary had passed away peacefully in her sleep.

## CHAPTER 24

# Making Things Right

HENRY STOOD FOR several moments staring at Mary's headstone without uttering a word. He felt overwhelmed by the circumstances and uncertain of how to proceed now that he was actually here. He had run through numerous scenarios in his mind but just being in her presence left him dumbfounded. Finally, after a couple of deep breaths he gathered himself slightly and looked down at the bouquet in his hand. He decided that a good start might be to place the flowers he had bought for her on her grave. He carefully stepped around to the right and nervously knelt to the ground.

"These are for you," he said softly as he set them against the front of the headstone. He stood and glanced at the bench, which was positioned just to the side of the grave and decided he needed to sit down. For a few more minutes he just sat quietly taking everything in and collecting his thoughts before he spoke again.

"Hello Mary. I am really sorry this visit is so long overdue. I can only imagine how you might feel to see me now after all of these years. There is just so much I need to say to you, that

I need for you to hear. I just don't know where to start ..." His voice trailed off as he looked into the distance.

"I ran into George a couple of months back. He and I hadn't spoken either in 40-some-odd years. He tried to tell me about everything then but I was hard-headed. I didn't want to discuss it with him. But yesterday, I finally gave him the chance to set me straight on things." Henry let out a deep sigh as he considered his new understanding of previous events, which had led him to come here.

"I guess I'm still in shock about it all to be honest with you," he said shaking his head and staring now at the ground between his feet. "That day at the Clairmont, I was so damn sure of what I saw and just so damn jealous to think about you and Bill going behind my back that I lost my mind. It was horrible. I didn't know what to do or where to go. Everything between you and I had gotten so screwed up by then ... You were always sneaking around and whispering on the telephone. We hadn't slept in the same bed in months. It all just added up. After I told George about it and found out that he knew you were with Bill that day, I had to run. It felt like my whole world was on fire. Of course after that, well, you know the rest," he stated, referring to the divorce proceedings and Henry's departure from the Schuetz Shoe Company and his life in St. Louis.

"I just couldn't see straight, honey," he said while shaking his head slowly. "I always felt bad about how things played out with Bill after the war but I always knew after that he wanted you back. In the back of my mind, I was always waiting for something to happen. Just living on thin ice. Aww, jealousy can make you so crazy, you know? It can also make it seem ok to do things you otherwise wouldn't and I did something a long time ago I'm not very proud of."

Henry paused for a few seconds and rubbed his hands together before continuing with his confession. "After Bill took off for New York I always wondered if or when he'd try to talk to you about everything. See if he could convince you to run away with him. That day on the phone it was just him and me; you weren't in on it so I figured at some point he'd want to see if you still had feelings for him, you know, get your side of things. I waited for him to show up or call again but as far as I could tell from you without coming out and asking, he never did. I wasn't wrong though. A couple of months later a letter addressed *only* to you with no return address came to the house. I just happened to have come home from the office early that day so by luck I was the one who got the mail. Anyway, I could see it was postmarked from New York. I didn't recognize the handwriting on it though. He was clever enough about that. He knew if I saw his handwriting on the envelope I'd recognize it right off. I guess he got a buddy to address it for him so I wouldn't notice. Who knows? Well, that's when my jealousy got the better of me and I opened it. Sure enough, the dirty son-of-a-bitch was asking you to come to New York."

Henry's remorse was now turning to anger as he remembered the incident as clearly as if it was just yesterday. Bill had been an innocent victim in an unfortunate drama before that moment. Now, *he* had crossed a line.

"Bill might have been the victim before that, but not after. He said he was in love with you. He understood that you had been shocked when you thought he was dead and had fallen in with me out of grief. Said I was no brother of his and any man who would backdoor his own brother would surely do the same to a wife someday. I didn't know what you would say or do and things had just started to get back on track between us, so I burned it without ever telling you it even existed."

Henry paused again as he reflected on the whole episode and the guilt he had experienced afterwards about his deception and actions regarding the letter.

"God I'm sorry Mary. I truly am. I should have told you. That was the only time I've ever lied to you. I'm also sorry I ever saw that damn letter because from then on I always wondered if there were others. Were there? Bill sure likes to write letters. He's been sending me three or four a year for over a decade now. No idea what the hell they say though. As soon as I see his handwriting on the envelope I throw them away. Since I never answer, I guess he keeps trying. I don't know, I just can't forget what he did. Anyway, I'm right with George now and I've come to do the same with you, but Bill can rot in hell for all I care." Henry looked at her headstone and the name upon it. It made him return his attention to her and the matter at hand.

"In any event, what's done is done and no one can change it now. We just have to live with it and that's why I've come, Mary. I have so many things to apologize for. George helped me to see what a fool I was and I wanted you to know that I realize that now. I am sorry for getting so caught up in my work that I didn't pay attention to how upset you were when we weren't having any luck with kids. I should have been there for you and I wasn't. I'm also sorry I ran out on you after I saw you with Bill too. I truly wish I had given you a chance to explain. If only …" He slipped into regret again as he pondered what might have been.

"I guess it all worked out for the best though, right? George told me you married a swell guy and had three beautiful children. I'm truly happy for that because you wanted it so much. I am so sorry that I couldn't give you children. I realize now it was because of me you couldn't get pregnant. I guess everything happens for a reason." Henry's eyes welled up as he spoke. It was hard enough to accept responsibility for his actions let alone come to the realization that his own infertility was to blame for the circumstances that ultimately led to the end of their marriage. He pulled a white handkerchief from his jacket pocket and lightly blotted his eyes.

"I'm truly sorry you got sick too, honey," he said as he thought of her illness and ultimate demise. "You deserved better, you really did. I should have been there for you." He hung his head for a bit and sat in silence with his eyes closed considering what she must have gone through. He was thankful that she had a husband and children by her side in her final days and wondered if David Anderson had been as devoted to Mary as George had been to Claire.

After some time had passed, his thoughts moved on to lighter topics such as Oak Forest, Millie, and Joe. He described all three in great detail and told her several stories of Joe's antics including the time when he had flown across the yard like a maniac chasing her only to end up in a heap, face down in the grass. The recollection made him laugh at himself and helped to lighten his mood a little bit. His discussion of Millie was equally light-hearted and he assured Mary that had they ever met, they would have been fast friends. In all, his visit to the cemetery consumed nearly an hour and a half before he began to say his goodbyes.

"I guess I should go," he said, looking around and feeling stiffness in his legs from having sat for so long in the cool air.

"I just wish … I just wish I could know what you were thinking. I really do. I wish I could somehow know that you forgive me, that you understand why I did what I did and that we are ok. I know it isn't possible and that's the price I have to pay for what I've done. I'll never forgive myself. I'll carry it with me until I'm in the ground too." Henry's eyes welled up again as the emotions of the morning started to get the better of him.

A lone dove, without reasonable explanation, flew over and landed near Mary's headstone. It looked directly at him, for just an instant, and then flew away. Henry was stunned and awed by the event as he recalled Mary's belief that doves were messengers from God. It was as if she had reached across from the other side and relieved his burden with a gesture that only he would understand. Suddenly, Henry felt a warmth inside himself and an inexplicably strong sense of peace overtook him. He was certain that Mary was there with him and that she had forgiven him for the past. His spirits soared.

As he was leaving, he could have sworn that he heard Mary's voice. Whether it was her or his imagination he would never be able to say with any degree of certainty. However, he heard her and did what she advised before heading on his way back home, feeling better than he had in years.

By the time Henry pulled into the driveway he was gassed. It had been a sleepless night followed by a gut-wrenching morning and he was in need of a nap. He made the decision to deal with putting the car away later and for now parked next to Millie's Ford along the side of the house.

Henry walked inside and was greeted by the sweet smell

of bread baking in the oven. Joe heard him enter and immediately sauntered into the kitchen to investigate. At the same time, Millie was walking down the stairs with a basket of dirty laundry in hand.

"Hey there, Henry," she greeted him. "Are you hungry?" she asked, noting that the wall clock indicated it was 12:28 p.m. and past time for his lunch.

"Nah, I think I'm just gonna take a nap and wait on the food. Say, are we good to go for dinner tonight?" he asked as she reached the bottom step. It was no small gesture for Henry to invite her to dine with him as they still had never eaten a bite of food together at the same table in all the years they had known one another. Apparently, that morning, Henry had decided it was time to end the streak.

"Yes sir! Thank you so much for the invitation. I'm going to make chicken fried steaks with green beans and mashed potatoes. I've got bread in the oven now and after a while I'll whip us up a pie for dessert!" she declared excitedly.

"Man that sounds great! Oh and here, these are for you," he said as he realized he had not yet given her the bouquet he held in his hands.

"My Lord, are those for me?" she asked in amazement as she accepted the flowers from Henry. First the dinner invitation and now this; she was completely shocked and wondering what had gotten into him. In 24 years, these were the first flowers he had ever bought for her.

"To what do I owe the flowers? You're not sick or something are you?" she asked without a hint of humor.

Henry chuckled. "No, those were Mary's idea. I bought them for her but she only kept the yellow ones and sent the rest along for you. She thought it was high time I gave you some flowers. I'd say she's right," he explained, recalling the incident at the cemetery that had prompted him to bring the bouquet home.

Millie realized that in all of the excitement over dinner and flowers she hadn't yet gotten any news about the most important event, his meeting with Mary.

"So ... how'd it go?" she inquired.

Having dropped his jacket onto a kitchen chair, Henry was already climbing the staircase on a mission to find his bed. He paused and addressed her question directly. "You know what? It was really good. It's a long story so how about I tell you everything right after my nap. I didn't sleep at all last night and I'm whipped. Give me two hours and then please wake me up and I'll tell you all about it."

Henry found his bed and was sound asleep almost before his head had completely come to rest on the pillow. When he awoke, just after 3 p.m., he couldn't recall the details of his dreams but he had a sense that he had been sitting in a park with Mary and holding her hand. He could still feel her touch and rubbed the fingers of his right hand together as he became fully conscious. There was an instant of sadness when he realized it all had been just a dream. The warmth of Joe's body, which was pressed against the back of his leg indicated, however, that though Mary was not there he wasn't alone. The same sensation of peacefulness he had felt after seeing the dove, again washed over him and he smiled knowing that everything was ok. Henry took a few moments to reach down and pet his pal who gratefully rolled over and accepted all of the affection he was willing to offer her.

Still dressed, Henry sprang from his bed and straightened himself up a bit before heading downstairs feeling remarkably refreshed by the power nap. He was excited to tell Millie all of the details of his conversations with George and Mary over the past two days and catch her up on things but was disappointed to find a note indicating she had gone to Lewis.

"Went for apples. Be back in a jiffy – Millie" the note read. He decided that having to wait to tell Millie his story was a small price to pay for one of her scrumptious apple pies. Next to the note on the kitchen table, Millie had arranged the flowers in a vase and displayed them prominently. He felt a sense of satisfaction with himself knowing that he had made her happy with the kind gesture.

"Good call, Mary," he said aloud as Joe looked up at him. He noticed the time on his watch and decided to stretch his legs with a trip to the mailbox.

"You up for a walk?" he asked his little companion. In recent weeks Joe had begun to once again brave the outer world and they had resumed their daily walks to the road together. He looked for his jacket and smiled when he saw Millie had hung it on the hall tree for him. He walked to the front door and put it on before stepping outside with Joe at his heels.

It was early March in Lewis, Missouri and perfect jacket weather. Winter was in the books and Henry was excited about the prospects for the future. He looked around at the island and grounds as he headed down the hill and felt true satisfaction with the life he had made for himself. Joe trotted along just steps ahead of him and he enjoyed seeing her happy and healthy and looking like her old self again.

As he reached the bottom of the hill he observed a lone red-tailed hawk soaring above him in total peace and solitude. He watched as it gently glided on the wind in a silent graceful circle.

*How lonely that life must be*, Henry thought to himself. To spend all day just with yourself, with no one to care for you or who depended on you seemed like a hollow existence to him now.

He reached the mailbox and retrieved a stack of items from within it as he watched Joe playfully pouncing on a moth a few yards away. He was happy to see the most recent issue of *Coin Universe* front and center as he closed the door to the box and thought it would give him plenty to talk about with George after he had read it.

"I'm heading home," he called out as he made his way back down the hill while sorting through the mail. Joe heard his voice and upon seeing him going back decided to release her prey, much to the delight of the moth, and scurried to catch up.

Henry fingered through the usual assortment of bills and checks before his eyes landed on what had always been an unwelcomed sight. It was yet another letter from Bill. He noticed that this time, when he saw it, there was no feeling of angst or anger associated with it. His conversations with George and Mary had diffused the power of these letters over him to produce painful memories and now there was only curiosity. What possesses a man to send countless letters year after year that go unanswered? *He might be a rat*, Henry thought, *but God love him the guy is persistent*. You had to admire that about him anyway.

"What do you think?" he asked Joe as he showed her the letter while they walked along. She didn't react or offer advice; he was on his own with this one. Something deep inside of Henry made him tear open the envelope and pull the letter out. He unfolded it and was surprised to find it was more than a couple of sentences in length. As he walked up the hill toward home, he read it aloud to Joe.

"Henry, I am writing to you again in the hopes that this might finally be the letter that produces contact between us. There is a lot I need to explain and tell you. A long time ago, after I first left for New York, I did something really stupid which has haunted me my whole life. I wrote a letter to Mary asking her to leave you and join me. It was a horrible thing for me to do. Thankfully, she never answered the letter and in '53 when I did finally speak with her, she claimed she never got it. I think she was just covering up to make me feel better about having done such a rotten thing. I'm sorry brother. I wish I could go back in time and change things but, of course, time is unforgiving that way. All I can do now is try to make things right between us. We are brothers. We're all the family we have.

I also wanted to tell you that I got married back in 1948 to a wonderful gal named Sue. We've got two fine boys, your nephews, named Bill III and Edward. I wanted you to know that our family name will live on beyond you and me.

I hope this letter finds you well and I pray that this is finally the time that you answer me. My address is provided below along with my telephone number. Please get in touch with me, I beg of you, and let's talk this thing out before it's too late. Your brother, Bill."

Henry stopped in the driveway just before the edge of the sidewalk and folded the letter before replacing it inside the envelope. "Well, what do you know about that?" he asked Joe who was already at the front door and wondering why he was being pokey about heading back inside.

Apparently Henry wasn't the only one who had been

tortured by regret. Bill had lived for nearly 50 years with the knowledge of his treacherous attempt to end his brother's marriage to Mary and it was still eating at him even now. Henry felt glad to learn about his nephews and was especially pleased that one carried the name of Henry's father while the other the name of his beloved uncle. Bill had certainly gotten that right.

As he walked into the house with Joe, he wondered what type of men they had turned out to be and hoped that they were men of character like their grandfather and great uncle before them were. Bill was wrong about one thing though; Henry had more family in the world than just Bill, his wife, and two boys. They were Engels, true enough, but Henry had a family of his own as well. He had Millie James and a little furry daughter named Hobo Josephine Engel to love.

It was a lot to consider. He wondered what Mary would have him do. He wished Millie was home so he could discuss it with her. He removed his jacket and hung it on the back of the nearest kitchen chair. He then put the mail on the kitchen counter and picked up the cordless telephone from its base before taking it along with the letter from Bill into the family room. Joe followed along sensing something was about to happen. Henry sat down in his recliner and once again removed the letter from the envelope and read through it a second time.

He stared out the window for a moment before realizing that putting things off was not in his makeup. He had acted with swiftness when reconciling with Mary and it had been one of the best decisions of his life. He thought about what to do and made his decision. In complete peace he looked at the number on the letter and dialed the phone. It rang three times before a voice on the other end answered and said hello.

"George? It's Henry. I wanted to tell you that I took your advice and went to see Mary this morning. Do you have a minute?" he asked as he sat the letter from Bill on the table beside his chair.

Henry had made his peace with George and also with Mary, and it was liberating. As for his brother Bill, he wasn't quite there yet.

# Epilogue

Love and Tragedy.

Loyalty and Betrayal.

In the end, there is only Truth.

## About the Author

Roger W. Buenger is an author and entrepreneur who was born and raised in St. Louis, MO. He is an avid numismatist, historian, movie aficionado, and sports fan. These diverse interests serve him well when he is crafting tales and pursuing his passion for writing historical fiction. Mr. Buenger resides in St. Louis with his family.

www.rogerwbuenger.com